MR. GO SLOW

A PICKLEBALL ROMANCE

NALINI WARRIAR

ISBN: 978-1-7774013—0-6

Created with Vellum

Yesterday I was clever, so I wanted to change the world.
Today I'm wise, I'm changing myself.

— RUMI, 13TH CENTURY SUFI POET

Dedication

To my bro and partner in crime, Phil, without whom this would never have been written

BOOKS BY NALINI WARRIAR

LITERARY FICTION

The Enemy Within, a portrait of a marriage-sequel coming

Fireflies in the Night, a coming of age historical novel set in 1960s India-
Next Generation Indie Award for Best Fiction 2017; Best Books 2016
Kirkus Reviews (starred review)

Karma's Slow Burn-a sizzling contemporary romance about a baseball player turned chef and a fiesty and independent sports journalist

ACKNOWLEDGMENTS

Pickleball is a big part of my life since I emerged from the dark ages of 2015. And lookee the darkness still here in 2020 due to entirely different circumstances. This book is for my fellow pickleball players especially those from the Bath Pickleball Club who can't wait the for the tail end of this comet. As the main protagonist in Mr. Go Slow, Priya Keelor, puts it: 'I can maybe probably live without a man but I can never ever survive without pickleball.' Some of us can give John McEnroe a run for his money when it comes to being a sick badass on the pickleball courts.

To my ever loyal ARC readers, so glad I found you.

GET A FREE BOOK!

https://dl.bookfunnel.com/zxcncddx5h

Get a free copy of my novella 'A Man of Substance.'

- Nimmy, a trauma surgeon, does the unthinkable. She chooses an arranged marriage . What she doesn't count on is falling for the guy.

ABOUT MR. GO SLOW

Life has taught Priya Keelor, a caterer, a Bollywood dancer and a pickleball player who flirts at being a PI, not to have any expectations. Stubbornly single, she's content to drift along the ocean of life for she does not believe in relationships. Or marriage.

Laid-back Dallas Crenshaw VP of Hovertek Inc, has a plan for his life. He's Mr. Go Slow. Fluent in Mandarin, he's captivated when he watches a sexy dancer in the house across his go through her moves. From the minute the two almost lock fenders at a turtle crossing to finding out Priya's the Bollywood dancer from his dreams, Dallas has only one goal: to make sure their paths are forever entwined and his dream world collide with reality.

There's only one problem: she's *so* not his type. Priya on the other hand is quite willing to let her feelings for Dallas go where they lead her. Preferably nowhere. She's not prepared to share her space with anyone. Been there done that. Her friends are her family. His family made him who he is. He makes her wish for things she never knew she wanted. They have their passion for pickleball, love of spicy food, Bollywood dancing and Rumi. Which should be enough, right?

In time, Priya changes her mind about Dallas for he's quite housebroken. She stops drifting and lets him be her anchor. Her safe harbour.

PICKLEBALL FACTS

Fun Pickleball Facts

It is the fastest growing sport in the world. The top four countries are: USA, Canada, Spain and India. Yes, India!

1. Number of places to play in 2017 was 5,876 and in 2019, 7938
2. 1st Nationals held in Arizona 2009: 400 participants. In 2017, 1300 players registered CBS sports network televised the event. In 2019, 2000 competed at the Margaritaville, California, for USA Nationals and $80,000 in prize money.
3. In 2017, 2.815 million players in the US alone an uptick of 12.3%. In 2019 there were 3.3 million players.
4. Core players in 55+ age range still dominate the numbers. 62% of players are men with average age of all players being 41. 84% casual players are 54 or younger.
5. 2020 marks the 55th anniversary of pickleball.

Source: SFIA Sports and Fitness Industry Association.

Game on, guys! You hit high, you die. You hit low, you blow. Paddles up!

CHAPTER ONE

PRIYA KEELOR STIRRED minced onion, garlic and ginger into fragrant butter and was just about to add spices when her phone rang. Putting the wooden spoon down on the plate, she picked the phone up and, grabbing one of the bottles lined up on the counter, began adding spices. When she could smell the spices, she added meat and broth. On her way to the pantry, she opened the freezer, grabbed a frozen banana and put it in the blender. She was doing what she did best.

Multitasking.

She finished her conversation with her supplier and threw in a handful of fresh spinach and a piece of ginger into the blender. Almond milk got it all moving along. While it buzzed-she had fifty-five seconds-she walked into the pantry to get the bag of flour. She reached up, hauled the hefty bag down from the shelf and nestled it against her waist. The air whooshed out of the bag and a cloud of white misted her face.

Bloody hell! One of her beautiful purple fingernails poked through the bag of flour. It had taken forever to get them growing just the right length and for once she'd been determined to have sleek fingernails, caving in to her own opinion about how long nails had no place in a kitchen.

"Bollocks!" She plonked the heavy bag on the counter which brought up another shower of flour to dust her face. Involuntarily she licked her lips, getting the bland pasty taste of uncooked flour into her mouth. "Aargh!"

Her assistant, Mark Bowers, raised his head from the tray of chocolate fudge cookies, the red velvet icing hovering.

"You could've asked," Mark's blue eyes twinkled as they leveled their gaze at Priya's powdered face and torso. "Or used the skinny ladder."

"That'll be the day," Priya mumbled and shook her head, thankful her hair was covered with a red bandana. A white dust billowed in the air, swirling and mingling with the aroma of spices. "Smoothie?"

"Sure. Hey, don't forget to show me what you planned for the fundraiser."

"No worries. I got it."

Priya poured the smoothie into two glasses and set one in front of Mark. Her mouth already salivating, Priya took a sip, anticipating the delicious taste of sweet banana with the zing of ginger. Instead, out poured the very same jet of green from her mouth and splattered on the floor of the immaculate kitchen, just missing the cookie tray.

"Byauck," she stuck her tongue out. Shuddering, she threw her plastic glass into the sink where it rolled and sprayed dots of green all over the counter and floor before it tumbled and rocked to a stop.

"What the hell?" Mark yelled and took a step back. He was too late. A splotch of green decorated his snazzy yellow sneakers.

Priya rushed to the sink, leaving behind a cloud of flour. She turned the faucet and held her mouth under it. Then she let water run over her face to get the flour off.

Multitasking again as usual. What the water did was create

rivulets down her face making the rest of the flour cling together in stubborn desperation. Mark gave one look at her and burst out laughing. Then he pointed at the smoothie.

"Not banana," Priya managed to form the words, all the while feeling thoroughly disgusted. "Sausage. Sausage smoothie."

"F…shit, Priya! You know you can't give me meat. I'm trying to be a vegetarian. Or vegan. Whatever. You shouldn't tempt me with a sausage smoothie of all things." He paused. "What kind?"

"Chipotle."

Mark smacked his lips and sighed. "My absolute favourite. It was the one thing keeping me from turning vegan completely."

"It was the last one too."

"What a waste." Mark's lips twitched, threatening to bloom into a quivering smile and Priya was just about ready to fall into a puddle at his feet.

He was gorgeous from the tip of his golden head to the broad chest, from the well-formed biceps to what she knew for certain were ripped abs and pecs. And he was stubbornly gay.

When she was done with cleaning up the mess, Priya checked the pot simmering on the stove before she went out the side door to back up the van. It was an eye-catching yellow with the Spice Haven's logo in raspberry pink.

"Done?" she asked Mark, pointing to the trays.

"Yep. All hundred and fifty of them."

"Okay. Let's load it all up."

When they were done loading, Mark got into the driver's seat. "See you there, Priya. In a bit. I'm sure you need to change into something less powdery."

"Give me twenty minutes and I'll be there. Layla and Mia will be there to set it up."

With a wave, Mark roared off.

. . .

After the gig and the cleaning up, Priya got out of her work clothes and slipped into shorts and a sleeveless T-shirt. She rolled her long hair together and stuffed it under a baseball hat. With heavy limbs, she got into her truck.

She drove down Princess past Bayridge, the AC cranked up and Metallica's *Until it Sleeps* blasting through her speakers. Coming down the hill, she sped up to pass the white SUV in front of her before the double lanes merged. As she was about to pump the accelerator of her yellow truck, the SUV in front of her came to a sudden stop, its break lights flashing red.

Easing her foot off the gas, she had seconds to act: either swerve to the side or hit the SUV in front of her. After glancing in the rear view mirror-thank God no cars behind her-she yanked the steering wheel. Her truck sailed to the right of the SUV and came to a screeching halt, making her head jerk forward and back. She'd only just missed the guardrails.

What the bollocks does the jerk think he's doing?

Priya unbuckled her seat belt and got out of the truck slowly. Emerging from the cool confines of her truck, a wave of heat hit her. The driver of the SUV got out of his vehicle too, stopping right in the middle of the road.

"Hey, great stop there! And lucky there were no cars behind you."

She could have killed herself and all he had was compliment her on her driving moves?

"What the hell was that? You almost made me drive off the road!" Priya balled her hands into fists, ready to pop him one should the need arise. Not only did she have to drive safely, now she had to watch out for nincompoops like him too?

She walked up to him. He was huge but that didn't deter her. She raised her elbow and poked it in his belly. He stood firm and didn't budge.

"Hey, you okay?" The deep and pleasant voice slithered into

her ears and into her body. "Sorry about that." His apology confused her.

"Bollocks! Sorry is not going to cut it. I almost hit the bloody guardrails."

Then she planted both palms on his chest and shoved! Hard. He didn't budge. She lifted her foot and kicked him in the shins. At least she tried to. Bending down, he reached out his arms and pinned *her* arms to her sides. No tough feat at all. She couldn't move an inch. Hell, not even one-eighth of an inch!

"Take it easy for a second, okay? Guess you didn't see the Turtle Crossing sign, huh?"

What the....oops! Plus he had a yellow 'I break for turtles' sticker on his bumper.

"And missed the adorable turtles crossing the street?"

Despite the heat, he did not even break into a sweat while she was panting like a dog.

"Stop squirming, will you? I'll let go of you if you just stop trying to hurt me."

Double fudge!

She detected a hint of laughter in his voice. He let go of her arms, stepped back and pointed to the sign. On the road in front of him, a dark mound with four tiny legs followed by a smaller one drifted slowly over with traffic on the other side at a halt too.

Turtles crossing.

Just like the yellow sign said.

What the hell was the matter with her? She was cool and collected when faced with tough situations. Could she blame Metallica?

Priya felt like crawling into a hole and disappearing. It was not like her to attack strangers. Furious at herself, she had no other choice other but to admit her mistake. And how she hated that!

She turned toward him, reluctant to utter the words stuck in her throat.

He was tall and broad-shouldered with dark, longish hair and a sexy beard. Dressed in grey slacks and a dark blue silk shirt tucked in, he was cool and collected, whereas she'd been prepared to do bodily harm to the gentle giant while in a hot and bothered condition. At least six feet two compared to her measly five-two. And bloody hot too! He was everything she wasn't.

"I'm awfully sorry. I can't believe I missed the sign." She tried her best to eat humble pie convincingly all the while aware the attempt was half-hearted at best.

Umm, pie. A huge slice of apple cinnamon would be nice. No, her favourite was rhubarb and ginger. Did she have rhubarb in her freezer? Saliva gathered in her mouth and his next words kicked her out of her sweet and tart trip.

"Are you okay? That was quite a stop you made there."

"I'm fine." She raised her right arm and rubbed the back of her neck, still floating on the rhubarb trip. She saw his eyes flicker over the butterfly tat on her wrist then catch the stud in her nose.

"No whiplash from getting your head jerked?"

"No, I'm good. Sorry, once again." She mumbled that last bit.

By now, the turtles had reached the other side of the road and disappeared in the surrounding wetland.

"No worries. Take care. And again, be careful about confronting strangers. You never know."

She shrugged one shoulder, got in her truck and he waved her forward, following her until the next turn.

~

DALLAS DROVE THROUGH the newly paved surface on Gardiner's in Kingston, on the shores of Lake Ontario, now an inky smudge disappearing into the hazy horizon. Kingston was once a busy port servicing the St. Lawrence Seaway. The day was hot like it never had been before and Dallas Crenshaw loved it. He was *made* for hot and heavy weather with his skin staying cool through it all. He even refused to have AC in his home despite the constant nagging from his brothers who were wilting wimps during Kingston's intense summers.

Exhaustion hit Dallas as he walked through the glass doors at Hovertek Inc. He was more exhausted from dealing with people than with his duties as an engineer for the city's project. He loved the latter and hated the former. The Veep and in charge of software-integrated design used in surveillance, search and rescue at Hovertek, Dallas did not usually deal with a lot of people. But heading the waterfront development the city had promised in the recent election campaign was turning out to be quite the juggle.

A mile stretch of the lake shore with two beaches, splash pads, three piers jutting hundred feet into the water and a tree-lined walk way, it was an ambitious plan he was proud to be part of. Not to talk about the countless people it took to make it all work.

The receptionist's desk area was a slab of polished wood in pale grey. A vase filled with fragrant white blossoms occupied a spot near the telephone. Marion, pretty in a pale blue sundress, was up and about with a blue tooth headset, inspecting the plants.

"Hey, Marion," Dallas stopped by her, sniffing as he went by the white blossoms. "Are these peonies from your garden?"

"Aren't they gorgeous?" She took a deep breath. "They smell heavenly. To think we can smell them for only two weeks. Two weeks!"

"Beauty is fleeting, I'm afraid," he grinned at her, his dimples showing.

She nodded to him and raised a finger as she answered a call. Dallas waved to her and strode to his office down the corridor.

Settled behind his desk, his fingers fiddled with the wings of a delicate mechanical dragonfly while his mind was far away. He went home distracted and out of sorts, his mind playing the almost fender-bender over and over again. It was not like him to be captivated for it had indeed been the case. Since his breakup with Kate about two years ago, he'd put his ability to be charmed and captivated on the back burner.

No, his mind was playing tricks on him. It was five years ago since Kate.

Fuck!

Time had flown by and he hadn't even noticed! Was he so out of it? Didn't he want the whole crazy basket of a wife and kids anymore?

The memory of the encounter with the tiny, angry and kicking truck-driving person made Dallas smile. Her truck was so yellow he had closed his eyes behind the sunglasses. She was lucky he was a calm and pleasant guy, which had not impressed her in any way.

Anyway, who says 'bollocks?'

When he got out of his car, he'd welcomed the heat on his chilled skin. He had to stop cranking up the AC. As the door of the yellow truck opened, Metallica's *Until it Sleeps* blasting through the speakers assailed his ears. The driver got out of the truck slowly.

She got out of the truck slowly. And it was a tiny 'she.'

He'd been relieved when she appeared to be regretting her outburst. And being the nice gentleman he was, he accepted her apologies.

She'd hitched her shorts up, pulled at the sleeves of her T-shirt and re-positioned the Blue Jays hat on her head. Her face had flushed a pretty colour, the pulse at the base of her throat beating rapidly, drawing his eyes to it and then down to where a vine tat peeked out. He noticed the butterfly tat on her wrist and the flash of a nose stud.

Images of the angry yet hot package rolling before his eyes, Dallas sat on the deck in his new house nursing a cold beer. He was eager for the deadlines and meetings for the opening of the Breakwater Park in July, a month down the line, to be over.

Everything was under control, but tell that to the nervous staff, fluttering about like jumpy grasshoppers.

It had been a stressful eight months dealing with a shit load of people who didn't know a thing about engineering and even less about software. If not for the cool and laid back approach of the mayor and the support of his engineer brother Houston and marketing bro Austin, Dallas would have given up months ago. The mayor was an insightful politician with just the right words at the right time. Like all great leaders, she was the pacifier and the soother of egos.

CHAPTER TWO

PRIYA, EAGER TO put the turtle incident from her mind, got home in time to receive her bestie, Marie Nilsson who was in town for a few days. Marie came in an hour later, all chic and swanky in skin-tight jeans, a cropped top and silver earrings dangling from her ears.

"Missed you, babe," Marie put her arms around Priya and gave her a hug.

"Missed you more." Priya returned the hug. "You tired? Want to unpack before we hit the town?"

"Tired? What am I, fifty? I'll just wheel my clothes in and we can have a drink before the Uber arrives."

"Wine? Beer? What?"

"Tequila? Only if you have lime."

They licked salt off the back of a hand and knocked back a couple of shots of tequila each, finishing each gulp of tequila with a wedge of lime.

"You got hold of Mia?"

Mia Tucker their friend from college days, also Priya's catering business partner.

"Yep. She's going to meet us at The Boat."

"Great! Haven't seen her in ages." Marie rubbed her palms together.

They walked in the door of the dry docked boat with the bar/restaurant/pub in its humongous hull. Priya stopped before a wall of glass, all blue and green, separating dry humans from wet fish, her eyes darting from one magnificent specimen to the other: from the colourful fish to the wondrous impossibly perfect anemones; from the swaying carnivorous plant-like creatures to the tiny crabs and shrimp hovering over the grains of sand. She could stand and watch the inhabitants of the aquarium all day and was almost getting comfortable when Marie yanked her arm and pulled her toward Mia.

As they made their way to the booth passing by the bar, quite a few of the male patrons turned their heads to look at them. Marie, tall and blonde, in four inch heels and a short red skirt with a black silk blouse and Priya, a petite and dark brunette, also in four inch heels but jeans and a cropped top.

"Hey, girl! How are you?" Marie said to Mia who was in a booth. She slid on the blue vinyl seat and leaned back in the corner of the booth.

"Great!" Mia pointed to the pitcher on the table. "Some for you?"

"Sure."

"You too, Priya?"

"Right on. How's Josh?"

"He's great. Always so thoughtful, always so considerate. And..."

"Always my soul mate," Priya and Marie said in unison.

"Can't help it guys, if he's the most wonderful person in the world. I just adore him. I'm so lucky."

A deep sigh made its way through Priya's chest. At one time, Priya thought Simon had been the one. She had thought he was her soul mate too.

After they emptied the pitcher, they got hot wings, fries and more tequila shots. As she was downing her second shot, Priya's eyes met dark ones from across the room. She looked away, not interested. Even though he looked quite delectable: hair to his ears, neatly trimmed beard and T-shirt tight across his broad chest and jeans.

Priya just could not drum up even a smidgeon of interest since she'd broken up with Simon. They'd been together for five years, the latter two being the longest. She'd stopped counting the months first, then the years. Now time didn't even have the whiff of relevancy.

She poked Marie in the ribs. "You interested? There's a hot guy over there checking us out."

Marie leaned back and sighed. "No. I've given up men."

"Given up? As in celibate?" Priya's eyes almost popped out of her head. "What about Jason?"

"Time out for a bit. Been a few weeks now. After Jason, I need a break. He was too much of a man. Maybe he's spoiled me for all others. I just don't find the thought of sex exciting any more."

Priya's jaw dropped.

Mia let out a soulful groan. "Here we go again."

"Maybe it's not exactly sex but the person you associate it with." Priya was an expert on how chemicals in the female body came together with just the right person to create an addiction she'd never succumbed to. It had never been this mythical explosion for her. She was convinced it was all fiction. "This is the second time you've split up. Maybe you need someone quite unlike Jason. A change of scenery."

"I'll say. Scenery sounds like an apt way to describe it."

"Jason will be hard to match." Priya scrunched up her face, recalling a few choice details about Marie's sex life. "He's considerate and so tuned into you. Time you gave him back some consideration too."

"Yeah, I know. Like that Tantric stuff you're always harping about. I don't think it's for me though."

"You don't even know what it is." Priya was a theoretical expert on the Tantric stuff too.

In her bedroom, she had a carved box full of tools intended to take the physical pleasure to the theoretical interstellar level but she'd been too chicken to try it out with Simon. Sometimes she'd been very tempted to try the Tantric stuff on herself but then again she clucked and hid her head under the covers.

"Why don't you tell us then? Right Mia?" Marie drained her glass.

"Right," Mia fanned herself with a napkin. "Then I can teach Josh more of the sexy stuff and then we'll never get out of bed. Ever."

"Not in the mood right now to spew innocuous sexual information to non-believers. Maybe another time." Priya signalled for another round of shots.

Mia's phone pinged with a text. She quickly glanced at it and said, "Gotta go. Josh's home and we're going to make a baby."

"So it's that time of the month then?" Marie stared at Mia's crotch.

"Yep. Tick-tock. See you guys later."

"Looking forward to whatever you're going to pop out when you've been securely knocked-up," Priya twirled her glass in her hand.

"So guess what?" Marie reached for the glass of water and drained it. "Jason has a best friend here in Kingston."

Priya shrugged. "Hot?"

"Don't know. Only heard about him. Dallas Crenshaw. Maybe I should look him up."

"Thought you'd given up men."

"It's a flexible notion. Not actually counting on myself to *actually* adhere to it. Depends."

"On what?" A fry dipped in hot sauce disappeared into Priya's mouth. "Hah," she breathed, expecting fire to spew out.

"On how hot the candidate is."

Priya giggled. "So what else is new?"

"So what d'you think? Should I get in touch with him?"

"What the hell do I know about relationships? You do what you feel like. You've always done so anyway."

"Right. So nothing of that sort going on with you?"

"Not a chance in hell."

"What about that sport you play? Pickle cock? Pickle dick?"

"You forgot the most important one: Pickle*ball*. I love it. I hang out with oldies. Besides catering and Bollywood dancing, my first two passions, I can add pickleball to it."

Pickleball was her safe haven. A place she could turn up and not expect questioning looks thrown her way. The courts were her comfort-zone. She kept her final proclivity, the licence to snoop, to herself. Marie would only laugh. Make a snarky comment about her being the Jack-of-all trades. She might be but she certainly wasn't just master of none since she excelled at everything she did. Which was the problem. She just could not give any of it up.

"But there are single guys around, right? Who's running this town anyway? They can't *all* be retired."

"Well, there is one over there. Can't say if he's single though," Priya jerked her chin toward the bar.

"So you go for it."

"Nah. Feeling a lack of enthusiasm. I want to be excited. Be exhilarated at the thought. I want my heart to pound when I think of him. I don't want the wishy-washy, low level dopamine and endorphin state of arousal I had with Simon. I'm waiting for the ULTIMATE supernova."

"Maybe we could make a cocktail-hah! A cock *and* a tail of that."

"Already here. Called morphine."

"Aw fuck! Give me something I can use, Priya! I'm still not over Jason."

"What's that about Jason? Thought you guys broke up."

"Nah. Just taking a break."

"Right, as in breakup."

"As I said, nah we're just taking a time out. See if it's absence makes the heart grow fonder or out of sight out of mind. It's been a pretty intense ride with him. He wants to make it permanent, me not so much."

"Whoa, whoa. Back up for a minute. He wanted to make it permanent? Did he propose?"

"I stopped him before. Wasn't sure it was the right move for me."

"You're not sure after four years? How much time does it take?"

"I think it will take a bit more than a few weeks. How are your Bollywood lessons coming up?"

Marie and Jason were Priya's template for the perfect couple. If they couldn't make it, what chance did she have of achieving the same? When she didn't even want the same. She was not cut out to be someone's wife or someone's mother.

She was a drifter. Once she hit a rock and stumbled, she changed course. Look at what happened with Simon. She'd tried, telling herself he was the right one for her. For three years, she'd convinced herself he was her soul mate. Then she'd spent another two unconvincing herself.

She was free now. Free to drift along as she pleased. Play pickleball, put together fabulous menus for her catering business, dress in Bollywood style for her dance lessons and when all that was not enough, she put on her trench coat and was a PI for a bit, drifting from one interesting thing to the next.

"Classes are a hit. I always have a waiting list. I'm thinking of getting a bigger studio. But then I'd have to cut back on either the catering or my pickleball hours. Don't want to have to make a choice. So I might just leave the lessons as they are."

"Just thinking about all that you do makes *me* breathless. Don't know how you can keep it all together and still be good at *all* of it. You're so talented."

Priya waited for the snarky comment but it did not come.

"I accept your compliment with humility," Priya flashed Marie a smile. "My assistant Mark works with a charity: a women's shelter. He's asked me to plan an event with Bollywood dancing for the charity's next fundraiser."

"That's great! Right?"

"Hmm, yes. More opportunity to do the thing I love most, which will involve more shopping."

"So you planning on coming to Toronto?"

"Yes soon. Hopefully, the charity's board will be as enthusiastic as Mark."

After Marie left, Priya was blue for a day or two. On the low point of her blueness, she sat in the office of the catering kitchen, going over the schedule: the mayor's gig was up next. Her calendar had just the right amount of empty spaces to keep it from becoming routine.

The mayor did not want dessert: only fresh fruit. And just like that inspiration hit her and the low blue point of her days was over. Berries, arranged in a pretty row with orange and yellow melon chunks, danced in front of Priya's eyes.

She even thought she could make it to pickleball. It had been a week since she'd played and she was looking forward to getting back to it again. When Priya got home from pickleball, she took a long shower and sat on her deck reading until the stars came out.

Then Priya changed into a long, blue skirt with sequins, a short, matching bustier blouse and a transparent blue diaphanous veil. She tied bells around her ankles and Indian jewellery around her neck, arms and head.

She slid her favourite Bollywood epic into the DVD player and selected the songs to play. She danced with the images flickering on her TV. She swayed to the songs, the music seeping into her blood, alone in her fantasy world.

Or so she thought.

CHAPTER THREE

DALLAS SAT ON his deck in the quiet of the night, the sky still glowing with the last embers of the setting sun. In a few minutes the sky turned dark and the stars popped up one by one. He rolled the cold bottle of beer across his forehead. Light poured out of the house opposite his. His deck was at a higher level and he had a clear view right into the living room. The patio doors were open as were the windows. Soft music drifted out. Something tinkled.

Bells?

And then he saw her. For there was no doubt it was a woman. In a flowing glittering dark skirt, she moved to and fro, hips shaking, arms moving. He leaned forward. Her body undulated, her shoulders shook, her hips swayed and his breath caught in his throat. It was so beautiful. It tugged at his insides. It was damned sexy to say the least.

There was something familiar about it though. He knew this. It took him a few minutes to wade through his memories.

It was when he'd been at the UofT. His roommate, Nikhil, had a sister who was a dancer. He'd invited Dallas to her performance. He recalled now how fascinating the performance had been. How sensual.

How could he have forgotten such a beautiful memory?

He sat for a long time after the dancer had finished, staring at the sky yet seeing nothing, his whole body still vibrating from the sounds of the bells and the music. The sensations began softly in his belly, sending goose bumps down his thighs and legs, radiating warmth up to his chest. When the feelings ebbed, he was left with something vague tearing at his inside, yearning for what he couldn't say.

The next morning, Dallas woke up early as usual. He quickly kicked the thin sheet from his body and got up, stretching. He heard the coffee machine rumbling and soon he smelled the enticing aroma of the fresh brew. He sat down at the desk in front of the window, cradling the coffee mug. Pink fingers of dawn tinged the fading dark sky.

He flipped open his laptop and pulled up the book he was working on. Not that there was much to go on. It wasn't a book yet. He was an undisciplined writer, moody and erratic. He hadn't even thought about what he was going to write: fiction or non-fiction. He'd been doing this for a few weeks now. Every morning, he got up, sipped his coffee and sat at the desk. And every morning all he did was write drivel, which he could do, pages and pages of it.

He was not ready to draw from his experiences in Afghanistan. Somehow his fingers refused to connect with the words bubbling in his mind and stubbornly refused to flow. He now stared at the drivel on the screen, then stared at the blossoming dawn and finally gave up. He shut his laptop and got ready to go for a run and then to play pickleball.

At pickleball, Dallas clipped his bag on the chain link fence. He noticed someone on the far court carrying a bag holding the frame and net, losing the struggle to prevent the bag from scraping her legs as it bounced to and fro with her stride. She began unzipping the bag and taking out the green metal frames.

As his shadow fell over her, she looked up.

She wore sunglasses and a Blue Jays hat tucked low on her head. She was wearing tight black shorts and a sleeveless top. Roses climbed up the side of her neck and disappeared behind. There was the butterfly tat he'd seen before, all green and red on one wrist. Another vine crept from below her collarbone and came out on the other side of her top. He couldn't help but stare-thank God for the dark glasses-at the gold pendant swinging to and fro, almost dipping into her cleavage and at the shiny nose stud.

"Need help?" he asked, his eyes hidden behind bug-eye sunglasses. They glinted with blue and yellow colours.

"Sure," she said, holding out her hand for a shake.

"Dallas Crenshaw," his hand engulfed her small one. He held on to her hand, frowning. "Turtle crossing? A few days back?"

She cringed. Her hand tensed. "Oh, God. It's you! Never thought I'd see you again."

She gave a nervous laugh. He could almost read her mind. She'd probably hoped to put the wretched incident out of her mind. But obviously, it wasn't going to happen.

"Well, this is a small town. It's been known to happen."

"Priya Keelor. Nice to meet you. Wait a sec. Crenshaw? You know a Jason Briggs?"

"Yes. My best friend since we were yea high." His palm stretched about three feet from the ground. "Do you know him?"

"Yes. He's my best friend's ex or something. Don't know for sure."

"Small world."

"You see him often?"

"He comes to Kingston a few times a year. I visit him in Toronto a couple of times. We keep in touch."

"Indeed. Know how to set up?"

"Yes, I do."

Together, they finished setting up two courts. When they were done, they got ready to play. Dallas grabbed a paddle from his bag and trotted over to her on court three.

"Start over? Like this is the first time we've met? I want to forget the duck incident, I mean turtle incident."

"All right. No problem with me. Truce then? No more trying to knock me down?"

"If you behave, I'll have no problem either."

She flashed him a gorgeous smile.

"Been playing long?" Priya asked, her gaze protected by the sunglasses.

"Couple of years, mostly at the Y and a bit at the drop-in courts. Not many places in Kingston. Then I heard about this place. Fabulous courts. You live here, in Bath?"

"No, in Kingston. Been playing here a few years, though. Welcome to the club."

Even with the sunglasses on he felt the intensity of her gaze. It was something to be tackled later.

Just then she cupped her hands around her mouth and bellowed, "Two more on court three."

Dallas took a step back, stuck a finger in his ear and wiggled it. She had some voice on her for such a tiny person. He muttered to that effect under his breath.

"I'm sorry, what?"

"Nothing," he shrugged, something he was very good at. He used it to convey myriad of sentiments.

Priya giggled. "Sorry about that. Peeps are not paying attention. Let's go. Let's go guys!" She waved and, putting two fingers in her luscious mouth, she whistled.

Her giggle charmed him into a smile. Two more players joined them and Priya got ready to serve.

"You playing in your sandals?" Dallas pointed to Priya's feet, silver anklets around her pretty feet.

She kicked off her sandals. " Oops! I'll just play without shoes."

"Sure?" he bent down and touched her toenails. "Interesting colour."

"It's called Deep Purple Haze."

"Very original," he grinned at her.

She looked like she was trouble with a capital T.

"Zero zero two," she said and launched the ball over the net, deep to the base line.

The player across the court stood too close to the base line and scrambled back, back pedalling.

"No, no," Dallas heard Priya say. "No back pedalling. Please don't fall."

The ball came back to him and he missed it. "Sorry," he said.

"There is no sorry in pickleball," she replied, adjusting her hat, making him wonder what was beneath it.

A bit more of the vine tat became visible. His eyes zoomed in on it immediately. An on-site perusal was what he had in mind. But being Mr. Go Slow, he slapped his leg with his paddle instead.

Sharply. The paddle bit into his thigh.

"Concentrate, moron. Focus!" he muttered under his breath.

"I'm sorry, did you say something?" her voice boomed from her side of the court.

"Nothing," he waved his paddle in the air.

The next ball came through the middle.

"Yours!" Priya called out, the soft jingle from her anklets told him she'd moved forward too soon.

"Hole in the paddle," he mumbled to himself.

"What?" he heard her say.

He called for a time out. She shrugged, the tat on her neck stretching with the uplift of her shoulder. He knew that shrug. It wasn't quite as disdainfully eloquent as his but she still managed to convey quite a bit of nonchalance. She was going to make pickleball interesting.

"Look, Priya. If the ball is in the middle, the one whose forehand it is gets it." He kept his tone out of the lecture zone. "And maybe, just maybe, you need shoes to play pickleball."

"Oh yeah? Is that a rule?" It was obvious to him his tone brought out the trouble in her. She stood with hands on her hips, looking up at him, her chin up in the air.

"Sorry to disappoint you, but yes it is." It felt good to be staring down at her from behind his sunglasses. He briefly thought about crowding into her space with his body but decided against it. He grinned at her, determined not to make an issue of it.

If it isn't, it is now.

"Okay. Got it," was her mild reply. She backed off, rubbing the back of her neck, as if she was getting a crick in her neck.

She surprised him. He'd expected her to be argumentative. Maybe even get physical and jab him in the side. Most of all, he expected her to be sore at losing the point. He saw her lips curl before she turned away. He couldn't make out whether it was a smile or not. A brief glance over his shoulder told him she was looking at him. Her felt her eyes burn a hole in his back as he walked to his side.

A barely there tickle ran up his spine.

This was going to be pretty interesting. He hadn't had a reaction to a woman like this since his breakup with Kate. And there it was again: the soft sound from the anklets she wore.

Fuck, that's sexy.

At the end of the game, they returned their paddles to the stand. Priya took a swig from her water bottle and moved her chair to a shady spot. Dallas plopped down next to her on the bench.

"You mutter a lot to yourself, don't you?" she squirted water on her cheeks. It dribbled down her chin and dropped into her cleavage.

His eyes followed the path of the water before he took off his glasses and hat to wipe his face with a moist towel. A gentle breeze lifted the heat from his face.

"Helps me get things in perspective."

She made a snorting sound and packaged it in a 'Pfff.'

"And what's that supposed to mean?"

He stole a glance at her. He felt naked without his glasses. She did not take the glasses or the hat off. All he could see were the tantalizing tats.

"Nothing," she shrugged, taking a page out of his own playbook.

Dallas appreciated all the various moulds a woman's body came in, each one an individually wrapped chocolate truffle, deliciously decadent and sweet. And their minds: forever mysterious and always a wonder.

He was going to enjoy playing here. If it meant seeing more of this intriguing bundle of contradictions, he'd make sure to come out here. He was always up for a challenge.

And this one appeared to be yanking his strings quite a bit.

CHAPTER FOUR

PRIYA BRUSHED HER hair back, tied it in a tight ponytail and secured a few loose strands with pins. She slid a net over her head. Over this came a blonde wig in a Coco Chanel style. She did her eyes and lips using the magnifying mirror and when she was done, she did not recognize herself.

Now came the fun part. She was a sometime PI who sometimes liked to snoop, feeling secure behind her licence. Since it did not bring in much revenue and only a huge lot of fun, she stuck to her catering business and the Bollywood dancing lessons. She pulled on shorts and a tank top, slipped her feet into sandals and she was ready to see what Hovertek was up to. She needed something for her blog, 'Things you should know about,' she put out every two weeks.

Every Tina, Diane and Mary had one so she began one of her own too. She was on her fourth issue. The first couple she'd written about the waterfront project, Breakwater Park, a project Dallas was part of. His name was right there. And that of his company too. As she re-read what she'd written-in her pre-Dallas days-she thought about how weird life was. After having played pickleball with him here she was going to snoop at his facility where he designed those design-oriented thingies. But that was Kingston for you.

Six degrees-three seemed reasonable-of separation.

In a smallish town like Kingston, everything was everyone's business. The sparkling glass and steel façade of Hovertek Inc. drew her attention like no other. Spread over at least two acres, it hugged the ground like a predator waiting to pounce. She'd read about it in *The Tribune* and wanted to know more.

She parked in the lot at Hovertek and walked through the door, looking around the white marble foyer. A curved tiled wall separated the security counter from the reception desk. Two security guards, in beige uniforms, were at the front desk. One stared at the monitors. The other didn't look up from the magazine he was focused on.

"Listen, my dog just ran into your lot and I can't find him. Would it be okay if I looked around outside for him?"

It was amazing how gullible people were. They didn't seem to realize the world was full of liars just waiting to take advantage of them. But she couldn't blame them. She did look the part. She even had a leash in her hand.

"That's okay. You go right ahead, Miss."

This was too easy. He didn't even look away from his monitor. Maybe he'd seen her coming and had already assessed her honesty. She was a bit disappointed. She'd wanted to show off her makeup. She wanted to flick her blonde hair at them, flutter her fake lashes at them.

Outside, there were no windows to peer in, as they were tinted *and* high above the ground. There was a door to the side marked 'Deliveries'. She strolled slowly to it, hoping to catch a delivery truck pull up so she could find out how their system worked.

She wanted in.

It was a large facility and she expected frequent deliveries. Ten minutes passed without a single delivery. She circled the complex once again and widened her inspection. She walked to the end of the grass-covered lot. By now, she was afraid the men in uniform would get suspicious so she hid behind a berm. Behind her, a chain link fence rose several feet into the air. On her belly, she peered at the building, her chin resting on her fists.

Finally, a black truck rolled toward the door. A man in brown uniform opened the back of the truck, rolled out a dolly piled with cardboard boxes and touched the wall next to the door. It slid open and he walked in with his load.

She wanted in badly.

In the thick hot air, a fly buzzed near Priya. Perched low as she was, a blade of grass poked up her nostril. She saw an ant scramble down one of her fingers into the thick network of grass. A trickle of sweat rolled down her cheek. The wig itched. She sat up, got a pencil from the pouch hanging from her belt and, sticking it in her wig, scratched.

That was her downfall.

One itch started another and before she knew it, she was on her back, all ten fingers in her fake hair. It was unbearable, like a literal itch in her pants. Only now she did not have to look for a private corner to indulge in it. She back-crawled down the berm and quickly made it back to her car. A brief glimpse in the mirror showed her wig leaning to one side and mascara streaking down one cheek. At home, in the bathroom, she yanked the wig from her head.

"Ah good," she moaned as she scratched her scalp.

Then she hit the Internet where she learned more about Hovertek than she'd done with the field trip. They were into design and software of all kinds of things related to surveillance, search and rescue. Backed by heavy defence contracts, Hovertek was also the lead engineer in the development of the waterfront Breakwater Park, which she'd known. It hadn't interested her until now.

Clicking on the 'About us' tab, she saw a picture of her pickleball partner Dallas Crenshaw. He was VP and one of two responsible for design and software, the other being Houston Crenshaw. A third Crenshaw, Austin, was in charge of marketing. The president was Joe Crenshaw and from the photo she figured it was the father.

Fingers poised on the keyboard, Priya began a draft of her blog. An hour later, *all* she had was a tentative title. Abandoning her blog, Priya went instead to the pickleball courts.

There were three other players setting up. Priya put her folding chair in the shade of the large maple, changed into her court shoes and went to join David Matheson, grabbing another net, a smile on her face.

Priya set up the nets near the gate. Bob Marshall was on the far courts. A few A-listers walked by.

These were the couples who only hung out with other couples. They lived in large waterfront houses, had a boat or two, jet skis and speedboats. They had boat parties, house parties and wine parties where a wine cellar was an absolute must. They did not look at her and did not offer to help.

Yep, she didn't care for them either.

Priya was a buy-a-bottle-at-a-time kind of person. Okay, maybe two because she hated to be out of wine. Her doormat said 'Home is where the wine is.' As she now took a swig from her water bottle, a shadow fell over her. She looked up.

Dallas Crenshaw.

"Ready?" Surprised at his short greeting, Priya nodded.

There was an edge about him today, his body giving off tension. He'd appeared so laid back and relaxed the other day. Even at the turtle crossing he'd given off a cool and unflustered vibe, laughing off her attempts at kicking him in the shin. She followed him, shamelessly looking him over. Dark hair peeked from under his hat. He wore a loose T-shirt over baggy shorts. Not much to see there. The large hand gripping the handle of the paddle was wound tight, the muscles in his arms tensing.

It wasn't a bad game. The last shot was aimed at her and she lunged at the ball, just barely missing it. The paddle flew out of her grip and clattered on the ground. The lunge brought her to one knee. Afraid of injuring her knee, she went with the fall, rolled into it and stopped flat on her back, getting back her breath.

They lost 13-15.

"You okay?" His shadow fell over her, the voice deep and pleasant, doing forgotten things to her body.

It brought him to her. It was worth the effort of almost scraping her knees. "Absolutely. Just needed a rest. These oldies are giving me a hard time today."

His lips twitched. She liked that. The tenseness she'd sensed earlier was gone. The next time, she'd get a laugh out of him instead of just a twitch of the lips. A very expressive mouth-um lip-it was. He reached down and pulled her to her feet.

"Good game." She draped a towel around her neck. This evening, she'd be taking care of the crick in her neck if she continued looking up at him.

"Was okay. Could have been better."

"You mean like win? That a better game?" She spoke to his chest.

"Yep."

"So you're one of *them*." Now she looked away as she spoke.

"One of what?"

"The competitive. The ones who *have* to win."

"Oh *that* kind! Yes, I do like to win. Otherwise where's the fun?"

She saw Bob Marshall on his way over after having finished his game too.

"Well then, here comes another one of your kind." She thrust her chin toward Bob making the rounds, stopping to chat. "He hates to lose even more than he loves to win."

"Is there a difference?"

"A big one. I think it's a man thing."

He threw back his head and laughed out loud, his body relaxed and his legs stretched out in front of him.

Two zip for her!

"You saying women don't like to win?"

"Oh, we do. Just not with paddles. Our ways are subtle. You'll never know until it hits you."

"Okay, O wise one. I'll give you this one."

"Good to see you, Papillon," Bob gave her a bear hug on his way.

"Me too," Priya wrapped her arms around him and returned the hug. Then Bob was on his way to socialize with the other members.

He was a charmer and a born salesman. He could charm a banana out of a monkey's hand even before it took a bite.

That was the other thing about pickleball: the players were all something. They all had successful careers and knew who they were while she did not even know what she was. She was into so many things nothing and everything stuck.

"So Papillon is for the butterfly on your wrist, I presume?"

His words brought her back before her thoughts began to wander.

Dallas took his hat off and rubbed a towel over his hair. He had the dark looks Priya found appealing. His hair was a deep brown, reaching below his ears. Sunlight hit the lighter streaks giving it a burnished tint. He had a sexy beard: it was clipped short and followed the curve of his jaw. It stopped at his ears where it faded into the short shorn hair of his sideburns. A moustache followed the contours of his upper lip and swooped down to meet the scruff on his chin.

"Yes. So you speak French? Papillon is French for butterfly."

"Yes."

"I shop at the Atwater market in Montreal a few times a year.

I love it there. It's so great to hear people jumping from one language to the other."

"So you speak French too?"

"Sure do. Bob used to live in Montreal. Actually many club members are from somewhere else. Bob was one of the first people to welcome me into his fold."

"He's a great player too. Been watching him."

From where she sat, she saw a straight nose and the beginning of-was that a dimple?-on one cheek. She asked him something trivial so he had to turn to her to answer. Threads of gold in his hair glinted as he turned his head her way.

"Yep, he is. What do you do, Dallas?" She knew of course, but still.

"Am a design-oriented engineer."

"Thanks for explaining it so well. But, here's the thing: what does it mean?"

"I put parts together from a design and then write the software to make the thing work."

"What thing?"

"Oh, anything from surveillance cameras and drones for search and rescue."

His eyes were a rich grey with flecks of chocolate and gold. He wore baggy shorts so it was impossible to form an opinion about the state of his butt. But no matter. She was more of eyes and shoulders kind of gal. He lived in a house in the west end.

"Family?" she raised her eyebrows. A swift glance at his fingers told her she was unattached. But maybe he was the type to not wear a ring.

"Have two brothers. Mom and Dad. *All* here in Kingston. Grew up here. You?"

He did not mention wife or kids.

"*All* alone. Used to live in Toronto. Moved here about five years ago after the death of my parents."

Actually it was after she'd broken up with Simon. But why bring that up?

"Sorry to hear about that."

"Don't be. They gave me my freedom," was her enigmatic reply.

She felt he wanted to ask more but just then Bob pulled up his chair beside her.

Bob said, "I see the important people have come to hit a few balls. Hmm. Hmm. No volunteers, eh Papillon?"

Priya shrugged. She didn't care. She was there to play ball. "It's okay, Bob."

"I'm home later. Drop by," he said.

"Not today. Tomorrow. Will text you before."

Mark sent Priya a text message.

YOU'RE IN! PROPOSAL A SUCCESS!

Priya was thrilled. Finally, some actual use for her dance lessons.

She plundered the boxes in her closet and laid out all the Indian dresses and dance costumes she had on her bed. She spent the remainder of the evening trying one outfit or the other, sliding jewellery on her arms and wrist, hanging gem-studded rings from the side of her nose, foregoing the Friday evening ritual of dancing to music, re-creating the times she'd been on stage.

It had been a long time since she'd performed, largely due to Simon's disdain. All she could manage was to get dressed up on Friday evenings and sway to the unforgettable rhythms.

Even now a flush rose to her cheeks when she thought about the day she'd dressed up in the swirling skirt, short blouse and jewelled veil intending to surprise Simon. He'd taken one look at her and burst out laughing.

And that had been the beginning of the end.

The unravelling lasted two years. It had been building up ever so slowly despite her best efforts to ignore the inevitable demise of their relationship. Simon's efforts to get her into a more sedate life style were in vain despite her willingness to be roped in.

Sighing, Priya folded the delicate fabrics back into the boxes and spent the remainder of the evening blasting her ears with Beethoven's Third, a sensual thirty minutes as the tempo increased and reached an orgasmic crescendo, before she crept into bed and fell asleep in a music-induced coma.

The next day, while her skin was still dewy with moisture, Priya inspected the contents of her pantry. She always took something spicy for Bob when she dropped in. Nothing caught her eye. Nothing inspired her until her eyes fell on the bunch of fresh cilantro sprigs.

Just as she was about to reach for it, her phone pinged with a text from Bob: **PLEASE SEND ME BILL'S NUMBER.**

She sent it to him.

Bob loved anything spicy so she took care to add seven green chillies. It was her magic number. Anything below was too mild and anything above scorched the ears. After buzzing the chutney, she opened the lid of the blender jar to transfer the content into a glass jar. The pungent fumes rose up to her nose and a wave of coughs hit her. She spent a few minutes getting over her lapse in judgment.

A riot of barks greeted her as she rang Bob's bell. She heard steps on the other side and then Anna's voice said, "Stop barking, Bella. Now."

Bella ignored her. Soon a tinny bark joined Bella's robust one. Chili. The smallest dog she'd ever seen. He'd fit into her handbag.

Then Anna was at the door. Tall and willowy with a short platinum bob and gorgeous grey eyes.

"Hi," she said, all smiles. "Come on in."

Priya stepped in and hugged Anna. She was the big sister Priya never had. They'd just had their patio re-done and Priya was eager to see it. Bella jumped at her, claiming attention. She bent down and scratched behind her ears. Before she went into an ecstatic swoon, Priya stopped.

"I brought chutney and samosas." She pointed to the bag she was holding.

"Yummy," Anna rubbed her belly with one hand while Chili nestled under her other arm.

"Don't be too happy. The chutney is very spicy. Maybe too hot for you."

"But I can have the samosas, no? With ketchup?"

"God, Anna. Ketchup? And samosas? It's a sacrilege."

"Gotta eat it somehow. Come on out. Bob's in the back."

"Why no pickleball today Anna?"

"Oh, the usual. Went to yoga. My dad called. So had to go and see what he wanted. Something with my mother. Came back. My neighbour next door called. She'd fallen and couldn't get up. So went over there. Called her daughter. She hasn't broken anything but I thought she should have it checked out. When that settled, my brother Art came over and stayed for ages. Then I had to take Chili to the vet. And now I'm going to enjoy your samosas."

"Why couldn't Bob take the dog to the vet?"

"He was busy with the yard."

"Hrmph," snorted Priya.

In the backyard, Bob was flicking through his phone. "Hey, Papillon. You made it."

"Brought you something. Anna is prettying it up."

She looked around. Bob looked up from the tiny screen. "Looks great, right?"

"It's beautiful, Bob."

The stones were greyish with yellow and red flecks. There was a gas fire pit.

"We'll get the plantings done next year. Beer?" Bob asked, putting his phone away.

"Sure."

He brought it in a frosty glass. Priya sighed, leaned back in her chair and took a deep swallow.

"None for you?"

Bob shook his head. "Gin and tonic a bit later."

Priya made a puking sound. "Don't know how you can drink that."

"One man's food is another man's poison."

"Hey, that's *my* line. Where did you get it?" Priya couldn't believe he was becoming literary.

"Fortune cookie. Had Chinese last night. Here check out the new pics of Billy. God, I miss him."

Just then, Anna strolled out, a platter in her hands bumping the door with her hip to close it. Hearing Bob's comment she said, "I'd love to see my new grandson more often too, but I rather like the buffer zone."

"Buffer zone?" Priya thought of the buoys on the water. Of waves crashing on the beach.

"Yeah. Between my daughter and us. Keeps us from getting too familiar. You know, absence makes the heart grow fonder kind of sentiment?"

"Or out of sight out of mind?"

"No, definitely the first one. The other one makes no sense. No sense at all. Unless it meant you were forgetting something. Or putting something off. But sometimes procrastination is good too, you know. Bob, can you bring out the other stuff I have on the counter?" she chattered on, taking control of the conversation as usual.

"I'll do it," Priya jumped up to get the food. Or she assumed it was. It could very well be candles.

With Anna, she never knew. But it was cheese, crackers and pasta salad. Then she went back for plates and cutlery.

"I'd like a large G&T, Bob. Bob!" Anna's stringent voice cut through the cloud in Bob's ear.

Bob had gone back to fiddling with his phone. Priya smiled. It was just like having a child: a big, grey-haired 60-something child. A child she could spend time with, spoil and then leave the monster she'd created without looking back.

"G&T. Chop chop!" Anna clapped her hands.

This was enough to distract Bob from the screen. "Coming right up, dear."

When they were all settled again, Bob dipped his samosa in the green chutney and took a bite.

"This is so lovely. So good." He dipped into the chutney again. "Delicious."

Priya saw Anna take quick looks at Bob. Could almost visualize her thought process. It could be like this: It seems delicious. Look at his face. Maybe I will try some. At its worst, I'll have to sedate my taste buds.

Her eyes followed Bob's hands: piece of a cracker, stuck deep into the fiery chutney scooping as much as the cracker could hold, then stuffing it into his mouth. The smacks of his lips did much to egg Anna on. "How bad can it be?"

Oh. it was bad. Very bad. One G&T-big mistake-two glasses of water *and* a bowl of plain yogurt, it was still bad. Her eyes watered, her nose turned red and she kept sticking one finger in her ear.

It was ear-burning bad.

Yet she insisted, "It wasn't too bad. Not bad at all." She refused to admit defeat. She was not a quitter.

"Hrmph!" Priya snorted.

She went home, content and at peace. Bob and Anna did that. All she had to was pop in and voilà! Her blues were blown away.

CHAPTER FIVE

DALLAS WALKED DOWN the glass walled corridor to the testing area in the Hovertek basement. The latest design, the Dragonfly, was not working as he'd programmed it. If it were human, he'd have said it was being stubborn. It was an in-ground camera with extremely sensitive motion and heat sensors hard-wired into the frame. Coupled with the software, it should have been a piece of cake to make the fucking thing sink down into the ground after sending data to the mainframe.

He fiddled with the drone. The wings fluttered delicately, reminiscent of a real dragonfly. Dallas sent it up to the ceiling of the underground testing laboratory. When he finished with it, he stopped by the unit monitoring the exterior of the facility. The team was going over the feed from one of the exterior cameras.

"What's that?" He pointed to the monitor on his left.

His tech whizz, Gus Anders, punched a few keys. "Someone on the berm, trying to stay hidden."

"Can we get a cleaner image?"

Gus punched a few more keys then shook his head. "This is the best."

"Is the camera not working properly?"

"No, it's not the hardware. I have to go over the software and tighten some of the areas. I'm on it."

On screen was the grainy image of a figure with blond hair. Even after cleaning the image, it was difficult to say whether it was a man or a woman. There was brief glimpse of something round after which it was only grey sky.

"Any idea who would be interested in our affairs?" Gus swivelled in his chair to look up at Dallas.

Dallas shrugged. "Could be competitors or just a curious citizen. Either way, we have to improve the feed from the cameras." He patted Gus on the shoulder. "I know you're on it. Okay, Gus. Talk to you soon."

Glad to have the respite of the weekend in front of him, Dallas did not take his troubles home with him. Instead he immersed himself in another kind of trouble: the sensual image of a dancer in an exotic costume, her moves pulling at him, reeling him in.

To what, he couldn't say.

On a scorching Saturday, Dallas drove to Hovertek in response to a text from a weary-sounding Houston. Other than the engineering and software of their products, Dallas put together proposals, reports and press releases, all involving anything to do with writing. He'd been just about to head to Bath to play pickleball when Houston texted him about needing his fast and furious word skills.

As he walked in through the door, Marion pointed to the corridor. "He's in there, pacing as usual."

Through the glass insert, Dallas saw Houston walk to one end of his office, hands clasped behind his back, turn and then walk to the other side. He swung open the door so suddenly Houston had to jump out of the way. It was a large room, with a bank of windows looking out the front of the building. On one side was a long drafter's table.

"There you are! Been waiting all morning."

"You just texted me about fifteen minutes ago. Where's the fire?"

Houston handed him a file, then pointed to the screen. "Go ahead. This is what you're good at. Do your thing with the words."

"Then move." Dallas shoved Houston out of the way, sat down in the fabulously ergonomic chair and adjusted *all* the settings on it. He stuck wireless earbuds in his ears, plugged in the stick-like MP3 player and hit a button.

"Wait a minute, wait just a sec," Houston waved his hands in front of Dallas's face.

Dallas looked up, removed one earbud. "What?"

"Why're you blocking your ears? What's with the earbuds?"

"Music. I need it to write. Plus then I can't hear anything you say. Blocks out the white noise, you know?"

"I'm white noise? You need to be somewhere?"

"Sure. Pickleball first. Then later it is uncle's day with the Emma and Olivia. You've forgotten as usual. It's Saturday! Remember?"

"No I haven't. I thought it was Austin's turn with the girls."

"He had them last week. Now it's my turn. I'm missing pickleball. Now skedaddle." Chuckling, Dallas stuck the earbuds back in and hit the play button.

After he got back home, Dallas took a shower and put on fresh clothes. His hair still damp, he got in his car to go to pick up his nieces.

As soon as his car turned into the driveway, they rushed out of the house to greet him. Emma climbed into his arms and onto his shoulders as if he were a tree while Olivia waited patiently for him to untangle himself from her sister's limbs and hair.

He took Emma and Olivia to the Playtrium where it was cool

inside. Emma, eight years old, and solidly built, had long, curly blonde hair and her grandmother's grey eyes, while Olivia, the wise ten year-old had his father's dark hair-cut short for her swim team-and amber eyes.

Inside, the barriers fell off. Olivia became the child she still was. They climbed the ropes with other kids. They ran and chased each other while Dallas liked to tell himself he was working when all he did was stare into space with his laptop open.

"Uncle Dallas, we're hungry." Emma jumped from one leg to the other as if her hunger was trying to get away, chewing on an end of a blonde, loose strand.

"What about you, Olivia? You hungry too?"

"Yes, me too," she said, quite the lady now where only seconds before she'd been running around screeching.

"Right. But you know what you're allowed to have?"

"Fries and water."

"And why?"

"Because everything else is crap!" Olivia leaned against him. "Crap! Crap!" she repeated, delighted with words forbidden at home.

"And what else?"

"No slush."

"We'll stop for ice cream on the way back home." He gave them money and they ran off to get their fries.

While they sat munching their junk food of the moment, Dallas untied Emma's hair and tried to get it tamed. He ran his fingers through her long and silky curls, lifting it up and tying it with an elastic band high up on her crown. When they were done, the girls ran back to the playground, full of energy again.

Dallas could have worked on something. Instead he sat there, fingers idle and mind busy with thoughts flitting from the grainy figure on the berm to the exotic dancer across the street and to Priya Keelor on the pickleball courts. It would be easy to find out the identity of the dancer but he was reluctant, content to let it be his fantasy. The Mr. Go Slow at work again.

When the girls were done, Dallas carried Emma in his arms while Olivia hung on his back.

"It's good to be outside," Olivia's hands almost cut the air off to his lungs. "It was noisy in there."

"Too heavy, too heavy," Dallas groaned and stumbled for effect as they almost got to his SUV.

"You're sure, Uncle Dallas? You're so big. And tall. Like Daddy. You must be strong." Emma wiggled in his arms. "Don't you eat meat? Meat makes you strong."

"You smell so good, Uncle Dallas," Olivia stuck her nose in his neck. She dug into his sides with her knobby knees. "Come on. You can make it. The car's just there."

He opened the door and threw Emma gently on the back seat. He untied Olivia from his back and neck. They got in and buckled their seat belts.

"I see you guys are too tired. And sleepy. So we go straight home, right?"

"No, no," Emma jumped up and down in the seat. "You promised ice cream."

"Yes, you promised. Cross your heart and hope to die promised," Olivia wiggled.

"Did not. Just said we'd stop."

"No, you promised." Now both of them sang it out loud in the close confines of the car. "You promised."

"Ouch! Okay girls. We'll stop. Now please stop shouting. My ears hurt."

"I want strawberry swirls," Emma announced.

Dallas was relieved. Emma usually chose one of those horrific blue and purple flavours. Blue stains were impossible to get out of clothes, according to Houston since Emma usually looked like her cone after she finished hers.

"And you, Olivia?"

"I want praline. Hmm...Yummy."

"Are you getting ice cream too, Uncle Dallas?" Emma asked.

"Am too. Chocolate chunks for me. Anytime."

They got cones-covered with sprinkles for the girls-and sat under the shade of a tree after Dallas armed himself with a wad of paper napkins. When they were done, he rinsed Emma's hands with water he had in the car. Olivia did not have a sticky spot anywhere: not on her body and not on her clothes.

Houston was in the yard mowing when Dallas drove up and Lara was on the deck reading, under the shade of the parasol with a glass of iced tea near her. Houston lived in a spacious, beautiful Craftsman style house on two floors. It had a wide covered porch in the front and sat on a two-acre lot with landscaping done by Austin of course.

"Got to use the printer, Lara," Dallas stuck his head out of the patio doors.

"No problem. Go ahead."

Dallas went down the hall to Houston's office, stuck the USB stick in the port and printed the files he'd just completed for Houston. He collated the papers and stacked them in piles on Houston's desk.

"You staying for dinner?" Houston, done with mowing, stood in the kitchen chugging cold beer, a towel tied around his waist. "Boy! It's really hot out there. Just took a shower and I'm sweating already. How about a beer?"

"No can do. Gotta go." Dallas wanted nothing more than to get home, have a cool shower and lounge on his couch with the TV on.

"Can I please play with my iPad, Daddy?" Emma was ready to tackle the next activity.

"Twenty minutes. I'm setting the timer. When it rings, iPads off. Okay?"

"Okay, Daddy." Olivia ran to her room.

"In here. You do that in the living room, please, girls."

"Okay."

Dallas left them doing their things and drove home where, after yet another cool shower, he lounged on his couch listening to music deciding on a plan of action about Priya. There had to be one since she was not his usual type. Decision made, Dallas popped a bottle of cold Corona and ordered a pizza. When it arrived, he bit into his oozing oh-not-so-good-for-him delicious piece of hot heaven.

Then one thing led to another on YouTube, and before he knew it he was listening to Sufi music. If he'd thought the sitar was an amazing instrument, the Sufi voices were an amazing gift to his ears. The rhythm, the harmonics, the voices all came together to give him goose bumps.

Hours later, he got up and stumbled upstairs to his bedroom. It was as if he was drunk, intoxicated from all those waves of music in his ears. He plopped on his bed fully clothed and fell into a deep and dreamless sleep.

The song of a lonely robin woke him up around 3 a.m. As sleep relinquished its hold, a new awareness came from the rumble in his belly: he was starving.

In the kitchen, he made himself a bowl of cereal, the sweetest one he had in his pantry and sat on his deck, eating and watching the shroud of the night sky give in to the faint amber glow of the day.

His eyes still awash with sleep, swept briefly over the patio doors across his yard on the other side, not registering anything concrete. Going back inside, he put the bowl in the sink, ran water into it and went back upstairs to bed. This time, he took off his clothes and slid under the sheets in his boxers. This time, vivid dreams painted his sleep. Dreams filled with haunting melodies and a body moving to the sounds.

CHAPTER SIX

PRIYA, READY TO storm the Hovertek fortress, was in full combat uniform: baggy pants with numerous pockets filled with useful stuff.

The star of her storm trooper arsenal was a Swiss army knife, though why the Swiss had an army was beyond her. It had twelve gizmos including a toothpick *and* everything except a gun. It sagged in her pocket, its weight dragging it down. So she clipped it to her waist.

Around her thigh was a lock pick set. Though it would do shit with electronic keypads. She wore a lightweight belt with pouches in which she carried night goggles, a can of pepper spray, a smoke bomb, a plastic bottle with vegetable oil and darts. She had bags of marbles weighing her down, a wad of gum and a pen that lit up. Because she couldn't bring her baseball bat, she brought her switchblade. She also had a squirting ink pen, a metal knuckle, some rope, a hammer, nails, a battery operated mini-drill and a thingamajig with three prongs.

Her combat T-shirt was short and skimpy. Where she showed skin, she smeared black makeup. There was a spotlight in her headband. In one of the loops in her belt, she slipped a water bottle filled with sweet mint tea.

It was easy enough to get through the delivery door. She didn't need a key card or a code. She just pressed a button and the doors opened. Priya puffed her cheeks up and blew out air. It wasn't what she expected from a facility involved in top-secret activity.

Diffuse light poured through the row of tempered glass transom windows. She was in a storage area with large blue bins and floor-to-ceiling metal shelving filled with boxes. As she padded softly around, she came upon a large recycling bin near the door. She peered into the mouth of the bin. Her headlight illuminated a small box in the far corner. She leaned over the edge, the sharp metal edge cutting into her belly. She wished she had worn the padded camouflage jumpsuit.

Ow! Ow! She screamed silently.

Balancing on her belly did not give her the leverage to reach the box. Rather than have her belly cut open, she pushed herself over the edge. On the way down, her head made contact with the side of the bin. She landed with a metallic clunk and lay for a moment with her eyes closed. Her head hurt a bit, so she slowly opened her eyes to darkness.

Oh my God! She'd turned blind!

"Stupid ass," Priya scolded herself, shaking her head, realizing the fall had switched off her headlight.

She flicked it back on and turned her head so the beam illuminated the corner. Crawling on all fours, the bin was that big, to the box, she whipped out her pocketknife and cut off the side with the shipping label. She put the label in her fanny bag and pulled the zipper shut.

Just as she clambered out of the bin, there was a loud *thunk* ending in a metallic click and the lights came on. She blinked and froze.

Fudge! Heat activated lights!

She switched her headlight off. Angling her head, Priya tried to get a sense of what was coming at her before she had to get out of there fast.

She still heard nothing.

She now moved in slow motion. She didn't know the point of that. The best thing would have been to run away as fast as she could. But there she was taking small, silent steps to the back of the aisle.

Now she heard footsteps. She was still on the long end of the shelves. The door to the warehouse opened. She froze again. She reached into the pocket on her leg and pulled out something.

Pepper spray? Or the smoke bomb?

There were two of them. Trapped, she waited in the corner crouching, ready to jump. She heard one of them come down her side of the aisle. She turned the bottle in her hands, her eyes glued toward the end of the aisle. She felt for the nozzle of the spray can with her fingers and turned it.

Good, got the pepper spray.

The soft steps were very close now. She jumped out, pressed the knob, her breath stuck in her throat. She bit her lips to prevent the scream rising in her throat combining it with words she never uttered.

She'd fucking sprayed herself with the fucking pepper spray!

She allowed a whimper or two to escape before she crouched and sprayed her face with mint tea. Thankfully, her finger had partially covered the knob and the spray only reached her cheeks and chin. Still, her eyes burned like shit.

She quickly yanked the other can out of her belt, released the knob and watched it roll away from her. Smoke billowed out. Then she darted out, squirted oil on the floor and emptied a bag of marbles on it. The man came round the corner, running at full speed.

Not a good idea. He would have been better advised to move in slow motion like her. She heard a crash and a thud. She slowly stuck her head around the steel truss. He was in the middle of a Bugs Bunny routine incorporating flailing arms, sliding feet and rotating hips.

"Ai, ai ai..fuck!" He yelled as he went down.

He bumped his way over the slippery marbles, hitting smack into the stinging vapours. Priya zipped out, his whimpering echoing in her ear.

The second one was waiting for her on the other side of the doors. He even had his gun drawn. She'd forgotten about him! His finger was on the trigger, the hand resting on the palm of the other hand, steadying the barrel.

On the count of three she was going to do the pelvic punch.

She'd never hit anyone before. And now she had to stick her fist into the man's soft spot? A man who was holding a gun pointed right at her! She hesitated for a second before she remembered how the element of surprise was always the best.

Oh, shit!

So Priya increased her speed, clenched her hand into a fist and ran straight at him. Her hand hit his soft belly and she felt it go deep. His face reflected the pain she knew he was in and he dropped the weapon. Leaping in the air, she jackknifed her legs. While one leg was on its way down, she kicked the other out.

She'd seen ballet dancers make such a move. She did one when she did her Bollywood dance routines, but it was a softer version. She hadn't known then that it had other uses too. Her foot made contact with his chin. His head whipped back and he dropped to the floor, clutching his middle. She bolted through the door, out into the lot and cut across it to the grounds, the sound of her breathing exploding from her chest. She expected to hear the wail of sirens at any moment.

But nothing.

. . .

At home, she wiped the black makeup off before she got in the shower. A while later, she plonked down on her couch, a glass of wine in her hand. It had been an exciting adventure. It had been thrilling. But she still had *nothing* for her blog.

In Kingston, life was much slower than in Toronto. It was a fresh start for her after the Simon debacle. Rush hour was twenty cars on Princess Street. And the lake was at her reach as well as the fabulous Sandbanks for sun-drenched days. But from time to time she did need a jolt of something.

The next day, in Spice Haven's kitchen, Priya went over the list of platters she was preparing to be loaded into the van for the gig at the Mayor's office. She was wondering where Mia was, when she got a text from Mia.

Have flu. Help.

She texted a thumbs-up emoji back.

Mark there?

Yes. No prob. I got this.

Priya dressed in black trousers and a long-sleeved buttoned-up white shirt just like the others. She tied a black and white apron with her business logo around her waist. Her hair was pulled back into a tight bun, hidden under a white head cover. She pulled her non-prescription glasses from her bag and slipped them on. A great protection against food splatters.

A text from Bob came in as she was on her way out. **U home? Can u send me Don's number please?**

She sent it to him because he'd said 'please.'

Wait a sec.

She was his personal phone book? Why? All these numbers would be in his call log. All he had to do was to add them to his contact list. Plus he talked to them *all* the time. Some were on the board of the Bath Pickleball Club just like he was!

She texted him that.

No matter. A while later he texted: **Can you please send me Kelly's number?**

Priya gave up and shouldered the added responsibility of being his phone directory.

She met up with the rest of the team at the Town Hall lobby. It was standard fare. To this, Priya added her spicy touch: tomato and fiery coriander chutney squares with a flagged warning near the platter saying, 'Spicy' and the image of three green chillies.

What the hell, might as well.

Priya set the platters on a rolling cart and glanced at her watch. Good, still thirty minutes left. She rolled it out to the hall and unloaded the platters. Mark came in with a second cart and together they set the food out. The two servers they'd hired took care of the water pitchers and glasses at the individual tables. The final touches were fat bundles of hot pink roses wearing cream tissue paper jackets in bud vases.

"Suits coming in now," Mark said, grabbing the last two platters and used his butt to open the door.

Priya, afraid the tower of sliders would topple, held the door open for him.

They took their places, the servers and Mark in the hall and Priya in the kitchen. Peering through the door, she saw the mayor and her husband walk in, followed by a gorgeous eye-candy: tall and dark-haired with broad shoulders and a crisp white shirt. His hair was longish, reaching below his ears and combed back in an understated yet elegant style.

He wore the pale grey suit well. The jacket was open, showing off a silver-buckled leather belt. A very sexy bit of scruff adorned his face. A straight nose, lips curved in a smile.

He was too far for her to see clearly but there was something familiar about his smile. As he moved around the room shaking hands, his face in profile, she became certain she knew him from somewhere.

Drat!

It would *all* she'd be thinking of.

Fudge!

At the end of the evening, Priya noticed there were only three tomato and coriander triangles left. She never ate when she was on a gig but now she couldn't resist. She stuffed one of the remaining triangles into her mouth.

It was bliss.

She closed her eyes. A slight moan escaped her mouth. It was just the right balance of spicy and tangy and sweet.

Mark nudged her. "Now, now. No need for all that. Don't want you in a puddle at my feet."

Priya shoved him back. Then she looked into his deep blue eyes and breathed cilantro breath into his face.

"Not. For. You."

He was Apollo. He was Michelangelo's David.

But for the fact that he was gay, she would indeed be a puddle at his golden feet.

She briefly wondered who the spice lover was. And hoped he or she did not have a belly ache later.

It only hit her later: the eye-candy was Dallas Crenshaw.

Priya threw the light quilt aside and got out of bed. And stepped right on the dratted earring she'd dropped the night before but hadn't been able to find. It was one of those dangly things with a hook. The hook conveniently settled in the sole of her foot.

Double fudge!

Grabbing her iPod…yes she still used it…she scrolled through the list of songs until she came upon her latest favs: Sufi songs. Plugging in the speakers, she set about making her breakfast, dancing her way from tea to toast.

Another thing she could do every morning: have toast for breakfast. None of that balanced, nutritional, healthy crap to start her day. Toast made her happy. Slathering peanut butter and honey over the two slices made her happy. It might have been four slices if she had a four-slice toaster, but no need to push it.

Happiness came in bits and she took it as it came along. Life had a way of screwing it up for her if she expected too much.

On the courts, she met up with Kelly Roberts who was vertically challenged like Priya. Built like a tugboat, she was gorgeous with pixie cut hair and beautiful grey eyes. After finishing her administrative duties for the club, Priya got ready to play against Bob and his partner.

"Zero zero two," she slid a long one over the net to Bob.

It hit the corner of the base line. Bob was standing a bit too forward. His return was weak and it bounced into the net.

"Jeez! Great serve, Papillon," Bob yelled. "Where did you learn that?"

"*You* taught me. Don't you remember? Last summer we had a clinic and you coached a few of us."

"Well then, kudos to me for being a great teacher." Bob was never one to skimp on compliments.

Priya had discovered pickleball by chance and never looked back. It was the one thing missing from her life. She could live alone. She could cook for herself. She could *possibly* live without a man, if the life situation demanded it. Proof was in her fifth year without one. It would be tough. Very tough. Just the thought of a naked flat chest and broad shoulders, characteristics she did not possess, was enough to give her premature hot flashes. But she could never ever give up pickleball. It was made for her.

Thinking of flat chest and broad shoulders brought to mind Dallas Crenshaw. He hadn't come to play today. Wasn't surprising. He was young and had a job. Unlike Priya, his job probably made him who he was. Then about an hour before pickleball play wrapped up for the day, Dallas turned up.

Yep, the sight of him did cause her pulse to beat faster. Just a little bit. There were five other players left. Priya and Dallas teamed up with Anna Marshall and Kalle as their opponents. It should have been a laid-back and friendly game. It began unravelling when Priya missed a shot from Kalle, the fourth one, coming down the middle.

"Yours," she yelled, her face turned toward Dallas, moving out of the way of the ball.

Dallas missed. "No, it wasn't," he approached her, pointing to the court. "I was there. And you, here. My backhand, your forehand. So much easier for you."

"You think so?" Priya growled and moved toward him. His calm demeanour rubbed her the wrong way.

"Not only do I think so, I *know* so."

"Yeah?" She flung her sunglasses to the side with so much force they hit the fence and bounced back onto the court. In a heartbeat, she closed the distance between them.

"I can't believe this!" Priya heard Anna say. "Kids on the playground. Oh, God! I hope she's not going to clock him. I wouldn't put it past her. She might be small but she can do it."

"Yeah." Dallas flipped his sunglasses onto his head, straightening his body to his full height. "And if you're thinking of using your leg to kick my shins-let me rephrase that-*try* to kick my shins again, you better think it over."

Fudge!

She'd been planning it. In fact, her foot just moved a bit to the back. One glance into his eyes, got her rethinking her plan. His eyes blazed at her, golden specks flashing, jaw tight and hand clenched on the grip of his paddle.

"Oh yeah? What if I was planning that? What're you going to do, huh?"

"Just try it and you'll see." He put his paddle gently on the ground.

They would've been nose to nose if she had a step stool. As it was, her nose was up in the air somewhere in the region of his chest while his pointed down to her. What was up with this guy? Didn't anything rattle him?

"What are you twelve?" Priya couldn't stop. She wanted to see more of the sparks lighting up his intense grey eyes. Trouble was, she had to look up. Way up, that crick in her neck acting up again.

She pulled her leg back and took aim at his shin. The instant her foot stuck out, Dallas held her arms tight to her side, his large hands clamping around them like a vice.

"What are you ten?" she could almost hear the grinding of his teeth if the movement of his jaw was any indication. "Don't even *think* about it."

The golden speckles in his eyes turned to liquid gold. His sculpted lips curled. It did not deter her at all. Instead she took a deep breath, prepared to do him some serious bodily harm. Priya did not question her actions. They were primal. Something about him got her all roiled up.

"Hey!" Anna stepped in. "What are you guys, six?" Then she squeezed herself in between them, pushing them apart with her hands. "Stop it! Or I'll have you benched."

Still glaring at Dallas, Priya backed off, thoroughly pleased with herself. It had been so much fun getting into his head, covered with unbelievably itching-to-run-her-hands-through dark hair. They finished the game in a reasonably friendly manner, Dallas even smiling at her when they got off the courts.

Priya shrugged. Okay. It was over. Too bad.

CHAPTER SEVEN

Dallas sat in his living room, his thoughts swirling around, all featuring Priya and the heated exchange on the courts with her. He felt it in his body.

He hadn't been able to see her eyes when she'd taken off the sunglasses. The sun was high, hitting his eyes, blinding him. So even if she'd planned to shin him, there was a good possibility he would have missed grabbing her arms.

There was something about her and those intriguing tats. She drew him into her orbit, exposing little flashes of her temperament he found so irresistible. She was so unlike Kate.

And there it was: the crux of his growing attraction. It was the mystery of what else was hiding underneath all the turbulence. It was the thrill of discovery, of finding the unexpected. She sent all the right signals to his very receptive brain, which couldn't stop thinking about her. But he had to. He had a job to go to. Deadlines to meet.

With regret, he put Priya out of his mind. For now.

After reading the report about the break in, Dallas Crenshaw stopped by the developing station where Houston was in front of three monitors hooked up in a series. A three dimensional image of the Dragonfly danced on the screens.

"We need to beef up security," Dallas tapped the report in his hand.

"Yeah, I heard. Any idea who it could be?" Houston did not take his eyes from the monitors.

"Not yet. But Gus is on it. What d'you think about increasing the photosensitivity of the cameras? Of *all* of them? And the lumens of the motion detectors?"

"Good idea. We have to get to the bottom of this before it escalates." Houston pushed his chair away from the design table and raked his fingers through his short hair.

"You think it could escalate?"

Houston shrugged. "Might not. Then again it's better to be safe than sorry. We have too much invested in this. And we're almost at the finish line."

"Okay. On it."

"You taking the girls out soon?"

"Yes, tomorrow."

He turned back to the screen. "Ah, delegate responsibility for a day. That's what fathers do. Enjoy."

"I always do. And bring them back spoiled. That's what uncles do."

~

PRIYA WENT SHOPPING in the Cataraqui Mall where she walked from end to end, first on the upper floor then the lower floor, wandering the aisles aimlessly. She grabbed a salad at the food court. Usually she liked to shop. But her heart was not in it today with Dallas Crenshaw creeping into her thoughts.

It took a certain kind of man to capture her attention. With the right one, the one who tugged at her heart, the one she couldn't stop thinking of, that kind would not take long. Was Dallas even her type? She didn't know.

It was beyond her why she couldn't have been happy with Simon. He was smart, successful and good-looking. Not eye-candy good-looking. Still, nothing to sniff at. He treated her well. Except for laughing at her dance get up, she could find no fault with him. He had even wanted to marry her and have a family. But she'd said no, left Toronto and never looked back. She'd even surprised herself when she heard herself say 'no' to Simon's proposal.

Perhaps his ridiculing of her love of Bollywood had hurt more than she cared to admit. It was part of who she was. She'd devoted years to learning the intricate steps. In making fun of her passion, Simon was rejecting her soul all the while accepting her body. Bollywood was part of her, her heritage and it was like he was rejecting her.

How could that ever work?

They'd been walking along Harbourfront, her hand in his. Suddenly, he'd pulled her close to him and whispered the words she'd wanted to hear. Or so she thought. She hesitated. Immediately, the light in his eyes dulled, his smile faded. She could still see his crestfallen face. He looked as if she'd sucker punched him. But wasn't her happiness important too? She wouldn't have been happy with Simon though he'd been housebroken. Too bad it had taken her two years to find that out. The next day, he packed his things and moved out. They hadn't exchanged a word since.

Glancing at her watch, Priya realized it was time to pick up her car from Canadian Tire.

~

AT THE GYM, Dallas finished his last round of muscle curlers and stretches. He hit the shower next. Pulling on a white T-shirt over his still damp head, he slipped on a pair of faded soft blue jean shorts and drove into a free spot in the Canadian Tire parking lot. As he turned away from his SUV, his eyes fell on an unusual yellow truck.

Isn't that Priya's truck?

Needless to say, he did walk the aisles up and down *and* to and fro in the hope of catching her. Rounding the fishing rods and weapons-of-the-woods counter, he heard a familiar laugh. He'd have recognized it anywhere. It could only be Priya's laugh. He wouldn't have admitted it if his life depended on it, but he jogged the remainder of the aisle to the end of the store. And there she was, chatting with this dude in a red shirt.

"So true," he heard her say.

If not for the laughter, he wouldn't have recognized her. She wore no hat and her dark hair spilled down to her waist in lustrous waves. Sunglasses on her head held them back.

She wore a short flared skirt in blues and greens. Her feet were not in sneakers but in sexy heeled silver shoes. A skinny strapless top in a soft blue material showed off her tanned skin. It barely reached her belly button. A strip of skin peeked out below. The rose tat was in full bloom before his eyes. The other vine was complete now, not broken by clothing. She darted to the side and grabbed an item off a hook. As she reached up, her top hitched upward, revealing yet another tat on her back.

How many did she have? And yes, he wanted a closer look at *all* of them.

Bracelets jingled on her right arm.

He thought she said something but nothing registered. All he heard was her melodious voice. It was very different from the one she used to bellow when she was on the pickleball courts. His breath stopped in his throat.

Good grief! She's the dancer!

She was the one he dreamt about. She was the one disturbing his sleep. Some part deep inside him had been quite content to leave her in his dreams.

Aw, fuck!

Of course it *had* to be her. Like there was no one else left in the world. How could he have missed it? Unable to look away, he watched as she turned toward the cash register to pay, luscious lips still curved in a smile.

He had to face it. Dream became reality. It was never a good thing when these two worlds collided. Confusing emotions roiling inside him, he approached. If she was the stuff his dreams were made from then he had to get closer.

"Hey, Priya," he stood like a schoolboy, hands stuffed in his pockets, appearing more relaxed than he actually was.

She turned toward him. Light flashed off her nose stud. And that was it for him. Dream and reality fused and became one. Thick lashes surrounded gorgeous green eyes in a sun-kissed face. He was close enough to catch the golden tips of her lashes. Her lips were magenta and there was an irresistible aura about her. He was awash in sensations he hadn't felt in a long time. It was too much for him. He took a step back.

His fantasy dancer was stunning! And a pickleball playing beauty.

"Hi, Dallas." Her lips now curved in a smile. "Didn't see you at pickleball today."

He swallowed, feeling like a hormone-controlled teenager. "Took a shot at the gym. It was pretty hot on the courts yesterday. Did you stay long?"

She shrugged. His eyes were glued to her naked shoulders, watching the play of the tat on her skin.

"No, I held out only for an hour. Plus I had errands to run. But Kalle was there. With Milla. He was not letting anything get by him. He's such a great player."

"Indeed he is. I'm playing with him in Cobourg."

"I know. He told me. I'm sure you'll do well."

"You playing?"

"Mixed doubles with Bob Marshall and women's doubles with Kelly Roberts."

"She's great. I've played with her."

His mind was scrambling to find a way to keep talking to her. But innocuous banalities refused to pass his lips. He did not want her to leave. But leave he must. He was going to see Emma and Olivia. They were back from their camp and he hadn't seen them in weeks.

"That she is. A bit nervous though before the first match."

"Would you like to grab a coffee?" The words popped out of his mouth before his mind latched on.

And there went the banalities down the drain. The first concrete and spontaneous phrase ever to come out of his mouth. Directed at her. His nieces were waiting! Instead here he was, rushing forward. It wasn't his style. He liked to take it slow. He liked to prolong the anticipation. He was Mr. Go Slow.

"I'd like that. There's a coffee shop right next door."

Her scent, something heady and flowery, filled his nose. As she walked by his side, he stuffed hands in his pockets to hide their trembling.

What the hell was the matter with him? A grown man quaking at the sight of a woman. But this was not just any woman. This was one who intrigued him. One who made his worlds collide. After getting their coffees., she made for a table in the corner where he pulled out her chair and watched as she sat, her hair falling across her cheeks.

What would it feel like spread over my naked chest?

The thought rose like a flame in his head and he extinguished it just as quickly. His hand whisked over the bare skin at the nape of her neck and he drew back, as if scorched. It did not stop him from taking another spontaneous step. In a bold and deliberate move-quite unlike him-he brought his nose close to her hair as she sat down, inhaling her beguiling fragrance. Was it lavender perhaps? She unsettled him.

He watched her stir the coffee and lick the stirrer before laying it on the napkin. The small movement of her mouth sent crazy signals to his body. He sat with his arms on the table, holding his coffee between his hands and twisting the cup. For a brief second, he caught himself falling into the mesmerizing green of her eyes. He took a gulp from his cup before he fell any further.

Bad move on his part. The coffee was scalding hot. With stoic indifference, he focused his attention on her, ignoring the discomfort.

Despite his inner turmoil, she was able to put him at ease with her vivacious manner. It was not the persona she carried on the courts. Or perhaps it was her intriguing scent? Whatever it was, she soon had him laughing and chuckling, just like she had on the courts. He relaxed and just enjoyed being with her, looking into her pretty eyes, trying hard not to lose himself in them.

"So what happened to your truck?"

"Remember the turtle crossing incident?"

"Sure do." Like it had been yesterday. Her trying to shove him and kick his shins the first time.

"Well, apparently the hard breaking loosened some unpronounceable parts. So I had it fixed."

"Good. So now you can break to your heart's content." A chuckle rose in his throat.

She giggled. "What does that even mean, Dallas? It doesn't make any sense at all."

She had an infectious giggle. His smile mirrored hers.

"Talking about that day, you used a British word. Bollocks I believe it was."

"I went to school in England."

"You don't have an accent." A statement rather than a question.

"I just pick up whatever accent is around me. When I'm in England, the other accent comes back. Other than the odd 'gobsmacked' or 'bollocks', my English is North American." She picked up her stirrer and began to swirl it in her coffee. "So you are the VP of Hovertek?"

"Indeed. With my brothers, Houston and Austin. My younger brother, Austin, is in charge of marketing with my dad as president."

"Wow! A family business." A wistful look crossed her face.

"You mentioned you had no family?"

"Yeah. Am an orphan. And no siblings either. My friends are my family."

She was an intriguing package waiting to be unravelled, to be savoured. One day she was combative, the next her sexy allure had him all in a jumble. Afterwards, he couldn't say what they talked about. All he remembered was her scent. And those pretty green eyes.

~

PRIYA THOUGHT HE looked scrumptious in those soft-washed tight shorts, cinched around his narrow waist with a silver belt. Other things she hadn't noticed about him came into focus: the way the white T-shirt stretched across his flat chest; his well-defined biceps and arms dusted with dark hair and the way the shorts moulded to his body.

Drool worthy.

He was indeed a cluster of marvellous manhood. A whiff of his cologne wafted to her nose. *Dior's Eau Sauvage,* if she wasn't mistaken. Knowledge gleaned from her stint in a Parisian parfumérie.

Strike one!

Her heart beat faster. His hair stuck to his head. Wet? She immediately pictured him in the shower, soap suds....strike two! The sexy dimple began to bloom on one cheek. Strike three and she was out.

He was delectable from the top of his wet head to the strong-looking feet in Birkenstocks. Grey eyes stared at her with unwavering intensity. From where she sat, she could see the light and dark amber flecks in his eyes pulse rapidly.

She did not fall in love often, but she fell in love easily. Just a look, a glance, a touch and she would be head over heels. It took that special man to catch her eye. And she had a feeling Dallas was going to be one of those. She couldn't remember if it had been that way with Simon too. There were a lot of things about Simon she didn't care to remember. She wiggled in her chair now delighted at the prospect, stretching her feet in the glorious silver Manolo Blahniks. They easily added another three inches to her height.

The journey was almost always much more beautiful than the destination. Was that another quote from Rumi? Or a Sufi one? It was going to be a glorious journey. But, her mind warned her, she fell out of love just as easily.

CHAPTER EIGHT

TWO HOURS LATER, Dallas was on his way to see his nieces, Stained blaring from the speakers. He was not going to think of *her*. But he had to take a last sniff of her with him. As she climbed into her truck, he breathed in deep and took her fragrance with him. He'd only barely resisted the urge to touch her hair.

He could hear his nieces as he got to the house. They were in back: in the pool, probably. They still liked to play with him. They liked to climb him as if he were a tree. Although Emma was more open about it, Olivia did it when she left her lady-like manners behind her.

He pulled the tiger mask and, using the mirror in his car, he adjusted it over his face. He slipped his sandals off and stripped down to his swimming trunks, making sure he had his phone in the pocket. He slowly walked around the side of the house.

They *were* in the pool.

Olivia was sitting on the edge while Emma somersaulted into the water from the other end. When Dallas got to the fence surrounding the pool, he crouched behind the shrubs, unlatched the gate and, hugging the ground, crept toward them on all fours.

As he approached them, he pressed the app he'd downloaded on his phone. A terrifying roar erupted from his pocket. He leaped into the air, Olivia screamed, Emma swallowed water and it was one big noisy party.

Olivia jumped up, running to the other side of the pool, screeching. Emma forgot she'd swallowed water and splashed around in place, unable to move, roaring at Olivia.

"Run, Olivia, run! He's close."

At which, Dallas abandoned Olivia and jumped into the water, forgetting he had his phone in his pocket. The roar became a gurgle as the phone drowned. Dallas used his own voice and roared, splashing and churning water toward Emma.

"Uncle Dallas. Uncle Dallas," Olivia shouted as she too joined the fray in the water. "Catch me."

She took off using the long strokes of a seasoned swimmer. Dallas, hampered with the weight of Emma hanging onto his neck, her long hair tickling his nose and the mask disintegrating and floating in the water, was not fast enough. Moving Emma to his back, he swam to the shallower end. He caught up to Olivia just as she was escaping out of the gate. Sliding Emma down his back, he raced after Olivia, followed by Emma egging her sister on. They rounded the house, back through the gate. Olivia had long strong legs, but he was bigger and stronger. He caught her just as Houston was coming out of the house with a platter.

Dallas grabbed a laughing Olivia and pulled her into his arms and up into the air, twirling around until she yelled for mercy.

"Stop! Stop, Uncle Dallas. No more."

"You give up?"

"Yes. I promise. I give up."

He let her go and grabbed the next one: Emma. He lifted her on his shoulders so that her belly was against the back of his neck and turned round and round until she too begged him to stop. Olivia ran into the house. As he let go of Emma, Dallas stumbled and bumped into Houston.

There was another yell, this time a manly one. The platter went one way, its contents the other. Dallas, dizzy, sat down on the wet stones. He was hot and the stones felt good.

Lara came out carrying a tray with pitchers and glasses. She was tall and slender with short blonde hair and eyes the colour of molasses. She set the drinks on the table, picked up a wayward piece of yellow pepper and put it on the grill. As she turned away, Houston grabbed her by the waist, pulled her to him and nuzzled her neck. Lara raised her arms, knotting them around Houston's neck.

They did not say 'I love you' like some couples did. They did not say it when they got off the phone with each other. They did not say it when they left in the mornings. Instead, they said it with actions. Like now, Lara turned her head and caught Houston's lips in a deep kiss.

The girls came out wearing dry clothes. Olivia, ever the preteenager said, "Eew! Mom, Dad. Stop that."

Her parents did not get angry with Olivia for saying that. Houston tightened his arms around Lara and lifted her off the ground, before letting her go.

Dallas got clothes from his car and went into the house to change. His phone was dead of course. Still, he used the hair dryer to blow hot air on the phone, hoping it would still work.

"Is Austin coming?" Dallas asked. "Don't know if he texted me." He pointed to his drowned phone lying on the table.

"Try it," Houston tapped his own phone. "He can't make it. There's a project-a small one-he's working on: house on Princess. He's doing it when he can fit it into his schedule."

Dallas pressed the button on his wet phone and it whirled to life sluggishly. The screen looked okay. All the icons appeared to be there. There was indeed a text from Austin.

"All the more for me, I guess," Dallas said, biting into a succulent sparerib. "Hmm. These are good. Come on, girls. Let's eat."

"No ribs for me, Uncle Dallas. I'm a vegetarian." Olivia announced.

"Since when?" he raised his eyebrows.

"Since I got back from Grams and Gramps."

"What will you eat? I mean right now?"

"I'll have the roasted veggies, salad and rice pilaf."

"What about you?" he asked Emma.

"I'm going to eat *all* the ribs I can. I can eat more now. I don't have to share with Olivia."

When they were having ice cream, his phone whirred and farted. As they all watched with wide eyes, it belched a small flame. A puffy cloud of white smoke wafted up then it was still.

"Is it dead?" Emma asked, her curly hair all over her face, some strands even sticking to the sparerib she was sucking on.

"I guess. I'll have to get another one."

"Can I have this one then, Uncle Dallas?" Emma could not contain her excitement.

"It's dead. You saw it. It won't work anymore. There's a battery inside and it could be leaking toxic chemicals. Besides, I have to take it to a special place and have it buried."

"Really? You can bury phones too?" A wild gleam came into her eyes.

There had been a time, about a year ago when Emma had been very curious about death. She searched for signs all around her, collecting dead insects and once even a bird. Dallas wondered now if she still had that morbid fascination.

"No, you silly," Olivia jumped in. "He'll take it to an electronics store where they get rid of it. It will be taken apart into all the tiny pieces it once was."

"Like in WALL.E and the dump he worked in?"

"Something like that," Houston replied, ending the discussion about a dead phone.

Later, as Dallas was home doing laundry, his phone pinged with a text from Austin.

Need help. Landscaping @ 1232 Princess. Tomorrow @ 7? Before heat hits?

Tomorrow being the weekend, Dallas was free, able and willing.

THE MORNING WAS awash with a breeze blowing in from Lake Ontario. It was a welcome break from the sultry heat of the past week. After her morning run, Priya chugged a glass of cold water at home, stripped and stepped into an even colder shower. Then she picked up the fundraiser tickets for Mark's charity from the printer.

On the pickleball courts later, she handed them out to those who had placed an order. And there were plenty who'd done that once the emails had gone out.

Dallas alone bought a dozen tickets. He was going to come with his whole family.

"I'm sure people in my office will be very interested," he stuck the tickets in his bag. "Can I have more? If I get a good response?"

They were standing under the large maple tree, its branches hovering and whispering above them every time a breeze came through. His sunglasses hung from the neck of his T-shirt. The breeze picked up the strands of his hair and layered them on his forehead. He was indeed beautiful. Tall, dark and beautiful, in her league *and* out of it. She clamped her hands to her side to stop them from touching him. He was becoming impossible to resist.

"Absolutely. Just let me know," Priya detected a subtle change in Dallas's ever since their coffee together.

She couldn't quite put a finger on it. Sometimes, it appeared to her as if he sought out her company. At other times, he seemed to back away from it. She had trouble trying to decipher the mixed messages he was sending. Anyway, why did she want to decipher it? Sure he was gorgeous in bits and spurts. But did she want something serious right now? When her life was going just the way she wanted? She was in that special place where any stumble would take her off course. There was nothing to beat drifting along.

"So you're going to be performing Bollywood dances?" he looked at the pamphlet.

"Indian, yes. Have been training and learning for a number of years now. I love it. You know about it?" Priya's eyes were innocently wide as she looked up at him.

She knew it was Dallas on his deck watching her dance. She'd known for some time. Right after she'd walked over to the house with the silhouette on the deck, moonlight flashing on the bottle he held in his hand, she'd known. She'd kept watch for a white SUV and had caught Dallas getting out of it. It had been a no brainer.

"No. But I did have an Indian roommate in university. His sister danced. It was something else." Dallas scrunched his forehead trying to pull out forgotten memories.

"Perhaps Bharat Natyam?" Priya focused her attention on his hands, the arms dusted with soft hair, as manly as the man himself.

She had to stop before she made an ass of herself. It wasn't what she was looking for. Not at this stage in her life. She was reasonably happy and mildly content. It would do for now.

~

SHE SAID IT with a strange smile on her lips. When Dallas looked at those lips, heat suffused his chest. All he had to do was to lean down and kiss the living daylights out of her. But here? Under the maple? Sounded romantic enough but with fifty potential onlookers? He fought the urge to touch her. The more he saw of her the greater the urge.

"Bollywood dance perhaps?"

"Maybe." A breeze lifted strands of her hair, swirling them over her head and face.

"Looking forward to seeing you on stage." He leaned down and whispered in her ear. "You don't know how much."

He tucked a strand of hair behind her ear, relishing in its silkiness. He felt a shiver shimmy through her body. Good. She didn't have to say anything. As it was, she made him do things. Feel things he wasn't ready to accept. Yet.

He closed his eyes and inhaled her fragrance. That was all he was going to give himself. Raising his head, he made the mistake of looking into her alluring green eyes. Usually calm as the lake but right now glittering with subdued emotions. Hiding secrets only she had access to. And he was a goner, pure animalistic tendency gripping him.

In two shakes of a donkey's tail, he closed the distance between them, bent his head and brushed her lips with his. It was the softest of touches, like the kiss of a butterfly or the brush of a flower petal.

There was a sharp intake of breath-his. There was the smallest of gasps-hers.

Then he stepped back and it was over. Her hands were tensed into fists, her jaw tight. He took another step back, almost anticipating a hard slap. Her cheeks flushed and eyes shuttered, Priya turned around, got into her truck and drove off with a roar.

That's that then.

Not for a second did Dallas regret his impulsiveness. For once, he went with the flow. For once it wasn't wine and dine first. For once he forgot he was Mr. Go Slow. And it felt great.

Question was what was Priya going to do about it?

He was a no-woman or one-woman kind of guy, either alone or in a committed relationship. He aimed for the latter but so far his aim was off. With Kate, he'd never been able to put the broken pieces together again and so they began to drift apart.

He'd wanted to be with Kate and start a family and he'd wanted it bad. So bad, he missed the warning signs.

~

PRIYA PUT THE kiss out of her mind. Or tried to. It was not an easy task. She had to focus on the upcoming pickleball tournament in Cobourg. Yet, she could still feel the delicious pressure of his lips on hers.

How strange when all the rest of him was hard and strong. And, to top it all, he hadn't touched her with anything other than his lips. Another second later and her legs would have given away. And still another second later, she'd have wrapped herself around him.

Question was: how was she going to face him?

It was too late to slap him. Water under the bridge, a done deal. He hadn't done anything she hadn't wanted. Besides, slap Dallas? Thoughtful, polite, considerate Dallas? She'd just be herself. And see where things took her.

If she only knew how she could do that.

In the first year of her breakup with Simon, Priya wallowed, her gaze aiming daggers at every smooching couple she came across. By the third year, she'd mellowed enough to get her BOB-battery operated boyfriend-to comfort her. She'd been on her own for so long, she didn't know how to share her space. She was not looking for forever. She wasn't even sure she was looking for a hookup, tenuous or otherwise.

The barely-there kiss rocked her senses like nothing else had in a long time. She wished she could go back in time and do it over. Then she'd put her arms around his neck, rub the sexy scruff on his cheeks against her skin and press her body against his long and hard body.

Dallas would want things from her: the commitments and promises to being a couple. Things she didn't do. He had a family, brothers and parents who were a big part of his life. She was a loner. She had friends, true. But in the end they all went to their homes and she slept alone in her beautiful bed. She wasn't prepared to give up her placid life and get into the whole mess of a relationship again. Life was too short to complicate it with the baggage of a relationship. She'd tried it with Simon and look where it got her. Never mind that Simon had not been exactly compatible. Still, she'd been somewhat prepared to take the plunge. And then she'd hesitated and taken that step back. Simon would have been a drastic mistake. She wasn't going to make another one.

CHAPTER NINE

THE ADRENALINE HIGH from snooping at Hovertek only made Priya want more. She had to find out what was going on at Hovertek. Maybe they were working on something hush-hush for the military. Dallas as at the head of the project made it even juicier. She couldn't believe the man she was hot for was part of a sinister undertaking. What it exactly was, she had no clue. But she was going to find out.

Priya climbed the ladder leading up to the roof of the Hovertek Inc. The flat structure was more at home in the desert. She tried to lift one of the metal grids set in the grey concrete slab. It didn't budge. Over on the side of the building, a metal gutter ran out just where the tube ended.

"To evacuate rain water," Priya talked to herself as she continued exploring.

The setting sun flashed on something. A closer look revealed frosted glass skylights with hinges and latches. Priya lifted a latch. It clicked open easily. Arms straining, she swung open the dome of the skylight. Peering inside, she saw what looked like a sub ceiling. She lowered herself and to her relief, it didn't bend under her weight. She flicked the headlight on. Copper pipes, tubes and metal ducts hovered in straight lines on the sub ceiling under her feet. Aluminum brackets anchored large ducts to the wood. It was one place she had to bend a little to avoid hitting her head.

"I'm guessing the acoustic tiles are just below these planks," Priya went on communicating with herself.

She aimed the flashlight at the dark recesses beyond the planks, the beam of her light falling on the snaking pipes and tubes as she turned her head. How could she get inside the building?

She continued silently for some minutes, dust swirling in the path of the beam of light. There were no turns. It was one open pipe and tube land. One second she was wandering around without a clue as to where she was actually going, and the next she stumbled, kissing the floor. Fuzz balls and dust stuck to her lips and face.

"Yuck!" she said, sticking her tongue out.

Wrong move. Now dust was not only on her tongue but also inside her nose. Using her hands as levers, she heaved herself up. A faint tickle started to burrow its way up her nose. A powerful sneeze erupted. When it subsided, her hands came in contact with a ridge in the floor. She aimed her light at the spot.

"Ah, the opening to more interesting places, I hope?' she tugged at the latch.

Beneath her, she saw a grey corridor. She had to try two more doors before she saw the corridor, familiar from the photographs on Hovertek's website, made of glass blocks, black rubber and acoustic tiles. It was well lit. Perhaps there was a way from this one into more interesting places?

She switched off her headlight and prepared to jump down. Priya hitched up her pants and spat on her gloved hands. Then she squatted over the opening through which she could have lowered herself feet first. She could probably hold herself stable on her elbows, all her body weight resting on them. The thing was, she had not even a smidgen of confidence in them. They would probably wobble and spit her out, destroying her plans for a grand entrance.

She decided to give it the frontal approach. Sitting down, she dropped her legs through the opening. She walked forward slowly, on her butt. Sliding down on her arms, she held herself steady on the way down. This was going to be a piece of cake!

This was more fun than she'd imagined. Her hips came down, followed by her waist. Now she was hanging by her underarms. Well, then gravity decided to take over. Her underarms couldn't support her weight either. They buckled. She let go and tumbled down like a sack of potatoes. There was a burning sensation as her arms grazed the opening. Although the rubber flooring cushioned her fall, the thud reverberated in her head and teeth.

Lucky for her, she was well padded. She landed on her ass and sat there, stunned, shocked and surprised, the thud still echoing in her ears. She moved her limbs and wiggled her feet. She swivelled her head.

"Well, nothing seems to be broken," she muttered and got to her feet.

She dusted herself off and walked down the narrow, glass-walled corridor. As she moved forward, squares on the floor lit up.

Light boxes.

The walls on either side were glass blocks, some of which were coloured. It was really cool. The ceiling was made of black acoustic tiles. About thirty feet further down the corridor were doors. She tried each. Both were locked. The absence of electronic keypads made her bold. No sign of spy cameras either. Both didn't fit with the normal landscape of a defence contractor. Such set-ups usually had a lot to hide.

She removed a small tool from her Midas pouch, inserted it into the lock, closed her eyes and listened for the click. The door swung open and she darted in, closing it behind her. Lights went on automatically.

Unfortunately, there were no sinister-looking weapons of mass destruction. No incubators designed to hold terrifying bugs. She should have gone out the way she'd come in, but she wasn't thinking straight. She'd been so positive Hovertek was into something mind blowing. She strode confidently forward, when her ears picked up a sound. It was faint, perhaps a jingle.

Keys!

Like those hanging from the belt of a security guard. Priya turned back toward the door.

She placed her left hand on the door handle. But she didn't depress it yet. Leaning ever so gently against the door she held her ear against it. There was the jingle again. No mistaking it now. Definitely keys. Approaching.

Pressed against the door, she felt her heart racing. Adrenaline pulsed through her system, preparing her for another confrontation. Her mouth turned dry and her breath came out in shallow bursts through her open mouth. She clamped it shut before she became weak-kneed and crumbled like a well-done cookie. She forced herself to slow everything down by taking slow, deep and soundless breaths in through her nose and exhaling through her mouth. She swallowed rapidly, getting moisture into her parched mouth. She needed a drink badly but didn't dare take her focus away from the door. When her body was still, keeping her ear pressed against the door, she dragged the water bottle out of its pouch and took a deep swallow. Of course, it was too much. She couldn't down it without an audible gulp, so she swallowed just a bit and let the remaining dribble down her chin.

Now she could feel the footsteps through the vibrations in the door. They stopped. She heard a click, more jingling and then the footsteps faded.

"Whew!" She breathed out in a whisper. "All clear," she said and pressed the handle down.

She opened the door a tiny bit and peeked through. All she could see was the empty glass corridor. She stepped out and shut the door behind her. There was a soft click. It was very soft, but in the silence it was amplified.

"Oops!" She bit her lips. "It's okay," she reassured herself.

Still, just to be sure, she stuck to the glass wall of the corridor taking a couple of steps, then waiting and listening for any sound from the other side of the glass doors. As she crept forward, her reflection in the glass followed. When she took out a towel to wipe sweat off her face and neck, she noticed her shadow did not follow suit.

Someone was following her progress from the other side! She left the security of the wall and darted to the spot through which she had come.

Shit! She hadn't thought of closing it. No wonder a shadow was following her.

There was no way in hell she was going to be able to make it through the roof. Not without a ladder in sight. Then she remembered the thingamajig hanging from her belt. It looked like a mini garden tool with three retractable metal fingers.

The shadow on the other side of the glass was now pressed to the wall, trying to see through.

She threw the thingamajig through the hole in the ceiling and gave it some slack with the rope entwined around her wrist. The sound of it dragging against the sub ceiling was loud and then it stopped as it clamped onto something solid. Or so she hoped.

Priya crept up the metal rope as if it were a tree trunk. Finally, she got her elbows on the sub ceiling and gave a final heave. Pulling her legs up, she rolled to the side, and got to her feet. Like a cat, she slid through the opening, unhooked the thingamajig and wrapped it around her waist, a big grin on her face. She was so made for this type of thing. She could do this forever. It was perhaps time for a change. Maybe she should ditch catering and focus on snooping.

Okay. Talk was for later. She had to get the hell out of there.

She made her way to the skylight and clambered out. It was dark now. Yet she could see everything clearly. Spotlights aimed at the roof projected an enormous shadow of her over the grounds.

Too late. She was trapped. They were waiting for her down there.

"Oh, crap," she said. "Shit."

Crappola was what it was. She stepped down to the sub ceiling once again and made her way to the top of the glass corridor once again. This time, she had no problem with her descent from the ceiling. Maybe her muscles were getting used to the extra stretching. She landed on her feet, knees bent.

She nailed it! Perfect landing.

The shadow on the other side was gone. At the glass doors, she slid her fingers in the space between the two panels. She got two, then three fingers in and when she got a grip, she pulled. The door gave in easily and she darted through. She walked quickly, turned the corner and saw a figure at the end of the corridor. It could have been her shadow from the glass wall. She stood with her hands on her belt, ready to pull out a weapon.

The element of surprise, she again remembered Marie saying.

Instead of stopping, Priya ran toward her. The guard had no time to react. She jumped out of her way. It was that simple. In the lobby, she caught up with her. She ran around the fountain and through the seating area. Behind the leather chairs was a jungle of indoor plants in enormous terra cotta containers. She grabbed a planter and shoved it with all her strength. The branches of the small tree swayed and the leaves rustled, the reed-like branches pricking her in the nose. Then she felt the sharp burn from a cactus needle streaking across one cheek. She rubbed her face on her sleeve and shoved harder.

Damn! It wasn't enough.

She moved to the next smaller container and tipped it. She

ran to the door on the side, behind the front desk. Glancing back, she saw the plant container wobble crazily before it tipped over, hitting the potted palm next to it. The pot broke spilling earth all over the path of the guard following her. The potted palm tipped over, hitting another plant next to it, creating a domino effect. It stopped the guard long enough to give her time to get out. She opened the door and darted out without meeting resistance.

Before she could jump for joy, she ran smack into a solid body standing in her way. His cologne betrayed him. Dior's *Eau Sauvage,* the sexiest fragrance on earth and the sexiest man she'd ever met wearing it was standing in her way.

Crap! Dallas!

He slid his large hands down her shoulders, clamping her arms to her sides, like he'd done at the turtle crossing when she tried to kick his shins. And like he'd done on the pickleball courts. Then, bending down he was about to lift her when she jackknifed her legs. Her knees rammed his crotch. He dropped her like a hot potato. Priya balled her body and rolled over. On her feet in a jiffy, she ran like the wind only to discover he was close behind her.

The man must have a steel crotch. No way could he have recovered so fast.

CHAPTER TEN

DALLAS STEPPED OUT of the shower and wrapped a towel around his waist. He had not slept well. His mind was filled with images of a tat-covered neck and the sensations she made him feel. His attraction to Priya defied logic. She was not his type. He was more into the tall, athletic type of woman he was at eye-level with. This one probably didn't even hit five two! Fuck, did she pack a shitload of sexiness into her body and personality. He liked her. The proof was in the tent forming in the towel around his waist. And if he didn't stop thinking about her and her sweet lips it was going to be a problem.

His phone pinged sharply five times in succession. With a thumping heart he grabbed it, then plonked down on the bed when he saw it was not from his family. They were all from his security unit at Hovertek. One was from Gus.

GET OVER HERE, PRONTO! BREACH!

He hurriedly pulled on a pair of faded jeans and yanked a T-shirt over his head. Sliding his feet into sneakers, he grabbed his keys and was on his way out in three minutes flat. It was a circus at Hovertek. Lights streamed to the roof, cruisers were parked on the grass and the yard swarming with law enforcement. They focused on the front of the building and Dallas jogged to the side to the door, which was almost invisible at first sight. It blended so well into the exterior brick wall, it commanded no attention.

In the faint light seeping in from the floodlights, he saw a figure dart out. The next instant the area was flooded with light. He planted both feet in front of the door and took the full brunt of a body slamming into his. He reached out and when he steadied the person he realized it was a woman. A vague yet familiar scent assailed his nostrils. Did he know her? Before he could examine this thought further, a blinding flash of excruciating pain radiated from his crotch. He let go of her and sank to his knees.

"Fucking shit!" he roared.

From his crouched position he saw her shift and he knew more of whatever she was doling out was coming at him. She lowered her shoulders and would have slammed her body into his like a bulldozer bent on carnage if he hadn't jumped to his feet, his military training getting the upper hand. Seeing him on his feet made her turn. Then she was off. His long legs ate up the distance in a jiffy. In another jiffy, his hand wrapped around her ankle and yanked hard.

She tumbled silently and equally silently, Dallas pinned her to the ground with his body. She lay there with her chest heaving, the air coming out of her mouth in ragged gasps. As she lay panting heavily beneath him, his hands grasped her wrists and held them in a vice-like grip while he took deep breaths to counter the pain emanating from his crotch. She must have steel-capped knees for they packed a vicious punch.

When the throbbing between his legs ebbed into a dull ache, he relaxed his hold on her wrists. They felt delicate and small. He might have eased his body off hers too.

Big mistake.

He sensed her next move: her knee rising up ready to do bodily harm. "Oh, no. You're not going to do that to me again."

Her wrists were so small he could easily hold them with one hand. He raised them over her head and released his other hand. He used his weight to press her body down with as much gentle finesse he could gather. He ignored the sharp prick of something against his belly. There was the clink of glass.

It was the same person from the other day, the one with the blonde hair. He looked closely. The hair was askew and her forehead appeared broader.

With his free hand, he yanked the wig from her head. And even though the hair was pinned up and covered with a net, he saw it was dark. And even though her face was black, he knew it was Priya. Patches of lighter skin shone in the harsh light where the makeup had come off. There was a pale red streak across one cheek.

The second he realized it was Priya, his brain switched off and his body latched on greedily.

"What the hell, Priya! What are you doing here? In this… this…" he pointed to her getup with his chin.

He felt her move as she gave him a double shoulder shrug. Oh, he knew that. He'd used it often enough himself when he didn't want to reply. To gain time and to stall. He nudged her. She rolled her eyes.

"It's not going to cut it, Priya. Rolling your eyes and shrugging will not cut it. Do you understand? And don't nod. Say yes."

"Yes," her voice was just a whisper. "Can you get off me? Can't breathe."

Right. And all of a sudden he became aware of her. Of his legs wedged between hers and her chest pressed against his. This was not just some intruder. This was Priya with her body beneath his. As he eased his weight off her body, the weird pricks on his skin relaxed their pressure. Maybe this was going to be another moment of revelation.

"Not until you tell me what's going on."

"Snooping for my blog. Wanted to know what was going on here."

"And all this," he cleared his throat and pointed to the belt and other accessories hanging from her belt. "All this was for your blog?"

And just like that, his brain took over. He took a deep breath and let go of her hands. His body began shaking and he rolled off her. He stayed on his back, arms stretched above his head, chuckles pouring out of him. Bracing himself on one elbow, he looked at her, taking in her netted hair, the dark outfit and the thick boots. The chuckles became a laugh. Then two. Under the glare of the floodlights, he touched the various pouches on her pants. He looked into the pocket with the marbles. He examined the Swiss army knife. Taking special care when he handled the thingamajig, his eyes widened. His low laughter turned into a roaring waterfall when he saw the pepper spray.

He fell back on the ground, hands rubbing his face.

"Jesus, Priya. All you had to do was ask. I'd have shown you around." He jumped up and raised her to her feet, steadying her with his body when she wobbled and swayed. Tossing aside the curse rising on his lips, he bent and hooked his arm around her knees. "I'm going to get you inside first, okay? Then I have to talk to the duty officers milling about. I will be back, okay? No running off this time."

He carried her inside to the lounge in the back of the building and set her down on the sectional. Tipping her chin with a finger he made her meet his gaze.

"Stay. I mean it. I want to know more about the marbles." He couldn't keep the grin from his face. "Don't. Move." He punctuated the words with a tap of his index finger against her cheek.

She nodded, her lids shuttering her gorgeous eyes.

Fuck, how he wanted to kiss her. But, now was not the time for it. He turned away from her, all of his senses aware she was very still and, despite the paint on her face, still highly desirable.

The more he saw of her the more he liked her. She was small as a Jack Russell with all the spunk, energy and fearlessness.

When things were settled outside, he came back to the lounge and was relieved to see she hadn't moved. He was not going to let her off easily.

"Explain," he uttered the word in a tone he used with subordinates. It cleared his chest in a stark and raspy wave.

"Like I said, Dallas. I was doing research for my blog." She refused to meet his eyes.

"And the research warrants such a getup?" He was not going to ease up. "This is serious business, you do realize don't you? I could press charges."

"Will you?" The green eyes swung to his face.

He waved her question away. "Where do you get your ideas?"

"I have a licence, you know."

"To do what? To break into a secure facility?"

"A PI license."

"You don't get it, Priya. That piece of laminated shit is worthless. It does not give you permission to break into *my* facility and snoop. If you wanted to know what we're doing here at Hovertek, all you had to do was contact my PR department."

"*The Tribune* reported you have military funding. You're into spyware."

"Yep, it's true about the funding. We're developing drones for search and rescue in both military and civilian operations. If *The Tribune* wants to call it spyware there's nothing I can do about it. But *you* I can do something about."

He hooked a hand around her arm and pulled her up.

"Where are we going?" She stumbled on her feet, pitching toward him.

"Giving you a tour of the place. And maybe get you a drink first."

"Can I have my wig back please?"

She held out her hand. It was stuffed in his pant pocket.

"Don't know, Priya. It's a real ugly one. Doesn't suit you at all."

"How do you know what suits me?"

"Just a lucky guess. Anyway, you can have it back." He didn't want to see her being blonde again. Dark suited her. Dark waves spread out on a red satin pillow, his fingers threading through the silky strands.

Hell, she was doing quite a number on him. He was in deep shit. She surprised him, blowing down his stable defences. She was unpredictable and he quite liked it. From the dancer invading his dreams to this burglar, he was enjoying everything about her.

She took the wig from him and pulled it on her head. She walked beside him, jingling and clunking. He bit his lips to smother a grin. She sounded like a cowboy with spurs. In his office, he was his calm and collected self again. He poured her a glass of cold water from a bottle in the fridge. She chugged it down, drops of water running down her neck and into the collar of her black shirt.

"Sit," he pointed to a chair opposite his desk.

She plonked her behind in it, set the empty glass on the small table beside the chair and undid the top buttons of her shirt. A V of pale skin contrasted sharply against the black of the shirt and the dark makeup on her neck, the tip dipping into darkness filled with promises. A golden chain dangled enticingly, carnal thoughts sending inappropriate impulses to his groin just as his gaze caught the horribly out of place wig and brought everything to a standstill. But not for very long.

"You wanted to know about something…?" her voice was husky and it rolled right up his spine making him want more.

"What's in all the pockets?"

She stood up, walked to his desk and began emptying them. He saw a pepper spray, a Swiss army knife-when did they get an army?-a three-pronged hook, various mini tool kits including a mini-drill and a squeegee bottle filled with a viscous liquid. He picked it up and squeezed a bit on his hand and sniffed.

Oil. From the smell and texture of it, of the cooking variety. Wrapped around her thigh was a water bottle from which she drank deep. She smacked her lips and wiped them with her sleeve, removing more of the black paint on her face. He couldn't help it. A smile began to twitch on his lips.

"Tell me how you use these weapons."

So she told him. Involuntary chuckles escaped the tight control he kept on his emotions. But she was too much. It was impossible to keep a straight face as she described how she got away from *his* guards and how they went down slipping and sliding over the oily marbles.

A full-blown laughter series burst out of him. He'd known she was trouble. But boy, did she make him laugh. He showed her around the Hovertek facility with Priya not showing much enthusiasm, matching his strides to her short ones.

"What's the matter now? Didn't you want to know more about what we're doing here?"

She shrugged again. "I think..."

"You don't want to anymore, is that it? How're you going to post a correct blog when you're not even looking for information? What changed, Priya?"

"It was more appealing when I was snooping around. Now," again the shrug, "not so much."

He stopped in his tracks, his eyes locked on hers. There was a resigned set to the way she held herself, her eyes having lost their gleam. He got it. It had been exciting when she was breaking the rules. Now, not so much. The thrill of it was gone.

Vapourized.

CHAPTER ELEVEN

GETTING CAUGHT BY Dallas had not been Priya's brightest hour. He'd shown her what Hovertek was working on and it was very impressive. She wasn't tethered to her sporadic blog. Anyway, it wasn't as much fun as it had been. The Hovertek incident was never mentioned again. Neither was her blog.

A day later at pickleball, Priya was paired with Dallas against Kevin and Angela. Kevin was a pretty hard hitter and Priya was wondering if she should sit the game out. Yet it would do her good to play with Kevin. Perhaps her responses to his hard projectiles would be just as rapid and hard this time.

Kevin launched one low and fast over the net, coming hard at her. Before she knew it, the ball hit on the soft spot above her knee. She grimaced, rubbing the spot. It was like getting hit with a whip.

Sharp. No matter.

She got ready to get the next one. When that too hit her on her leg, she knew he was targeting her. She was the weak link.

By now Dallas was frowning. He was suspicious. "You okay?"

"Am fine."

"He's aiming at you. Let's switch at the next shot after you return it."

And that's what they did. After she returned Kevin's serve, she moved quickly to the other half of the court, while Dallas slid over to her spot. Kevin's shot came back hard and fast to Dallas who returned. The ball cleared the net and skimmed the sideline. Kevin lunged at it, to no avail. Priya and Dallas won the game.

"Great game, Dallas. Thanks to you."

"Geez Priya," Angela said, squeezing Priya's shoulders. "Are you okay? That guy wouldn't let me get a ball. He was always in front of me, poaching. Think we should suggest he play singles? Then he'd have the whole court to himself."

Priya giggled. Now that would be a sight: Kevin trying to make the shots from all over. She didn't think he'd survive.

"How does he get at my body every time?" Priya took a gulp from her water bottle. "I don't do that. I never target an opponent's body. Have yet to hit someone."

"Don't worry about it," Dallas touched her arm gently. "You're a great player. You know that, right?"

His touch sent a shower of goose pimples over her skin. It never happened when either Bob or Kalle touched her. But then again if it had, she'd be in even more trouble than ever. Anna and Milla would get together, chop her to pieces and feed her to the fish. She mopped her temples with a wet towel.

Priya smiled, something tugging at her heart, wishing for what she couldn't say. Seeing the softer side of Dallas, the caring side left her yearning for something she had never had in her life before.

When she finished her next game, Bob was sitting in his chair next to Anna.

At Priya's raised eyebrows, he said, "Got to take a break."

"Me too," Priya replied and flopped into her chair.

"Nice turn out. Plenty of new members. We'll try it at Cobourg in a few weeks," Bob said, going off in a tangent.

"Try what?"

"The switcheroo. If the man picks on you-and believe me he will-and hits smash after smash at you, I will not wait for the smashes. When he gets the ball back to us, you take my place and I'll slide over to yours and smash the ball right back at the bastard."

They were strategizing and it usually got Bob really worked up. Plus Bob wanted to win.

"I tried it with Dallas just now. Kevin, you know Kevin right?" At Bob's blank look, she described him. "Lots of grey hair? Grey beard and moustache? Likes to smash."

Thing was, there were quite a few with grey hair.

"Nope. Does not ring a bell."

"That's because you can't remember names," Anna came up with her bit of wisdom.

"Anyway, Dallas and I were playing him and Angela. First, he kept poaching her shots. Then he kept targeting me. I got blue spots all over my leg," she showed them the bruises. "Well, Dallas showed me this switcheroo thing and we did it and we beat him."

"That's *exactly* what we should do."

"And then Dallas told him off."

"He did, eh? Good for him. Yes, that's what we should do. If they lob a shot over your head, I'll run around to your side and get it while you scoot over to my side to cover the return."

"Got it. We should get a few practice sessions before the tournament."

"We should. And we will. You playing with Kelly?"

"Yes, of course."

They'd played together in a few tournaments. Brought home a few medals too. Nothing to sniff at. They'd beaten the Belleville gang. It was quite a feat as the Belleville gals were built like Mack trucks. Next to them, Priya and Kelly looked like ants, scrambling around. They were a good fit: Kelly the power player and Priya the strategic soft shot player.

Priya looked forward to beating the Mack trucks again this time around.

~

DALLAS RAN UP the stairs to his spare room. It was fabulous Friday. In the dark, his foot hit the wall, stubbing his toe. Hard.

"What the fuck," he said out loud with nothing but the dark shadows for an audience. Then for good measure he repeated, "Fuck." Words never permitted in his parents' house.

Ah, it was indeed great to live alone.

But the shit hurt like hell. He hopped on one leg, rubbing the toe until the pain subsided into a dull throb. Then he carefully navigated in the dark to the window overlooking the yard. He had a clear view into Priya's living room. He was not too late. He sighed deeply, living only for the moment, nothing but the now in his mind. Which was quite the turnaround for him. He lived for planning and taking it slow. But ever since Priya walked into his life, it had taken unexpected turns. She made it impossible to go slow. It was now or never. He felt it each time he saw her.

Like the kiss. It had been a now or never kind of moment. He'd just jumped right in. And it had felt good. Right.

Today, Priya's skirt was green. She wore a bikini type top, leaving the midriff bare. Her skin shone through the transparent piece of cloth covering her chest. Yet, it revealed everything. He wished he'd thought of grabbing his binoculars from downstairs. As it was, he was afraid to leave the window. Then quickly before he changed his mind, he dashed down the stairs, grabbed the binoculars and raced back up.

Her windows were closed: he couldn't hear the music she danced to and her body swayed and dipped, her feet moving quickly as the skirt flared out around her. He watched her, waiting for his favourite part when she shook her hips and undulated her body, the arms and hands doing a graceful dance of their own. She stood on one leg, raised the other up to waist height, bending it at the knee to cross her body. Both arms reached to the side of the raised leg, one pointing down, the other, up.

Dallas adjusted the focus on the binoculars. Her outfit came out more defined than her face. He could see all the little stars and mirrors on it. The long piece of cloth over her head and across her breasts sparkled with sequins.

When she was done, he went to his fridge and grabbed a bottle of Tuborg and emptied it in few frenzied gulps. Then he pulled on his running wear and ran ten times around his block. A quick shower and he dropped into bed, falling into a dreamless sleep.

He woke up in the early hours of the morning with the moon shining on his face. With the awareness of his surroundings came images: Priya's bare midriff glowing through the diaphanous material; her sensual body movements. And as usual, these images went straight to his groin. Not to speak of the early morning testosterone surge.

It was the fifth year after his breakup with Kate. She had not wanted a long distance relationship. She had not wanted to get married. She had not wanted children. There had been a lot of things Kate had not wanted. In time, they turned out to be things he wanted. Even the thought of a long distance relationship had not been a hurdle to him. They'd work it out. Eventually. He *did* want to marry her and have a family.

Ultimately, what Kate did not want outweighed what he wanted and that was it.

Splitsville.

Being alone was now part of his life.

Now, before things got out of hand or into it, he switched his laptop on and worked on a few more pressing matters. The trade delegation from China wanted information on Kingston and its investment opportunities. City Hall had requested his input.

Normally, such deals went to Vancouver, Toronto or Montreal. This time, it seemed as if the Chinese were ready to make a mark on small Kingston. Perhaps its proximity to the US border was a factor? Whatever it was, Dallas was on it. First with the Chamber of Commerce and the remainder would follow as the project advanced. He worked on the files until it was time to pick up his bestie, Jason Briggs, from the airport.

At the tiny airport, Dallas waited for Jason. As soon as he saw him, he waved.

"Jason. Good to see you, man." Dallas bumped him with his shoulder and thumped his back.

Jason nodded, the aviator glasses glinting in the sun. "Same here, buddy. Long time no see."

"Yeah. Been what? A year?"

They walked out to the lot.

"Something like that. Maybe closer to two."

At his place, once Jason was settled, and food was ordered, they sat on the shady deck and cracked open bottles of chilled beer.

"I can't remember ever sitting like this with you and having a cold one." Jason put his bottle to his lips and took a deep swallow.

"The last time was just before we left the army. I never looked back but you still fly."

"It's the only thing I know, Dallas. The only thing I'm good at."

"I get it. It's great you're still doing what you love. Tell me more about it."

"I fly private jets. It gives me the time to be with Marie or rather gave me the time since she decided we needed to take a break."

"Why? I thought you proposed?"

"I did and that's what did it. I think it scared her more than anything. And the thought of not having her in my life scares the shit out of me. Even more than the reconnaissance tours I did in Afghanistan."

"That sucks, man. Did you find out what she wants?"

"Time apart for starters. She's such a blitz of a woman. Always on the go. She's been spending time with friends. In fact, she was just in Kingston with her best friend Priya Keelor."

"Yeah, Priya did mention she knew you." He took a swig from his bottle. "Small world! I know what you mean by 'blitz.' Priya has so many things going on. It's like she's juggling five balls and I'm waiting for one to drop so I can pick it up just to get the chance to get closer."

"Exactly. Marie is this firecracker, popping all over the place. The thing is, we're perfect for each other. But tell that to her. She just will not admit it. You know they went to school in England together?"

"I gathered something like that. Priya does not have a British accent but her curses are British. You know her well, do you?"

"Sure. She's this tiny gorgeous, sexy Bollywood dancer."

"Right," Dallas chuckled. "You've summed her up quite nicely. Too bad I didn't know her when Marie was visiting."

"How did you meet?"

"She almost ran into my SUV at a turtle crossing."

"Almost?"

"Stopped just short. She drives this eyesore of a yellow truck. She tried to kick my shins and I stopped her."

"She's a hoot."

"Then I met her again at pickleball."

"Pickleball. Yeah, I've heard about it. The fastest growing sport in America."

"I'm playing tomorrow and I'd like you to come and try it out."

"Sure thing. Heard it's a bit like tennis."

"Tennis and table tennis mostly. And maybe racquetball too. You play tennis, you'll pick it up in no time."

"Have always wanted to try it out but never had the opportunity."

"Remember the time you flew out to the mountains?" Dallas leaned back in his chair, his voice soft and low as it drowned in memories.

"It was a beautiful space with spectacular views of untouched snow-covered peaks of the Hindu Kush in the Himalayan range. It's why I still fly. It's in my blood. I especially love flying at night. I get this feeling of awe when I'm up high with nothing but the endless sky above dotted with who knows how many fucking planets and wondering how Earth is the only viable one. Unforgettable. I flew to the edge of China and back. And then my radio caught the Chinese frequencies. You had to listen and translate."

"At least I tried to. My Mandarin was nothing like what I heard over the waves. At first I thought they were using a code. It took me a while to decipher what they were saying. Turned out they were speaking Cantonese and just enjoying a break and a smoke."

"Good thing too. I thought General Davidson was going to blow an artery. He was so tightly wound, so sure it was something really bad."

"There was a bit of chatter in Urdu too which, unfortunately I couldn't decipher."

The doorbell rang announcing the arrival of their food.

CHAPTER TWELVE

For a second Priya was startled when she saw a familiar blond head with Dallas on the pickleball courts. Then she remembered Jason and Dallas were best friends just like Marie and she were.

"Hey Priya." Jason gave her a hug lifting her off her feet while Dallas watched.

"Hi Jason." She looped her arms around his neck. "Lovely to see you. Sorry Marie is not with you."

Jason shook his head. "I'm only slightly concerned. I'm not letting her go this easily."

"I think you should not. You guys are perfect together. But tell Marie that."

Jason and Dallas joined in her chuckle. "This so called break will do her good."

"So, shall we?" Priya picked up her paddle from the stand and made her way to the court where Bob was waiting.

Despite it being Jason's first time, he picked up the pickleball moves quickly. It was a tough match but Dallas was no match for Bob's wicked down the middle and sideline shots while Priya did her bit to get in her nasty just-over-the-nets pokes. Bob and

Priya managed to hold on to their slim two point lead to finish the game.

Panting, they flopped on the picnic bench, Priya chugging from her water bottle as she mopped her face with a wet towel.

"That was great!" Jason slung a towel around his neck. "Wow! Bob, you have some wicked moves."

Bob smirked, shrugged and chugged his water. He took his cap off, rubbing a towel on his balding grey head.

"So how long are you staying?" Bob asked Jason the same time he took another swig from his bottle. A bout of coughs and he was ready to go again.

"A few days. Long enough to catch up with my best buddy here," Jason slapped Dallas on the back, "but not so long that I begin to get in his way. He's writing a book, you know."

Dallas frowned and looked away. "Actually I'm not. I'm *thinking* of writing. Totally different."

"Oh really?" Priya, slouching on the table, sat up straight. "What kind of book?"

"That's exactly it. I don't know. I haven't started yet."

"But watch out when he does," Jason grinned at his friend. "He has a way with words."

"Can we please change the subject?" Dallas voice rumbled in Priya's ears.

So he was touchy about this writing thing of his. Good to know. She filed it away for future use.

Pleased at having beaten Dallas and Jason, Priya went home, showered and made it to Spice Haven in record time. Mark and Mia were already in the kitchen, getting trays out of the ovens.

"What's the grin for?" Mia paused, balancing the cookie sheet on the edge of the counter.

"Win at pickleball."

"That's it? That's all it takes. A measly win at pickleball?" Sliding the tray on the counter, Mia slipped the oven mitts from her hands.

"This was against two strong and young players. Scratch that. One and a half players."

"Half? How do you come up with that?" Mia plucked a cookie from the tray and took a bite. "Hmm. Priya, this is so good. It has just the right amount of chocolate chunks. Melting chocolate chunks. Hmmm."

"It was Jason's first game. So the half."

"Jason's in town?"

"Yep. Visiting Dallas."

"What about the breakup with Marie?"

"He's determined it's not a breakup. He's not letting her off this easily."

"Glad to hear it. She can be such an ass sometimes."

Priya tied an apron around her waist and got busy. With the menu up on the screen hanging at eye-level above the counter, it was a breeze.

"Who do we have for help tonight?"

"I will be there," Mark announced. "I'd love to see the inside of Hovertek. I've heard wonderful things about them."

Priya bit her lip, unwilling to reveal her suspicion about the gig. Surely this was Dallas's doing!

"Melissa and Jeremy have signed on too."

"Great! It's all set then." Mark rubbed his hands together. "And I guess, you Mia, will be handling the coordination?"

"You got it, Mark. Not letting this one go. I want a peek inside Hovertek too."

When they walked in through the glass-walled lobby at Hovertek, Mia shrieked "Crenshaw? This is Dallas Crenshaw's turf? As in the hunk you play pickleball with?"

"Hmm. So? What's there to shriek about?"

"OMG! This is so crazy, Priya!"

"Why? This is a small town remember? We all will eventually run into each other at some point. Six degrees of separation?"

A bit deflated at the logic behind Priya's words, Mia began to unload the truck with Mark.

Priya palmed the door from the hall where the event was taking place and pushed it open, an empty tray in her hand. As she came back with a full platter and rounded the corner, balancing the metal tray on the widespread fingers of her right hand, she stopped short.

"Do I have to thank you for this gig?" Priya looked up at Dallas.

He shook his head. "Nope. Am not involved in planning our bi-weekly lunches. My assistant takes care of it."

"Oh." And here she'd been so certain it was Dallas.

He was dressed casually in jeans, the T-shirt he wore stretching nicely over his broad chest. Visions of it bare and wet instantly rose up in her mind, as did the memory of his lips gently brushing hers. Her mouth went dry and her throat knotted up. All she could do was lick her lips and that innocuous movement drew his eyes to her mouth.

Moving faster than her exhale, Dallas closed the distance between them. She did not hear the platter drop from her hand, land with a muted metallic thud and, once emptied of its delicious content, clang its way merrily down the polished stone floor to hug a corner, waiting in vain to be picked up.

All she saw was Dallas, the fire in his grey eyes and those kissable lips approaching hers.

"Tell me you want this," his mouth barely touching hers, she heard the words flutter across her skin.

"I want this," she murmured, rising on her toes and looping her arms around his neck, sliding her eager fingers into his silky hair.

Dallas grasped her by the waist and backed her through a door and into a dark room where the lights came on. Kicking the door shut, he backed her against a wall. Then his mouth was on hers. It was unlike any kiss she'd ever had. He devoured her, his lips drinking and drinking deep, taking away her last breath and still she wanted more. A slow heat began to unfurl in her belly, the fingers licking their way down between her thighs.

"I'm going crazy with want for you." He cradled her face in his hands. "Do you feel it?"

He thrust his hips into the wedge between her legs. Then his mouth was on her again, skimming the skin on her neck, his hands rising under her skirt.

Warning pricks of reality prodded her lust-engrossed brain. She was here on a gig! Mark and Mia would be looking for her. And crap! Where was the platter she'd been holding not a minute ago?

She drew away from him. "Dallas, I've got to go. This is not the right time or place."

"When will it be?" He still held her by the waist.

She tugged her skirt down and straightened her shirt. She shook her head and shrugged. "Can't say. It's not something you plan, you know."

"Right. Okay, then this will have to do."

He yanked her to him and crushed his mouth to hers. Her mouth opened under his. His hot wet lips ravished her and when he was done, she could only stare at his back a he left her speechless and breathless. She was shaking so hard, she slid down the wall to the floor, legs stretched out in front of her, her listless arms by her sides.

What was he doing to her? Dallas made her feel things she had forgotten. He was screwing up her life by thrusting himself into it. He was rocking the raft she was contently drifting on. She did not *want* to be anchored down.

But she wanted him. God, how she wanted him!

His life was Hovertek, a family business. And family meant marriage and children. They were not the things she wanted.

Could she have one without the other? She was not cut out to be a wife and mother. She was almost certain she wanted a hassle free hookup and just as certain Dallas would not be the one to give it to her. Whatever his past relationship experience was, she was sure he still believed in a committed one.

WHEN DALLAS GOT home he could not forget Priya and their heated kiss when her body was flush against his, her fingers raking his scalp. She'd been hot and ready for him just like he'd been for her. He'd almost lost it then. If she hadn't stopped just then he would have forged ahead, lost in the sensations of her hot body pressed against his.

Scratch that. Sizzling body.

Was that his or hers? He'd been almost sure she was about to shin him when he put his hands on her. Like he'd said to Jason, she was a blitz, superbly multitasking her life, doing many things at once, while he could barely handle two. His type was the cool and collected woman. Not a firecracker on the verge of blowing his sedate life to bits. Priya made him feel he was more, more than he was as the middle son and the middle brother. She brought out desires and wants in him. She drew him into her orbit, exposing little flashes of her temperament he found so irresistible. She was so unlike Kate.

That was then when Dallas thought the woman called Kate was his soul mate. That was when Kate had been the Juliet to his Romeo. Perhaps he'd been naïve enough to believe Kate had ever been his Juliet.

This was now. Dallas was steadfastly single. Not necessarily by his choice though. Or maybe it was. He was getting picky, reluctant to spend precious time chasing after high maintenance companions. Reluctant too to relish the thought of one night stands. That was not him. At the most, the thought got a wince out of him and at the least, a disdainful shrug. He could do the shrugs very well, having had quite a bit of practice.

Houston wanted him to join the family man club while Austin didn't give a shit one way or the other. Although Austin's vocabulary did not include 'shit.'

Being the Mr. Go Slow, his goal was to peel layer after layer from the object of his desire, taking his time. He was a sipper while Austin gulped. It would take someone special to catch his eye, someone like Priya if there was a way he could breach the final restraint holding him back.

Dallas was not immune to female charms. In fact, he admired women and their strength, fearlessness and ability to blossom under the direst of conditions like the cactus flowers blooming in the Arizona desert. When he thought of their bodies-as in not any particular one-it was always accompanied by Beethoven's Third. In Priya, he encountered the one body encased in a beautiful mind-maybe it was the other way round-to capture his fantasy.

Then there had been her storming the Hovertek castle. What a night it had been! He'd been so sure it was espionage. Finding out it was Priya had been an anti-climax. It was amazing what she could do, all five foot two of her! Shocker of fucking shocker was the knowledge of her being a PI. Was that even a job description in today's IT world? Where did she come up with these ideas? If he had her imagination, his book would have been written by now. In a few years, he might be ready to write the book fermenting in his brain. He was not a disciplined writer. He scribbled things down when he felt like it and those times were not often enough.

He could not indulge in this distraction. He had to focus on his projects.

He'd just walked in the door and about to pop the cap of a cool bottle of Sapporo when his phone pinged. His older brother, Houston, sending him a text.

Boat. This evening.

This was followed by Austin's text.

Dinner where?

Food was always on Austin's mind. The youngest of three, he was ready to eat whatever whenever. Houston and Dallas were the cooks, just like their mother, and Austin was the eater just like his father. Dallas was the in-between guy, at thirty-four a perfect reflection of his karma as the in-between brother. Still in that place he'd left behind, still unable to look forward.

It was a beautiful evening and the sunset over Lake Ontario was going to be gorgeous. He had an hour to pack the cooler with food and drink before Austin picked him up. Spending time with his brothers relaxed Dallas. They eased the stress out of him like nothing else could.

Austin arrived to pick him up on time, roaring into his driveway in a humongous tuck. It guzzled gas like someone dying of thirst in the desert.

At thirty, Austin was also the tallest Crenshaw with the same dark hair but amber eyes. He kept his hair slightly long on the top and short on the sides. The wavy locks were brushed back in a controlled chaos style. A diamond stud glittered in one ear. At one time, he'd sported a nose stud too but now no more. A neatly trimmed beard and moustache framed his expressive mouth. Tats peeked out from the edge of the sleeves of his T-shirt.

Eyes followed them as they made their way through the aisles at Farm Boy. Blessed with strikingly good looks, they moved like the alpha males they were. Dallas piled items into the cart while Austin pushed. They loaded everything into the truck. Dallas's phone pinged again. Houston again. He ignored it. Then it rang. He had no choice but to answer. Houston again.

"Calling base station."

"What's up? Need us to get anything?"

"Just wondering where you guys are. Over and out."

"On our way, dude. Be there in thirty."

"Roger that."

Predictably, Houston associated his name with NASA Mission Control. He made sure everyone knew he had the name to live up to. He'd seen Apollo 13 at least ten times at last count. He could watch Star Trek forever.

In his truck, Austin punched a button and music filled the interior. Music from Dallas and Houston's teen years: Pearl Jam and Stone Temple Pilots.

"What's this?" Dallas asked as the digital display lit up. "Gerry Rafferty. The Cars. Toto?" He pressed the button on the player and read out loud the artist list.

"Remember when Mom used to make Dad nuts by listening to *Baker Street* over and over again?"

"Yeah. And ZZ Top. And U2. And Bon Jovi. And especially Styx and *Boat on the River*. He used to poke his head through the kitchen door and then disappear. She'd be baking: muffins, breads and cookies."

"She'd make two large loaves of bread and they would be gone by the next day. She couldn't keep up with the demand, right? Remember how we slathered butter over warm slices and scarfed them down?"

"Yeah, I remember. She gave up making bread and stuck to muffins and cookies."

"Well, I downloaded all those songs and now she can listen to them all over again."

"She stopped listening to them a while back, I think. At least I've never heard her play them since."

"Recently she's into sitar music. She says it's inspiring."

"She said that? Wasn't Ravi Shankar the greatest sitar player? The Indian musician? The Beatles went to visit him in India."

"Hmm. Maybe. Don't know. Music extends over all barriers of culture, religion and language, she says."

"When did you do this?"

"Last night. Thought it might make a great gift for Mom's birthday."

"Super idea, bro." Dallas slapped him on his shoulder. "No Emily?" he waded in carefully. Austin was sensitive about his philandering ways. And close-mouthed. Austin could sense his family's disapproval.

"Nope. We're not together anymore."

Dallas sighed and let it go. Plenty of time for that later on. When he was filled with food, Austin was pretty malleable. Dallas now flipped through the songs, reading the titles on the screen until he came to *Boat on the River.* They listened to it and the others until they reached the marina.

The boat, The-what else?-Enterprise belonged to Houston. There, Dallas and Austin hauled the food and drinks to the boat in one shot.

They found Houston, bare-footed at the grill, flipping burgers. At thirty-eight and without his customary suit and tie, he was less intimidating. He was shirtless, with smooth well-toned skin on a sculpted body. He wore swimming trunks hugging his narrow hips. His hair fell over his forehead in unruly strands.

Houston raised his eyes from the grill and gave them a wave with the spatula he was holding. Then took a jump back as hot liquid sizzled on the grill. But he was not quick enough: a drop hit his bare skin, and he uttered words not allowed in his home.

The Crenshaw boys were good at that. With two young children, they had to watch their mouths. But when they were together, all bets were off. They were their natural cussing selves.

"Fuck!" Houston yelled, throwing the spatula down.

From the storage bin under the cushions, he yanked an apron, threw his head through the loop and tied it around his waist. It belonged to Lara and said, 'Kiss the cook,' in red letters.

Austin stopped what he was doing and watched his brother's antics. In two strides he was by his side, grabbed him by the shoulders and plonked him a kiss on his cheek.

"What the fuck?" Houston stumbled back, rubbing his cheek. "Fuck!" he said again for good measure because he could.

"Says right there," Austin said pointing to the apron. "Don't tell me you've never been kissed before."

"No. Never by a bearded moron."

"Ah," Austin said, slapping Houston on the back. "You'll get over it."

As they were unpacking, Austin hummed under his breath. Then he said, "Forgot my MP3 stick in the truck. I'll go get it. Can't sail without music."

He jogged up to his truck, still humming.

"What's up with him?" Houston asked pointing the spatula at Austin. "Why's he kissing and humming?"

"Broke up with Emily."

"Ah! That explains it. He wants *us* to think everything's fine. *He's* fine. Wonder what he did this time? He always messes it up, doesn't he? Why can't he be happy with the woman he's with instead of being afraid of what he might be missing? He'll never be happy this way. Emily is a great woman. I think she's just his type. She's warm, intelligent and beautiful. Why is that not enough for him?" Houston rattled on.

"Maybe he's insecure. He has to keep checking if he's just as good as Emily thinks he is."

"What, he couldn't keep his pants zipped? Again?" Houston did not get his younger brother.

"Don't believe it was his roving zipper. He's changed. He's more mature. More focused."

"How d'you know? Has be been talking to you?"

If anything, Houston was the protector. The one who knew everything going on in all their lives. This included him as the giver of brotherly advice. He relished his role as the elder brother. What they did, he'd done it before them. The eight years between him and Austin did not help either of them. It was okay when they'd been younger. But now they'd caught up with him in size.

"Not quite. I've seen them together a lot. A lot more than you. He could be in love with her, Houston. You know how that is. Remember how it was with you and Lara? He doesn't realize Emily *needs* to hear it. *Really* hear him say it."

Dallas could dish it out as easily as Houston. Say all the appropriate things about what women wanted to hear when in fact he had no clue. He was big on fantasy and theory but came short on actually being able to keep the woman he loved by his side.

Houston remained silent, with the look of a man whose thoughts swirled like the sun washing over him. He wiped his brow with the apron and squinted at Dallas through his sunglasses.

"You're right. There was a time when I thought I'd lost Lara. We were so stubborn, neither of us giving an inch. But anyway, what about you? Anyone?"

Dallas shrugged, shaking his head. "Not quite there yet. Still going over the past."

Been there, done that. Dallas did not want to elaborate.

"Ah! Let it be, bro. Leave it there. Move on to new experiences with new people."

CHAPTER THIRTEEN

DALLAS SAW PRIYA huddled with Kelly under the shade of the big maple tree. He couldn't wait to finish his game and get over there. He played two games back to back with Kalle.

When he got to where Kelly and Priya were, he plopped down on the bench beside Kelly so he was facing Priya. Her sunglasses were propped up on her hat, a wet towel around her neck. She handed Kelly a frozen icepack. Kelly rubbed it on her neck, shoulders and temples.

"Hey, Kelly. Priya," Dallas did not look at Priya. He waited for a sign from her.

"Hi," Kelly said.

Priya gave him a smile, raising her eyebrows. He caught it when his gaze flickered over face briefly. Okay. Looked like it was all right. Taking a wet towel from his bag, he took off his sunglasses and mopped his face, not looking at her. He felt her gaze on him. Still he did not look at her.

Damn it!

He was prolonging the sweet torture, Mr. Go Slow at work again. It was so like him to wait for the reward. He was the hoarder, the one who kept the Halloween candy hidden way beyond Christmas. When finally grey eyes met green, something sizzled between them. Kelly's eyes shuttled from Priya to Dallas and back again.

"So are we good about our game? The strategy and stacking?" Kelly got up, handing Priya the icepack.

"Yeah, we're good. You free in the evening to practice a bit more?"

"Do we have a four? Maybe Dallas and Kalle could come too." Kelly looked at Dallas. "What about it, Dallas?"

"I can't make it here before seven. I haven't asked Kalle yet."

"I'm sure he can make it. He's quite obsessed with pickleball. You'll see. See you both at seven then."

"Okay." Finally, Dallas turned toward Priya. "Had a good game?"

"Was okay. I'd like to play against a stronger women's team. You know just to be challenged. Mixed doubles game was better. I play better if I play with better players. My game is better. Better for all of us," she finished with a laugh. "What about you?"

"Kalle and I did pretty well. So you want to ride together later?" Dallas stared into her unfathomable green eyes. "Pick you up?"

A ring of black surrounded the green. Minuscule flecks of gold scattered through the green and caught the light flickering through the leaves.

"Okay. Let me give you my address." The eyelids dropped over her eyes, as if hiding a secret.

He let her give it to him. He entered it in his phone. He did not say he knew it already. He had his secrets too. He took the opportunity to lock his eyes on the tat on her neck. Then he got up.

"See you later." He waved at her. He wasn't going to broach the subject of the kiss if she wasn't.

He got hold of Kalle just as he was preparing to leave.

"You up for some games this evening? A few of us are getting together to practice at seven."

Kalle looked at Milla before answering. "We have anything this evening, honey?"

"No, we don't. Not you at least. I can't. Anyway, *I'm* not playing in the tournament."

"See you then at seven, Dallas," Kalle waved and drove away.

At quarter to seven, Dallas was before Priya's house. He texted her.

AM HERE. READY?

BE RIGHT OUT.

She came out, hair tucked away under a hat, holding a plastic cup and a canned drink.

She climbed into the passenger seat, adjusted the height and incline. She clipped the seat belt on, leaned back and, turning to him she said, "Want some coconut water? I brought you a plastic cup. I could pour some for you."

"I've never tried it. Would like some. Thanks."

She poured coconut water into the cup and watched as he sipped from it.

"Well?" she asked as he set the cup in the holder.

"It's okay, I guess. Has no flavour, just a bit of sweetness."

"What did you expect?"

"It *is* coconut water. I was expecting this to taste of coconut."

"It's never that strong. I've had the real thing."

"You have? Where?"

"In Toronto. And fresh sugarcane juice too." She smacked her lips. "Now *that* has not only flavour, but it's also very sweet. Want to ask you something." She turned toward him.

"Go ahead."

"You were there at the mayor's office get together, right? A while ago? Did you get a chance to taste the tomato and coriander chutney sandwiches?"

"Taste? I gobbled up the whole tray. They were out of this world. A riot of taste in my mouth."

"No after effects? You inhaled twenty of them!"

"Nope," he patted his stomach. "Pretty good lining. Wait a sec! Did you make those?"

"Yes I did. They're my favs. I always slip a tray in at my gigs."

"So all that food was you?"

"Not just me. My partner too. We own Spice Haven."

"That's wonderful! I love spicy food."

"Yeah, I got that."

"Hmm hmm," he started the car and backed out of her driveway. "Ever been to India?"

"No. Why do you ask? Wait. Don't tell me. It's my name isn't it?"

Hah! That was the least obvious. "Actually it's not. In China, for example, many parents choose Western names for their children. It's," he touched his nose, "your nose stud."

And her pretty brown skin, all smooth and delicious as honey; the riot of black waves hanging down her back and her love of spicy food. The green eyes had stumped him at first.

"My maternal grandparents were from India as was my paternal grandfather, both my parents were born in England. They settled in Canada and I was born here. That's my connection to India. Other than that, nada. I love spicy food, that's true. And I do love Indian dresses-the traditional ones. As far as I know I have no family in India. My father married the love of his life he met while at Oxford. What about you?"

"WASP all the way. Great grandparents came from England."

"Why did you mention China?"

"Lived there for a few years after I finished college."

"Few years? You speak Mandarin?"

"Fluent in it. And a bit of Cantonese."

"Wow! That's something. I've always wanted to learn Mandarin. It's so complex and yet intricate at the same time."

"It's quite the challenge."

"Hey, maybe you can teach me Mandarin."

I don't think so.

Dallas was positive he did not want to do that. Be with her in close quarters? She intrigued him. He was fascinated by the complexity of the many layers she was wrapped in. He'd waited a long time and finally he was roused from his deep slumber. He'd kissed her twice. He wasn't going to charge in. He was going to savour it. He was going to take it slow, real slow like the Mr. Go Slow he was.

"Don't think that will be possible. Am too busy at the moment dealing with the upcoming visit of a Chinese trade delegation."

He got no response from her. He dared not say her preference for Bollywood dances made him think she'd been to India. And he certainly dared not say he'd seen her wearing traditional Indian dresses.

Then something just popped out of his mouth.

"About the kiss...Priya...I'm sorry."

"Why did you do it? Kiss me? Again."

"Just felt like it. Had the urge so I did it. I'm sorry if it offended you."

"No," her voice was low and soft. "Nothing like that. Just want to know why."

"Why not? You're gorgeous and sexy. And your lips were irresistible. I caved."

Whiskey. Tango. Foxtrot.

He didn't mean for it to come out like that. He was the laid-back master of slow. But the words were out and he couldn't stuff them back into the hat they'd popped out of. It had been so wonderfully spontaneous and he wasn't going to take them back. Sometimes it was smarter to ask for forgiveness later than for permission before.

"Twice?"

"Yes. Why not?"

Why not, indeed. Exactly what he was asking himself. The second time was even more fantastic than the first. And he managed to steal a third just as he let her go in the supply room.

"Tell me why you did it the first time. Under the maple tree."

Dallas swallowed, his eyes on the slender curve of her neck. He wanted to find out what her skin tasted like. He wanted it badly. "Again couldn't help myself. I just got lost in your eyes. Do I have to apologize for that? Because I could but I wouldn't mean it."

"Okay." She chuckled. He saw her swallow a mouthful of coconut water. "Guess I have to less irresistible then."

"I promise it will never happen again. Not without your permission."

He had to lay that out. It was going to be a one-time spontaneous act. Scratch that. Two-time thing. Nothing else was going to come out of it. Nothing she didn't allow.

"Unh huh."

And so subject was laid to rest.

Dallas found the games gruelling on the courts and was bushed after the evening session in Bath. He hit the shower and crawled into bed. He even switched off his phone.

The following weekend, Houston, Dallas and Austin took out the Enterprise again, the weather too enticing to pass. Houston directed the anchor with Dallas reeling it in. It was not good sailing weather with only feeble winds in the forecast. They motored to a shady bay off Amherst Island and Houston threw down the anchor while Dallas steered. Sleeping with the boat rocking on the water was going to be good for his soul.

Austin rummaged in his bag for the mini-speaker set and stuck the player in. The sweet sounds of *Brothers in Arms* by Dire Straits floated over the water.

Apt, Dallas thought.

"You're in the bow," Houston told Dallas and Austin. "I'll take the bed in the stern."

It was still scorching out in the open waters where the sun beat down relentlessly. But Dallas was not complaining. They stripped down to their shorts and dove into the refreshing coolness of the lake. Dallas swam to the nearest buoy and then to the pebbly bank with Houston and Austin following.

"Where are Lara and the girls?" Dallas asked when Houston plopped down beside him. He hadn't seen them in weeks.

"Visiting Lara's parents."

"Short or long stay?"

"Two weeks. Summer, you know."

"Right. Why didn't you go with them? You usually do. You whine and whine if they're gone for even a day."

"Work deadlines, you know that. It's not quite like your Breakwater Park project though. This defence contract is going to put us on the map. Dad is out of his mind with pride and joy. The weight of the responsibility this brings hasn't sunk in yet."

"The marketing department is ready to go," Austin added. "It's a big job. But not quite as fun as the landscaping gig I landed. Plan to do a bit of the heavy digging and levelling myself."

Dallas knew Austin was living his dream, working with the land and operating heavy machinery. He did the actual plantings and never passed on an opportunity to work with heavy equipment.

Now, Austin walked up the small dune and stood looking at the scenery before him. Something was up with his little brother. He rubbed his hands together, using both hands to comb his wet hair back, drumming two fingers on his lips. He came back to where the other two were, sitting down with his arms locked around his raised knees.

"You ready to tell us about the latest project?" Houston asked Dallas, poking him with his foot.

Dallas was stretched out on the sand, hands locked behind his head, taking in the absolute calmness of the evening. The sun was just over the trees, still casting hot waves over the lake. He took his time answering. He squinted as he looked over the water. Majestic pines towered over the lakeshore. Ancient willows dipped their long boughs, caressing the surface of the water.

"In a few weeks, I'll be ready."

"Good. Very good," Houston smiled and closed his eyes. "I can see that before my eyes: The Crenshaw brothers at it together. Again. It's going to be great. Don't you think, little brother?"

"Yeah, sure," Austin mumbled. "Let's go back. It's too quiet out here. I need some music."

He jumped up, brushing sand from the bottom of his shorts. Soon they saw him making his way to the boat.

"Guess we'd better go too," Dallas said.

Reluctantly, Houston agreed.

When they got to the boat, Pearl Jam poured through the speakers. From the bow, Dallas watched Austin as he lit a cigarette. His younger brother had been on the path to being smoke free. Now, smoke wafted back to where he and Houston sat. Austin had things on his mind. Probably the break up had hit harder than he'd imagined?

Dallas jerked his chin toward Austin and Houston nodded. As one, the brothers moved stealthily toward their younger sibling, feet still sandy from their swim to the beach. Houston grabbed the cigarette from Austin's hand and flung it into the water. Austin jumped up and turned. He hit the wall of Houston's chest.

"Hey! My life. My choice," he yelled out his favourite mantra. "And fuck you!" Austin added for good measure.

"Not if we have to breathe it in, little bro," Dallas growled.

Houston grabbed his arms from the back while Dallas pinned him with this arms from the front. Austin kicked and struggled. A single Crenshaw was a threat but two were impossible to stop. He was no match. With only his legs free, Austin kicked hard and thrust his body back, taking Houston and Dallas off their feet for an instant. Dallas scrambled to stay on board, arms flailing to grab onto something. Failing, he went over the rails with Houston. Austin planted his feet firmly, rocking on his heels from the impact, watching them go into the water. For a few seconds, there was nothing but ripples. When Dallas came up, he spluttered, treading water. He slowly swam stern side and got back onto the boat, dripping water all over the place.

And angrily silent.

Houston's jaw was clenched tight. Dallas saw Austin take a step back, his back hitting the rails. Austin knew them well enough. They were *not* going to let go of this. A wary look came into Austin's eyes.

Dallas jerked his head at Houston in a silent agreement. Dallas shook his head. Water dripped from his hair. He brushed his arm across his face, menace in each stride. The brothers circled Austin, then pounced, holding him in a tight grip. No movement was possible. They hauled him over the rails. Austin kicked silently. Grunting in unison, they got him over and down into the water he went. They did not peer over the rails to see if he came up.

Panting, Dallas flung a cushion to the side and sat down. When Austin was a no show after a few minutes, Dallas got on the ladder to check. What he did not see made his heart thud. Then he saw a yellow flash to his right.

The bastard!

There he was! Swimming away from the boat, to the middle of the lake. Would do him good to get it out of his system. The lake was good for that. Dallas had no qualms about it. They'd grown up with the rhythm of the lake woven into their lives. The lake was their backyard in the home they grew up in. In summer, they swam and fished. In winter, they fished and skated.

Chest heaving, yet relatively calm, Austin threw himself down on the cushioned bench. Dallas still stood on the ladder, one leg in the water.

"Is this about Emily?" Houston said softly, relating to the droop of Austin's shoulders.

Austin heaved a big shudder. "She said she couldn't be with a man who had the hots for every pretty woman he saw. All I did was look. What's wrong with that? Don't women look?" He asked desperate for some support.

He got it. And he didn't get it.

"Listen, bro. Lara tells me every time she sees an attractive guy. I always look over only to see it's someone who looks just like me! Not exact clones, you know. But similar. So yes they do look. But there's looking and then there's looking, you know?" Houston looked at Dallas, willing him to jump in. "We both just want to prosper. And live long." He put up his hand in the Vulcan salute and grinned.

Austin looked as if he was going to get caught up in his brother's Trek. Then a shadow fell over his face and in the fading light, Dallas saw a different side to his otherwise buoyant brother. His lips drooped and his whole wet body took on a dejected stance. Houston went downstairs and came back with towels draped over his arms. He threw one at each brother before he towelled himself off too.

Dallas moved over to sit closer to Austin. He put an arm around his broad shoulders.

"Kate and I broke up because we did not want the same things. It was stupid of me not to know that before, I guess. But sometimes you go with the flow. What about Emily and you? You were on the same page, unlike Kate and myself, right?"

Austin nodded, swallowing. His breathing became calmer.

"Emily wanted kids. A family. Every time we went out, we came back pissed at each other."

"Maybe it's like growing pains, you know. It takes time to get used to each other. Perhaps you should look into her eyes more. She is beautiful, don't you think? All that gorgeous black hair and grey eyes and perky breasts..."

"Hey! Okay, stop drooling over my woman."

"Now that's the spirit," Dallas clapped him on the back. "Just listen to what she's saying. Even if she's angry about it. She's giving you a map to her soul."

"Soul. Right." Austin gave a deep sigh. "I don't know how I'm going to face her again. Or where to find her. She left, Dallas. She's gone."

"Don't worry about that yet. You still have her phone number, right?" At Austin's nod, he added, "There are ways of locating her through the GPS system on her phone. If she hasn't switched the tracking system off."

"You'll find her in no time," Houston said, the towel wrapped around his head. Then all you do is apologize. And grovel. And hope she'll take you back."

"Apologize? I don't know how I can face her again, Houston. Let alone apologize."

"I'm certain you'll drum up the courage. You're not a wimp. You can do it."

"Sure you can," Dallas twisted the caps of cold bottles of Tuborg and handed one each to his brothers.

They slept with the gentle waves rocking the boat, hearts full of unfulfilled promises. The next morning, after a breakfast of smoked salmon on cream cheese bagels and coffee, they headed back to the marina and drove to their parents' home for lunch.

CHAPTER FOURTEEN

PRIYA GOT HOME at midnight, when the moon began to play hide and seek betweeN clouds. She sat on her deck in the dark, the sky ablaze with a million stars, head back on the cushions gazing at the night splendour. Her eyes fell on the light pouring out from the window across her yard.

Dallas. Another night owl like her.

She wished she had it in her to just go up to his door, knock and let it all happen. Dallas made her scramble for her breaks. He was the boulder in her path of drifting along. He was too intense, too focused. There had been something in his eyes the evening of her gig at Hovertek. He was all scorching fire just waiting to consume her. Recalling the look on his face made heat rise up in her and her heart thump. It was followed by a flutter in her belly and the inevitable tight clenching between her legs. He would want all of her and she couldn't give him that.

A warm breeze whisked her hair about her face and Priya's calm contemplation of the night sky vanished with the breeze. A riot of feelings crawled up her body. Truth was, she wanted him. Like she'd never wanted a man before. Wanted to feel his large hands on her body. But, she craved her freedom more. She was *not* going to tie herself down again. Then again he was not Simon. In fact, when he kissed her at Hovertek, Dallas looked like he wanted to eat her alive. He made her feel she was more. All the splintered parts of her became one and sank into him. She couldn't deal with passion like that. She would lose herself in him. She was happy where she was right now, once again at her pre-Simon stage. The time when it had been her. Only her. She did have it all at one time. Yet, she'd moved to this little town and never looked back.

Priya dropped her head in her hands and dug her fingers in her hair, yanking hard. All it did was bring sharp tears to her eyes and the image of Dallas holding her in his arms. A soft groan rumbled through her body.

She sniffed and raised her head. It was amazingly quiet for a city. She did not miss the blaring sirens or the hum of traffic of Toronto. She did not miss the hustle. What she did miss was the promise Simon had been wrapped in. If only she hadn't let him get so close to her. If only they could have just drifted together. If only she hadn't unwrapped him. Once she'd done that, she'd been disappointed and that was that.

When her parents were killed in a car accident, they left Priya the beneficiary of their substantial estate, giving her the freedom to do the things she only wanted to do. Like taking on only the catering gigs she liked. Like play pickleball every morning with grey-haired retirees.

Later, at her studio, Priya clipped pictures of makeup and henna designs on the pin board and pulled up the music on her iPod for the recital. She went through the steps standing in front of a large mirror. For Mark's fundraiser recital, there were five others, with Kelly Roberts acting as assistant and a sub. The others dancers were in various stages of getting ready.

The event was sold out. From Toronto, Jason and Marie now

together again and many of her pickleball friends would be present.

Not to mention Dallas and his family. Butterflies fluttered in her belly. It had everything to do with Dallas and nothing to do with the dance. She liked him. Liked his kisses. And the way he made her knees weak and her heart race. A small finger of want crept into her feelings, making her long for someone again, the longing tainting her usual contentment. It made her freedom less desirable.

"You look beautiful, Kelly," Priya gave her a hug. "Come on, let's do it. You start with Led Zeppelin's *Kashmir,* then the curtains open and two minutes later, you cut Zeppelin. Then we walk on stage....you know the rest."

Peeping through a slit in the red velvet curtains, Kelly whispered, "Not a single vacant seat, Priya! This is going to be great!" She did a little jig and danced her way into the side wings, her Indian skirt swirling around her.

Yep, Kelly was as close to being a BFF to Priya.

~

DALLAS COULD NOT wait to see Priya dance.

"Very interesting, don't you think?" Austin unfolded the program he was reading. "Look at the costume in this pic! This began as a devotional dance performed by women in Hindu temples before a deity. By the way," he thrust the pamphlet in Dallas' face. "That's her. The sexy, dancing queen."

"Hmm...yes, sure interesting." He was even more impatient than Emma and Olivia who were jumping from one leg to the other. He wished he could do the same and let off some of the energy building up inside him.

"This is so exciting, isn't it girls?" his mother, Madison, squealed in delight. "I've never seen it live. I've only seen it on the screen."

"Can we please go in and sit?" Olivia stopped jumping and rested on one leg.

"Let's go fast before someone takes our seat," Emma added.

"No need to hurry, girls," Houston put an arm around each one. "Our seat numbers are on the ticket. And, I believe we're sitting in the first row."

"Okay, let's go."

Olivia hopped her way to the seats with Emma following and doing the same.

"Be right back." Dallas told his family. He saw Bob coming in through another door, Anna by his side. Kalle was not far behind with Milla.

"Hello there, Dallas my boy," Kalle held out his hand. "Going to have a fun evening, right?"

"Good evening, Kalle. Milla. Nice to see you." Dallas shook their hands, one eye straying to the stage.

Bob and Anna joined them. "Anyone know what kind of dance this is going to be?" Bob asked, always ready to quench his curiosity.

"Read the pamphlet, Bob," Anna thrust one under his nose.

"Can't. Don't have my glasses."

"Oh, you silly man. They're on your head." Anna turned to Dallas. "Did you know Priya's into Indian dances? I didn't. And, look, isn't it lovely, students from a school of dance will be doing Bollywood dances too?"

"No." Dallas was not going to say anything further. Then he realized how rude he sounded. "I mean, I didn't know she was into Indian dances. I'm sure it's going to be a wonderful experience. A cultural journey of sorts."

He sounded like a damn travel brochure. No way was he admitting he knew about Priya's dancing.

"Let's go find our seats then." Bob herded them off.

"See you guys later." Dallas went to join his family.

Led Zeppelin's *Kashmir* poured out of the speakers as Dallas and his family took their seats. Dallas had a bouquet of yellow roses with baby's breath in his arms. He set it under his seat. The curtains parted illuminating a midnight blue set. The music stopped and Priya walked out on the stage, hands folded and palms touching together.

He watched with bated breath, eyes taking in her costume and the white flowers in her hair. He didn't know what to focus on. She dazzled him so. There were red dots on her feet and her palms. Jewels ran down the length of her braided hair. The costume was the kind of midriff-baring ensemble he'd seen her wearing before. He did not recognize her. He saw her eyes, etched in black, as they moved from side to side.

Still with the palms touching, she bowed before a framed picture. There was a brass lamp in front of it. Flower garlands hung around the frame. Then the rest of her troupe joined her on stage.

The musical arrangement sounded simple: a vocalist, a drum, bells and a violin? He couldn't make out the instrument. But the rhythm and beat were anything but. Everything moved: her feet, her head, her eyes as well as her expressive hands. It was quite unlike any dance he'd ever seen. The sight of her, the music and the rhythm all unfamiliar but so seductive and captivating, made him realize this was another part of her he couldn't wait to discover. She carried him to a place he didn't even know had existed before she came into his life.

The dances finished to thundering applause. Priya, head bent over joined hands, bowed to the audience and walked off the stage. It was a standing ovation and the girls could not have clapped harder and longer. She came back for the encore and danced a short bit and with that they had to be content.

Then followed a series of dances by groups of dancers from the dance school. The costumes were colourful and the choreography brilliant but Dallas found the music a bit generic. But what the hell? The girls loved it just like everyone else.

Dallas texted Priya when it was over.

Will I see you in the foyer?

Yes.

And his heart jumped out of its cage. He let out the breath he was holding.

They walked out to be greeted by delicious smells. There was familiar finger food among the more standard fare. Austin, Kalle and the girls made for the buffet line, while Joe, Madison, Houston and Lara chatted with Bob, Anna and Milla.

Dallas cast his eyes around, searching for Priya. Then he saw her, still in costume, in the middle of a crowd of people. He approached, the flowers in his hand and the crowd parted.

"Hello, Priya. That was wonderful." She was a glittering jewel he dared not approach. Up close, he saw a wide golden belt around her waist and bracelets on her upper arms. He stood holding the flowers, his eyes filled with the sight of her.

"Hi, Dallas. Glad you enjoyed it. For me?" she said as he handed the bouquet to her. "Thank you so much!"

She stepped forward, rose to the tips of her toes, threaded an arm around his neck and kissed him on both cheeks. He let her bring his face in the crook of her neck, her sultry fragrance enveloping him. It was the jasmine flowers in her hair, he realized.

His hands brushed against the slightly moist skin on her waist. He closed his eyes and breathed it all in, his senses all on high alert. There was fleeting warmth in his arms, so consuming and luscious, he almost didn't let go. Then it was gone.

"Guys," she turned toward the crowd. "This is Dallas. We play p…."

"Pickleball," they all said in unison.

"..together," she laughed. "Dallas these are my friends, Riley, Marie, Mia. You know Jason, of course."

None of the names stuck with him. Even Jason was a blur. All he could see was her. All he could smell was her. Her fragrance was intoxicating. The buzz in his head began to create ripples in other parts of his body. Priya knocked him out of his orbit, sending him spinning out of control.

"The girls would love to meet you," he said when he was able to speak. "They're over there, stuffing themselves with samosas and pakoras."

"Sure. I'd love to meet them too. Bye guys," she waved to her crowd. "Talk to you later."

Austin was the first to greet her. He did it with his usual flair and did what Dallas hadn't dared to do. He snaked one arm around her waist and then slung the other across her back and swept her off her feet.

"Oh, Austin," Dallas heard her breathe into his ear. "Thanks for coming."

"Anytime, my sweet." Austin flicked a finger on her chin. "It was fabulous. You were fabulous."

Dallas wanted to clock him one, preferably in the balls. But that was *so* not him. He was the laid-back one, the one without the flair. He stood back and did what he loved to do: watched Priya.

But wait a sec! "I take it you two have met before?" Dallas stepped in between Austin and Priya. "Because this, what he's doing, is much too familiar for just one meeting."

"Yes, we have. At the garden centre," Priya looked up at Austin. "I was shopping for mulch, right?" Austin nodded. "Ten heavy bags. And he was so kind to help me load them in my truck."

I'll fucking bet he was.

As if the garden centre did not have helpers. Dallas wondered if he should make a better point at staking his claim.

"And then I introduced myself. And then she remembered I was your brother. And the rest is history." Austin kept his arm around Priya's shoulder. It bothered Dallas very much, a whole lot.

Emma walked around Priya examining her from head to toe and Priya turned around with her making her giggle.

"Stop, please. I want to see what you have in your hair," Emma took Priya's braid in her hands and touched the jewels pinned onto it.

Priya went down on her haunches to Emma's level and then on one knee. With wide eyes, Emma checked out Priya's head, ears, nose, arms and neck. She tentatively touched the ring in her nose. The she touched the nose stud on the other side.

Olivia stood beside Emma watching and listening.

"Do you dress like this everyday?" Olivia wanted to know.

"No. This is only when I perform. Normally, I dress like everyone else, you know, jeans and T-shirt with sneakers."

"But that's how we dress."

"Well, then I dress like you."

"These flowers in your hair smell good."

Divine. Dallas corrected Olivia mentally. She was mesmerizing.

"Can I have a flower, please?" Olivia twisted her body this way and that as she asked.

"Me too. I want a flower too." Emma hopped from one leg to the other.

"Sure. I will need scissors though."

"Oh, Uncle Dallas has one in his pocket. He has it with him all the time. It has a lot of other things on it. It has a screwdriver, a knife…no three, a scissor, a…." Olivia forgot what else there was.

"Then it must be a Swiss knife. Let's go ask him if he'll lend it to us."

Olivia slid her hand in Priya's and Emma did the same with the other. They got the scissors from Dallas. Priya undid the jasmine garland in her hair and cut two pieces. She gave each of the girls a piece.

"What if I said I'd like a flower too?" Dallas bent and put his lips close to her ear.

He had a smile on his face but his eyes were serious. So she gave him a piece too and it disappeared into the pocket of his jacket.

PRIYA HAD ONLY met the second and the youngest of the Crenshaw brothers a few days ago. Austin's hug had not come as a surprise to Priya.

He was probably the most devastatingly handsome one. And that stud in his ear only made him look more dangerously sexy. He was so full of himself. Nothing daunted him. Yet, despite all of Austin's sex appeal, it was Dallas who made her senses hum. Dallas who stood to the side with his smouldering eyes on her, watching her every move.

He was all in black, in slacks held up by the silver-buckled belt combined with a soft-knit sweater. It was so soft it couldn't be anything but Cashmere. The gold chain twinkled around his neck, drawing her eyes to the strong column of his neck.

She had caught a whiff of Austin's cologne: spicy like him with woodsy undertones. He smelled good though Dallas' sexy *Eau Sauvage* buzzed her insides more.

"My dear, you were fantastic!" Anna bent down and gave her a hug so fierce, the necklace around Priya's neck poked into her skin.

"You were great, Papillon." Bob thumped her on her back. "Didn't know you could jump around like that. Think I'm going to grab a plate of samosas." He wandered off.

Kalle and Milla stood talking to a tall, handsome man, clean-shaven with a precision part in his dark hair and a pretty woman with short blonde hair. With them was an elderly couple.

"Come, meet the others," Dallas took her hand and led her to them.

The tall, handsome one turned out to be the other Crenshaw

brother, Houston and his wife, Lara. And of course his mother and father, Madison and Joe.

Now she'd met *all* the Crenshaws.

"Hello, my dear. That was lovely," his mother said, shaking her hand.

"Thank you all for coming. This has been wonderful. The local Indian restaurants stepped in with the food. Have you tasted it yet?"

"No, we were waiting to meet you."

"Please, go ahead." Priya glanced around and her eyes locked with Dallas's. She did not want him to go with them. Her heart began to thud when he did not.

"How're you getting home? Can I give you a ride?" He stood with his hands in his pockets, totally relaxed and totally cool while she sweltered under his intense gaze.

"I came with Kelly. So I will be going back with her. She's going to help me with getting all this stuff off me." She immediately wished she hadn't said that last bit. It projected images of his hands in...

She was not going there. At the end of the day, she went back to her home to her quiet and calm home where she had no one to answer to, no one else to consider.

"Priya," he moved toward her. "It was a glorious performance. Where did you learn all that?"

"In Toronto. I'm passionate about my dancing. And I love this dressing up." She touched the jewels around her neck.

"I can see that. It is indeed beautiful."

He clasped her by the waist and, pulling her to him, he whispered his goodbye. Back at home, Kelly and Priya helped each out of their dresses, Kelly still on a high from being on stage. Her grey eyes sparkled and her hands couldn't keep still. Priya sent her home with a cup of soothing chamomile tea swirling in her belly.

In her bed, Priya wondered what it felt like to be surrounded by so many loving people. Dallas was indeed lucky. It must be great to have someone to talk to when the need arose. Someone to lean on. No holidays spent alone. Especially Christmas, which was always a bitch with everyone else busy hanging out with their families.

He was intruding into her life whether she liked it or not. He'd looked so gorgeous in the slacks he'd worn today, the golden chain glinting on his skin. The dark cashmere he wore a perfect background for his sexy dark looks.

Life with Simon had shown her she was not made for marriage. She did not believe in it. What the hell did a piece of paper mean, anyway? Most couples lived together in sin before they got 'married.'

She preferred the journey much more. Oh, so much more.

DALLAS DROVE HOME, a sharp finger of disappointment flicking at his insides. There was nothing he wanted more than to take Priya home. Be with her a bit longer. If not with her then at least in her orbit.

But no matter.

He tapped the phone in his pocket with pictures of Priya. He sat with the feet on the coffee table watching photos of Priya flip through. Feeling his body heat up, he got up to change out of his clothes. On his way to the bedroom, he grabbed a cold bottle from the fridge.

He took out the piece of jasmine garland from his pocket and buried his nose in it. The aroma rose up to his head, spreading visions of Priya through his mind. Her sweet lips against his, her body curved against his. He'd never felt this way about a woman before. Kate and her cool blonde looks were not even specks in his mind. It was Priya all the way with the dark waves he wanted to sink his fingers into, her to-drown-in green eyes and her smooth skin the colour of rich latté just begging for his eager lips.

He was aware he had to tone it down. It was not like him to be all gaga over a woman so quickly. He just didn't know how to slow down when it came to Priya. Something about her made him impatient, his usual Mr. Go Slow approach getting blown to bits.

CHAPTER FIFTEEN

DALLAS GOT A text from Priya the day before the tournament.

WANT TO RIDE TO COBOURG TOGETHER?

YES.

Here was the break he was hoping for: more alone time with Priya. She showed up at six in the morning with Bob lounging in the back seat, turning his hopes into dust.

"Had a bad night," Bob declared. "Will probably sleep. So don't mind me."

"Why? Do you snore?" Priya turned the rear view mirror, getting Bob in her sights. "I *will* mind if you do. Will have to stop and throw you out."

"Bleh bleh bleh," Bob stuck his tongue out each time he said the word. Priya picked up the packet of Fisherman's she had in the cup holder and threw it at him. Then Bob rolled his eyes. "Have my blankie. All good." He rolled the fleecy grey piece of cloth around his legs and stretched out. "By the way, young man, did you notice she's driving a standard? I've never seen a woman drive a stick shift before." That said, Bob turned on his side and closed his eyes.

"It's an old model. I love it. He roars like a tiger. And purrs like a cat when I treat him right."

In the side mirror, Dallas saw Bob open his eyes, roll them and close them again.

"It's a he?" Dallas couldn't believe it either. She switched gears like a race car driver.

"Yes, he's strong. Powerful and utterly dependable."

Halfway there, Bob had to pee, so they stopped. In Cobourg, they signed in, got their name tags and the schedule. Dallas went to the men's locker room to change into his pickleball clothes and shoes. Then he went in search of Kalle.

PRIYA PUSHED THE door of the locker room open and stopped short. It was a bad idea. The door hit the wall and swung back to knock her on her ass. She stumbled forward and furious, she turned raising her foot to smack the door one in the face. But the sight of Bob pacing to and fro in the corridor stopped her as a prickle of unease hit her gut. This was not going to be good.

"Forgot my shoes," he said with a sheepish look about him. He rubbed his hand over the little hair he still had. "Can't believe it! What will I do? God, this sucks. Shit! Pardon my language."

Priya took a deep breath and shrugged it off. How many times had she said 'shit' when she missed a shot? In her mind of course. No swearing was allowed on the Bath pickleball courts. She usually yelled 'Oy' when she missed a shot she should have been able to reach. But here, in the hallowed halls of competitive pickleball, she promised herself she was going to be quiet. Very quiet. Not even a whisper of an 'Oy' was going to cross her lips. She'd bite her tongue off if need be.

How could a grown man-scratch that-a more than grown man forget his shoes? What was he, a child needing constant supervision?

"Okay. Calm down. Take a deep breath." She took another deep breath herself. "When is Anna coming? She can bring you another pair."

"We play at 10:30. She won't be here until noon."

"Then we'll have to get you a new pair. We can go to the mall and buy you another pair of shoes. Problem is, my game starts at nine. I won't have time to go shopping with you." She was beginning to feel like a mother in righteous snit. She wanted to smack him hard, grab him by the shoulders and shake him till his teeth rattled. Wait a sec? Were they real or false? Would they pop out if she shook him too hard?

Aargh!

"God. What'll we do? What'll we do? Fuck. Pardon my language."

Putting smacks and rattling false teeth aside, she looked around the hall and saw Dallas in deep conversation with Kalle further down the corridor. "Have an idea."

She ran toward Dallas and tapped him on the shoulder.

Dallas turned and his face lit up, dimples showing. "What's up?"

"Bob forgot his shoes. Anna won't be here until noon. So he needs to go the mall and get a new pair. What time are you playing?"

"Eleven-thirty."

"Great! Here's what we'll do. You take my truck and find a mall. Here are the keys. Good luck. Have to get to the courts," Priya dropped the keys in his hands and went to join Kelly in the gym.

Problem solved! Delegate, just a like a mother would.

~

DALLAS AND BOB got in Priya's truck. Or at least Dallas tried to. He had to adjust the seat, putting it as far back as it would go.

How did she drive this thing? He started the engine and the truck jumped forward, almost hitting the car in front.

Houston, we have a problem, was his first thought.

He looked down at the pedals of which there were three. He wondered what the extra pedal was for.

"What d'you think?" he asked Bob.

Bob was absolutely out of it, completely focused on his not having shoes. He kept tapping his knuckles on his forehead as if it was going to solve anything. With no advice coming from Bob, Dallas called Priya, hoping she'd not switched off her phone yet. To his relief, she answered.

"Have a problem. Your car has three pedals and I'm used to two."

"Here's the short version. Beginning with the long pedal on the right, accelerator, break and clutch. Right foot for accelerator and break as in an automatic, left to press down clutch all the way and simultaneously change gears with your right hand. That's all I can do at the moment. Gotta go. Oh yeah, listen to the sound of the engine. If he's revving up, you need to shift up. Or ease off the accelerator. Depends. Kay. Gotta go. Good luck."

How hard can it be, right?

With trepidation, following the gear notations on the stick, Dallas put the truck in reverse and backed out. With a horrific groan, *he* rumbled back.

Fuck! He hadn't pushed the clutch in deep enough.

Maybe.

Changing the gear again with the clutch pressed down as far as it would go, Dallas released his foot from it slowly as he increased speed, wincing in anticipation of another groan. This time he moved forward and a bit of the tension eased off him. By the time he got out of the parking lot, he managed to get the hang of it. Dallas glanced at Bob who was no help at all. He was still shaking his head and mumbling. Dallas hoped he'd get his act together before the tournament. He looked as if he was falling apart.

"Here we go, Bob. You'll have your shoes in no time." He tried to put more confidence into his voice than he felt. "Can you check on your phone where the mall is?"

Bob tapped his finger on his phone and soon had the mall's location. The only store open this early was Walmart. Bob got his shoes and they got back to the courts in good time.

After the excitement of the trip to the mall, the gym felt hollow and chilly. Dallas used the corridor to go through a series of warm-ups. Then he went into the gym to see how Priya and Kelly were doing. They were just finishing the last game in the second round.

~

It was game point for Kelly and Priya. Kelly aimed a serve toward centre court. The ball flew over the net, skimming the middle of the court. Priya saw the receiver back off, apparently thinking it was going to be out. All noise around her receded, everything in slow motion. The player had to use her backhand. She jabbed at the ball in a futile effort to get it over the net. And failed.

Kelly and Priya moved on to the next round. They went their separate ways.

Priya sat on a bench in the locker room, taking deep breaths. She chomped on a granola bar, took a swig of water and then took another bite. Kelly was probably somewhere doing the same thing. As a team, they found it worked better if they separated after the game and then regrouped five minutes before their next game began.

Priya emptied her mind of pickleball and concentrated on chewing and swallowing water. She did not think about the next team. She did not check the schedule to see whom they were matched up with. And she most certainly did not screw her mind with info on how the other teams in her group were doing. She played each game as if it was her last.

Like her life, she let it all drift by, taking her wherever it chose to. She chose not to think about Dallas. Every time her stupid mind did, she bit the inside of her cheeks and ran up and down the corridor.

"Hey, Priya," Bob called out to her as she was heading to the gym. "Can you keep my locker key with you?"

"Sure." She stuck his key in her lunch bag.

She and Kelly reached the bronze medal round. They were happy to have one last shot at a medal. Glancing at Kelly's face, Priya felt butterflies begin to flutter in her belly. Kelly had her tongue sticking out the corner of her mouth. She giggled her way through the game, which made Priya even more nervous because it was Kelly's biggest tell. The more nervous Kelly got, the more she giggled.

What was up with that?

They almost bungled it by letting the other team get way too far ahead. But they got control of the game back after a time out and a bit of mind-boggling strategizing.

Priya couldn't have asked for more when they won the bronze medal. The odd thing was Bob came every hour to Priya and asked for the key to her locker where his bag was kept. With the bronze medal around her neck, she went in search of Bob.

"Hey, Bob!" She caught him wandering up and down the corridor. "Why are you asking for the key so often? Why don't you just keep it?"

"No pockets. See." He tapped the sides of his sports shorts.

"No itty bitty slot around in your waist band for a key either?"

"Nope," Bob said checking his waist. "My shoulder's aching again. I'm full on painkillers," Bob gave a rasping laugh.

"Oh, I hope that's a laugh and not a cry. We're up in about twenty minutes."

Bob flexed his right arm. "I feel great!"

Most probably he was just plain numb, the dummy!

"You ready for this?"

"Am so ready. Okay, okay. I see someone I need to talk to. See you in a bit." And off he went to schmooze and socialize.

Bob and Priya reached the gold medal round and had just finished their first game when Anna came in. By the time she was off the court after handing over the scorecard to the scorekeepers, Anna was in a chair looking around. Bob was nowhere to be seen. Probably taking a leak.

"I didn't tell you, Papillon, but these Walmart shoes were slipping all over the floor," he said when he came back into the gym.

"Why didn't you tell me?" Priya was glad he was calling her Papillon again. It meant he was over the shock of having no shoes.

"Why? So you'd be nervous too?"

He was right in a way. No need to burden her with more.

They got silver. Of course, Bob had been angling for gold. However, Priya was thrilled.

"He was picking on you, Papillon. All the time." Bob jiggled from side to side, unable to keep still.

"That's the way the game is played. Hit the ball to the weaker player. But we got some good shots back. We did the switcheroo thing quite well."

"Bastard! Pardon my language. I'd like to pop him one."

"Oh, shut up and sit down, Bob," Anna snapped at him.

Instead of listening to Anna, Bob was off again, out the door of the gym, mumbling something.

"Hey Anna," Priya hugged her. "Lovely to see you."

"Where's Bob gone off to again? He told me to bring shoes. I thought he had them with him. I was so surprised to see them in the shoe stand. Then I thought maybe he had another pair. These are his only pair though. I'm certain."

"He forgot them."

"He forgot them?" Anna's eyebrows rose. "You know what? He packed his bag on his own today." She sipped from a water bottle.

"He doesn't do that normally? You do it?"

"I always do. Otherwise, he'd forget stuff. Look what happened today. How can someone forget shoes? Without them, he cannot play. How can he forget shoes? Anyway, how did he play without shoes?"

"I sent him to the mall with Dallas to get another pair."

"Such a child," Priya and Anna said in unison.

Then they looked at each other and laughed.

"Wait a minute. Dallas? The gorgeous young guy? Longish hair and sexy beard?"

"That's the one."

"I see. So you drove together?"

"No, I drove *with* Bob in the back and Dallas. Didn't Bob tell you?"

"Oh, he never tells me anything."

"I see."

"So this means you and Dallas will be driving back together."

"Why? How's Bob…oh."

"Yes, he will be going back with me."

Priya shrugged. "So what?"

"So what, indeed."

Priya was able to catch the last round of Dallas and Kalle's game. They played extremely well together. Dallas, standing way back, got all the smash shots aimed at them and popped them just over the net to land in the kitchen. Kalle covered the front half of the court and was unbeatable with his low serves. The other team was not able to return a single ball served by Kalle.

They got gold. All in all, it was a very productive event for the Bath Pickleball Club.

"Got my breasts squeezed today," Anna announced, as they waited for the medals to be given out.

Priya's jaw dropped. She imagined a lecherous individual, a man perhaps, pressing up close to Anna and doing the squeezing. How could that happen?

"Did you slap him? Knee him in the groin?" Just thinking about the assault drove Priya mad.

"No, you nut case. I had my mammogram. Got them between these plastic plates, you know?"

Priya shook her head.

"Oh, right you wouldn't. You're still a baby. Wait till you hit your sixties. The letters from the Breast Cancer Screening program will start coming every two years. You stand close to the X-ray machine, your breast gets arranged on a platter-like thing-one breast at a time-a plate descends on top of your breast..."

At this, Priya scrunched her eyes and winced.

"It doesn't hurt. The plastic plate keeps your boob in place. And then they take pictures of it. Of both. I guess it will get easier to put my boob on the platter as I age: my breasts will be losing to gravity. I do pity the small-breasted women though. Tough for them. The squeeze might be a bit more painful. Not much material to put on the plastic plate, you see."

Priya couldn't wait.

She said goodbye to Bob and Anna and got ready to drive back with Dallas. She took a lovely cool shower and was ready, her long hair still damp, in fifteen minutes. When she came out of the locker room, Dallas was waiting, chatting with Kalle.

"Bye, Kalle." She hugged him. "Congrats again. Milla will be so thrilled."

"Bye, gorgeous. See you back at home." As usual, he lifted her off her feet in a classic Viking power show.

When she turned, Dallas stood there with arms outstretched. "What? No hug for me? I won the gold too!"

With trepidation, she approached him and put her arms

around his neck. Not an easy feat. She had to stand on the tips of her toes and was careful to leave plenty of air space between their bodies. He did bend his neck and he did smell delicious. His hair was still damp. Strands of it stuck to his forehead.

He brought his arms around her and lifted her slightly off her feet, chests barely grazing together. When he let go of her, open strands of her hair got stuck in his beard. He released them one strand at a time while Priya watched the big hands move gently, his face blank and intent on the job at hand.

It did not feel like Kalle's hug at all. This one left her breathless.

"You have to re-adjust your seat before you get in the truck," Dallas said as he opened the door for Priya and moved around the truck to the other side. She got in, flipped through the music in her iPod, plugged it in and waited for Dallas to buckle up.

"What kind of music do you like?" She pointed to her iPod. "You want to choose something?"

"I like all kinds of music. D'you have sitar music? Ravi Shankar?" He was betting she did.

"I do." Her lips curved into a beautiful smile.

He couldn't look away. Didn't want to. She so needed to go to India. Her soul belonged there. And he was going to take her there. He wasn't sure when he'd decided that. He wasn't even sure if she'd ever been. But it was the plan. And he was going to make her fall in love with him. Of that he was certain because there was no going to India without that.

She scrolled through a list and tapped her finger on the screen. The sweet sounds of a sitar filled the interior. Plus, with whatever it was she used as a fragrance, it was the perfect combination. He leaned back in his seat and prepared to enjoy it all in sumptuous silence.

"This is a beautiful piece called East meets West. Three musicians: A Hindu, Ravi Shankar on the sitar, a Muslim, Alla Rakha on the tabla and an American Jew, Yehudi Menuhin on the violin making gorgeous music together. It transcends all barriers. Especially religious ones," her words startled Dallas. They echoed the ones his mother had used.

She'd felt wonderful in his arms. The touch of her silky strands on his face was bliss. He couldn't say if he'd actually felt the swell of her breasts against his chest, but whatever he felt was close enough to fire his fantasy.

She dropped him at his place. Before he got out of her truck, he leaned toward her, cupped the back of her head with his hand and drew her to him. Then he bruised her lips with his. Not saying a word, he got out, got his bag from the back seat and let himself into his house. Once the door closed behind him, he dropped his bag on the floor and leaned against the door, reliving the taste of her mouth.

CHAPTER SIXTEEN

WHISKY TANGO FOXTROT. What the hell was that?

Priya sat rigidly in her seat, finger still on the ignition, her lips burning with his kiss. Dallas was not going to let go. She had to prepare for war and not let him get close to her. No more hanky panky. She wondered how she was going to do that when he had every intention of winning this.

Aargh! Priya tossed her hair over her shoulder and drove home.

It was hot. By 9:30, heat waves rose up from the baked pickleball courts. Fingers of sweat trickled down Priya's temples and back. Behind her sunglasses, her eyes began to burn. The hazy branches of the trees in the park behind her turned into snakes weaving in the air. Halfway through the game, she got off the court.

"Kalle, take my place please." Priya shut her eyes. The courts began swaying in an alarming way. Her head was about to explode.

"What's wrong? You caving? Giving up already?"

"I'm winning, if you cared to notice. Just hot. Need a drink." She managed to get off the courts without falling.

A delighted Kalle grabbed his paddle and took her place. As she looked at Kalle, he spun crazily. Priya made her way to the shade, nodding to Anna and Bob waiting for a court to open up. She stumbled against Bob almost knocking him down.

"Hey, you okay?" He had her by the shoulders, her head drooping onto his.

"She does not look okay, Bob," Anna hitched her shoulder under Priya's. "I think she needs to get into the shade. It's so damn hot."

Anna pulled off Priya's hat. In the shade of the big maple, Anna and Bob turned Priya gently intending to put her down on the bench. She slid out of their hold and rolled at their feet.

"What's wrong with her? I'll call 911." Bob ran to get his phone from his bag.

"We're right next the firehouse! Just run over and get someone here quickly." Anna put her fingers on Priya's pulse. "Strong. Maybe just fainted from the heat."

DALLAS, PLAYING ON the far court, broke his play. He grabbed his bag on his way out, unzipping it as he made his way to Priya's side. Taking a cool, wet towel from his bag, he knelt down and pressed it to her hot forehead. A big, brawny, young firefighter came jogging toward them, a bag in his hand, followed by a panting Bob.

"I'm fine. I'm okay. Too hot," Priya stood up on wobbly feet.

The firefighter took her pulse. He looked in her eyes.

"Strong and steady. She's okay," he said. "Needs to hydrate and get into bed, though. Heat stroke can be dangerous. But I think she's just dehydrated. Someone should stay with her. If symptoms get worse, get her to the hospital. Don't wait."

Without saying a word, Dallas bent down and hooked his right hand behind Priya's knees. He lifted her up, despite her protests and carried her to his car. He couldn't say whether it was from embarrassment or something else, but she tucked her head under his chin. He definitely lifted weights heavier than her.

"I'll get her home, Bob. And Anna could you please get her bag? It's over there. The red one."

Anna went to do his bidding.

In the car, Dallas put Priya in the passenger seat and buckled her in. For the first time since he'd known her, he saw vulnerability peek through. Her breathing was shallow and fast. It was as if she'd just run a marathon.

"You okay, squirt?" He couldn't help it. The name just slipped out. She looked so small and forlorn. He wanted to engulf her in his arms and never let her go.

She did not protest but turned her head to the side. "Am okay."

He ran a finger down her cheek and turned her chin to face him. Green eyes with dark lashes stared into his. They were wary and guarded. She lowered her lids, dropping the shutter on them.

"I'm going to get you home soon." He used the fob to start the car and opened his side of the door, cranking up the AC. Anna brought Priya's bag. Dallas got Priya's keys out, took the car keys out of the ring and handed them to Anna.

"I got this, Anna," Dallas took off his sunglasses.

"I can see that," Anna looked into his eyes. Satisfied, she took the keys. "You take care of her. I'm *trusting*," she stressed the word again, "*trusting* you to take care of her. She's my little sister. You have me to answer to." She squeezed his arm gently and patted it.

"Don't worry, I'm on it." He put his sunglasses back on. "Could you please get Priya's car home? You can leave it in her driveway."

"Sure, no problem."

"Hope you can manage the stick shift."

"Oh," Anna paused. "Blast!"

"I can do it," Bob remarked. "Give the keys to me. I've seen Dallas *try* to drive it," he added with a smirk.

"Right," Anna's lips twitched. "The shoe incident. Okay. See you at home then in a bit."

"Wazzat? You're not coming?"

Dallas figured there was nothing worse for Bob than missing a game of pickleball.

"I'm staying for a few more games. Let me know how she is," she said to Dallas. "Looks like she's going to be all right."

"Right, see you later, dear," Bob said.

Dallas got out of his car and opened the door to Priya's house first, before he carried her in. He slid off his shoes at the door, tossed Priya's hat to the side, kicked the door shut and up the stairs he went. Her eyes were closed. He hoped it was just fatigue and not something more serious. Taking her shoes off, he got her into bed. Her skin felt hot to his touch. But her breathing was calmer now. She opened her eyes, groaning and sat up.

"Oh, my head." Licking her lips, she said, "Water, please."

"In a sec."

Dallas rushed downstairs, got a glass from the cupboard and filled it with cold water from the dispenser in the fridge. He got back, sat down beside her and held the glass to her lips. She gulped it down.

"In the dresser there, you'll find a bottle of Motrin. Can you get me two, please?"

After saying that, she lay back. Dallas got the pills, slid his arm around her back and held her up while she swallowed. Priya laid her head back on the pillow and closed her eyes. Dallas pulled the drapes closed, sat in the armchair by the window, got up again and texted Bob and Kalle.

Got her into bed. Sleeping. Will stay with her. Don't worry.

He could not sit down. He paced for a bit at first, his eyes registering the surroundings. Her bedroom! Well, at some point it would have been his destination. But this was definitely not the way he'd imagined it.

Done in a cool lime green, he saw her touches everywhere: in the deep lavender of the drapes; the icy blue stain on the furniture and the voluptuous satin bedding. On the dresser were pretty bottles on a glass tray. He looked closer. He picked up a slender dark bottle.

Sandalwood oil.

He sniffed and got a whiff of a familiar smell he associated with her. The mystery of her alluring fragrance solved. The light outside got dimmer. When she slept for a few hours, he began to worry. He put his palm on her forehead. Her skin was hot and clammy. She was burning up! Her hair stuck to her forehead.

"Damn it, squirt! Looks like you have a fever."

From the bathroom, he got a couple of washcloths. In a bowl, he filled cold water from the tap. He dipped the cloths in the water, squeezed the excess out and put them on her forehead. He removed her socks and wrapped her calves in cool compresses. He covered ice cubes in a towel and rubbed her arms and temples.

He had considerable experience with bringing down a fever. His nieces had been sick many times and he'd been there to help Houston and Lara. Priya's fever broke even faster. It took just two hours. She slept. He didn't. He sat in the armchair watching and waiting for her chest to move.

Finally, he couldn't bear it. He moved to the bed, where he sat down. He had a better view of her breathing. That too was not enough. He put his hand on her so he could feel the rise and fall of her every breath. He sat for a while like that. When the leaning over became uncomfortable, he rested his back on the headrest, his hand still pressed to her side.

His mind was blank, all his energy focused on the crisis at hand. He might have dosed off. When she began to shiver, his senses were on high alert again. Rising up from the bed, he got blankets from the closet and piled them on her. He wrapped the duvet tightly around her and took her cold hands in his, hoping to transfer some warmth into her. It did not help and she continued shivering in spurts.

Finally, he stripped down to his shorts and got under the covers with her. He pulled her shivering body over his and wrapped his arms around her. Gradually, the warmth of his body seeped into her shivering one. His eyes drifted close as he fell into a dreamless and exhausted sleep.

"HOT," PRIYA MURMURED and opened her eyes.

She couldn't say where she was. She was in her bedroom, wasn't she? In her bed? Her cheek was lying on warm skin.

A man! God, who was it?

A forgotten fragrant memory from the summer working in Paris, the smell of *Eau Sauvage* drifted to her nose.

It was Dallas! There was a thudding in her ear. It was pressed against smooth and taut skin. Reality hit her. The thudding was his heart. She was lying on him!

What the hell?

She dared not move. She closed her eyes, lying as still as she possibly could.

DALLAS FELT THE lightest sensation on his chest like the touch of a feather and he was awake. There was a tickle in his nose. He opened his eyes slowly, a bit disoriented at first. Then he felt the warmth of a body on his. They were chest to chest, her hair spread all over his face. Her body temperature felt normal and her breathing had settled.

Then he remembered.

He lifted her gently and moved her to the side. She sighed and turned to the other side. He felt her forehead. No fever.

He rose from the bed, got his clothes together and made his way to the bathroom in the spare room. He took a hot shower and, feeling energized again, he went down to the kitchen to find breakfast. While his coffee was brewing, he used Priya's laptop to find out more about sunstrokes.

He had done good.

Now, he had to find out if she was hungry. As he rushed upstairs, he heard water running in her bathroom. So he went back downstairs and made her toast and tea. His mind was blank, his actions on auto pilot. He slid the bread slices in the toaster, got out a plate and utensils. A mug for her tea. He had just finished buttering the toast when she came down the stairs, her head wrapped in a towel. She wore shorts in a soft material and a tank top.

"How d'you like your tea?" he inquired.

"Lots of milk. And sugar."

She sat at the counter, her chin in her hand, big green eyes looking at him, face shiny and devoid of makeup, faint blue shadows under her eyes. A smattering of dark freckles on the bridge of her nose caught his attention. When he'd gotten under the covers with her-a feverish her-there was nothing sexual about it. He'd been exhausted with worry. And then natural sleep had taken over.

But now he remembered how soft she'd felt in his arms, her silky hair teasing the skin on his chest. Now his body responded. His pulse quickened. Sharp fingers of desire flicked at him. He dragged his gaze away from her mesmerizing eyes. The dark flecks in her eyes turned blue.

Not the time, buddy.

Wait a sec! Did he just *talk* to his dick?

What the fuck was she doing to him?

He turned away from her and got his hands busy, pouring milk into the strong black tea. He put the tea in front of her and pushed the bowl of sugar toward her. He watched as she spooned sugar in, stir and take a sip. She swallowed, closing her eyes.

"Mmm. Good." Her soft voice did wondrous things to him. "You make tea the Indian way. Boil the bags in water first."

"For three minutes. Always like my tea this way, strong and dark. Houston was in India for a year with the Peace Corps and got hooked on it. Now all of us drink tea only this way."

"My mother used to make tea like this," her voice wavered.

"How old were you?"

"Fifteen. I was in school in England."

"Must have been hard for you."

"Yes," she whispered.

He'd never be who he was today without his family. Without them, he was nothing. Yet, here she was without the support of a family, living her life. Her single life. Dallas took his eyes off her looking for something to do. "Toast?"

"Peanut butter and honey, please."

From the pantry, he got the jar of peanut butter and honey. On a slice of toast, he spread peanut butter then squeezed honey over it, put it on a plate and in front of her. When he lifted his head from his task, he caught her staring at him. She quickly lowered her eyes and concentrated on the toast. Her lashes were inky smudges on her cheeks. He stared some more at her freckles.

When she was done, she said, "Thank you, Dallas. For everything."

"No prob. I'm glad to see you up and about." That wasn't difficult. He could make polite conversation.

"Crazy isn't it? How life can change in an instant?"

"Definitely. One moment it's fine and the next, it's changed."

"Aren't you having anything? You a no breakfast kind of guy?"

"No. Breakfast to me is the most important meal of the day. Just popped toast in. Hope you have eggs in the fridge."

"I sure do."

He opened the fridge, got out the eggs and got ready to make scrambled eggs.

"Would you like some eggs too?"

"No, none for me thanks." She touched the towel on her head. "I'll be right back." She went upstairs.

Dallas finished making the eggs. He ate it standing at the counter, sipping tea. When she came down, the towel was off her head. Her hair hung down her back in dark lustrous waves. He could smell her shampoo. Something flowery. He breathed in deep, his nostrils flaring.

Big mistake. It was his undoing. He poured scalding tea down his throat, distracting his body to cover another heat-propelled emergency. Relieved at the success, he drained his mug.

~

"DON'T YOU HAVE to be at work?" Priya asked.

"It's Sunday."

"Oh."

"How are you feeling? No dizziness? No heat wave?"

"No."

"Headache?"

"No."

"I guess you're okay then."

Her shoulders lifted. "Guess I am."

He put the last of the dishes in the dishwasher. He hadn't

combed his hair. It was still damp. He kept smoothing it back each time his hair fell across his forehead. He put on his shoes while she sat on the steps watching him, her arms resting on her knees. His grey gaze flicked over her before they caught hers.

"I'll be back in a bit. You need anything from the store?"

"You don't have to be back. I'm fine. You can text me."

"No can do, squirt. Be back in a bit." He was not going to take no for an answer.

Priya took a deep breath. She opened her mouth to protest then shut it quickly again. Thoughts rambled in her head. Apparently, he was going to call her that. Why prolong the inevitable? She was usually combative. She did not give in easily. Yet, she did not want to start a fight with him. Which surprised her. Plus no one had ever given her a nickname before. It was kind of nice.

"Okay, then. Thanks once again for everything."

Then he was gone.

Priya sat on the steps feeling grateful, thankful and also a bit worried. It was not going to be easy to resist him. He was going to be a tough one. All wrapped in a hard to ignore sexy package. She dropped her head on her arms, hair tumbling down like a screen.

"Fuck," she whispered for the first time ever.

It seemed so appropriate. It summed up the situation in one succinct exhale.

CHAPTER SEVENTEEN

DALLAS SAT IN his office, PHONE IN HIS hand. It was as if he'd come back from an arduous journey. He felt jet-lagged, groggy and disoriented. Priya had drained him emotionally. Being so close to her yet unable to make the next move was debilitating. Even recalling the warmth of her body failed to give him the usual buzz.

Something about her made him hesitate. And even though he was Mr. Go Slow, this was even slower. Wasn't it? Was *his* master plan failing? Priya treated him like she did everyone else. Hell, even Austin got more response from her than he did. The more he ruminated, the thicker the knobs of doubt in his gut grew.

Was it all one-sided? They had quite a few interesting exchange of words. A few searing kisses with none of it leading to anything more. The heatstroke incident only made him aware of how much he wanted her in his bed. Question was, what was he going to do about it? He just might have to go on the offensive and get her off her defensive mode.

DINNER? DALLAS TEXTED.

When and where? She made it simple for him.

GREEN MANGO. SEVEN.

MEET YOU THERE.

PICK YOU UP.

NOPE. MEET YOU THERE.

Priya could sense the expletives hovering on his tongue. He was probably puzzled by her insistence. She was glad he did not push her further. It was one of the things she liked about him. He took his cues from her. She still had not sorted her feelings out after the fever episode. He'd seemed so tightly wound then. Which was why she'd kept the counter between them. Though she'd wanted to brush back the strands of hair falling over his face, she hadn't dared to. There had been just the hint of tense control. She saw it in the tight sinews of his arms, in the clenched jaw and in the muscle twitching in his cheek. She'd been afraid of setting something loose she couldn't either handle or had control over. Both of which had been scary enough to stop her.

Yep, he'd definitely been tightly wound. And she had no intention of unwinding him.

If he picked her up then he'd drop her off too. She'd have to decide right then and there about her next moves. She was not up to it. Not right now. It was too much pressure. She did not want to be backed into a corner, looking for a way out when things got uncomfortable. She was going to take it slow and be prudent about it.

Dallas might be the one she was attracted to right now but it was not going to be the way it had been with Simon. She was going to be careful.

What *else* did the dinner invitation mean?

They'd rarely been alone. Now it would be just the two of them.

Dallas hoped he gave off a cool vibe when he was feeling anything but. He smoothed his hair with the palms of his hands. He rubbed his knuckles across his chin. He thought he should order a bottle of red. Then decided against it. Then changed his mind again.

Why did she insist on meeting him here when they lived almost next to each other? She was doing something weird to his confidence, running hot and cold like that.

Tonight they would be alone. Not right now, of course, but at least later. He wondered how ready she was for this. He sat facing the door. He didn't have to. His body went on high alert the instant she walked in.

A white wrap covered her red dress. Her sun-kissed skin had the sheen of sweet cinnamon, the colour fading as it ran into less exposed areas. She wore white open-toed shoes with spiky heels. It was still not enough to raise her height above his shoulders. He thought he caught a glimpse of red on her shoes. She took off the wrap and his breath hitched in his chest.

She was not going to make it easy for him to get through dinner.

A red sheath, strapless, moulded to her curves. Cinched tight at the waist, it followed the swell of her hips before it hit the calves. It might have been a simple dress. On her, with her hair pinned up, showing off her graceful neck with the exposed tats, it was stunning. He watched eyes follow her as she made her way to him. A necklace with a single stone dipped into her cleavage. There were large silver hoops in her ears along with ear cuffs and that stud in her nose. He heard the sexy sound of bracelets on her wrists.

He pulled out her chair for her and just as he about to sit down, her wrap slid to the floor. Dallas leaned over and picked it up, running the soft fabric through his fingers. He stood up to hang it back on her chair and took the opportunity to shamelessly fill his nose with her scent.

It was driving him nuts.

"So, Priya. Why didn't you let me pick you up?"

Dinner over, Dallas tilted his glass and took a sip of the red. It slid deliciously down his throat.

"So I could make that entrance." She tucked a straying strand of hair behind her ear, her bracelets tinkling softly.

"I don't buy that for an instant." He leaned over, his eyes intent on her face, daring her to look away. "I think," he took another sip of wine, "you're playing a game. A dangerous one, I might add."

"And why is that?"

"Wait. What? Why is what?"

"Why do you think I'm playing a game? A dangerous one at that?" Priya enunciated each word before she leaned back in her chair, sinking into the softness. She twirled the stem of her glass between her fingers.

"Dangerous because you can't predict what will happen. You will have no control over it once...." he paused, his gaze intent on hers.

"Once what?"

"Once I make up my mind about you." Actually, he already had. But he wasn't about to spill the beans. Not yet anyway.

She raised the glass to her sumptuous lips and he watched her mouth close over the rim, take a mouthful and swallow it. His eyes followed its trail down her throat and stopped at the pulse beating there, then drifted to the pendant shifting ever so slightly with her breathing.

A low sound bubbled in her throat. "Once *you* make up your mind? Isn't that a bit presumptuous? You are full of yourself, aren't you?"

"You just wait and see."

"Is this a challenge?"

He shook his head. "In no way is it that. A challenge requires two equal opponents. And that we're not."

"Are you saying I'm not equal to you?"

"We are up to 99% of the time. The one percent? That's where you are woman and I'm man. That's where we differ and thankfully not the same."

She caught his gaze. Her eyes sparkled. "Oh, I get it. You Tarzan and me Jane? Let me ask you something: you're not hanging out with me coz you think I'll let you get into my pants, are you? Coz I won't."

He chuckled. It rumbled up from deep inside him. Trust her to bring that up! Trust her to state the obvious.

"No." His lips uttered the words while his mind shouted something else. *Liar!*

"Liar." She echoed his thought, a deep bloom rising to her honey-toned cheeks.

"So what? Have I ever made you uncomfortable? Touched you inappropriately?"

She shook her head, for once at a loss for words. "You've been proper. A gentleman."

"I will never, I repeat never, touch you in that way without your permission." He filled her glass with wine, his lids shuttering his eyes. "Never. So be careful how you look at me. Permission can be given without words too. When I have it, there will be no holding back," he promised.

~

PRIYA NOTICED IT was 'when' and not an 'if.' She looked at his large hands lying casually on the table, one holding the stem of the wine glass. She wondered if he had callouses, imagining the rough skin sliding over hers. And right then, all she wanted was for those hands to be all over her. She bit her lip before the words spilled out.

She leaned forward on the table, her arms resting on the white tablecloth, not touching his, desperately wanting to close the space between them and run her fingers through his dark hair. She wanted to feel the brush of his beard against her skin. Her belly clenched, her imagination running away with her, jolting awake the slumbering parts of her body.

Her lips parted and her gaze dropped to his mouth. When she raised her eyes, his were dark, a black hole into which she was falling, amber flecks covering the darkness, a supernova ready to erupt and to swallow her whole.

"Don't." A pulse throbbed in his clenched jaw.

"What?"

"Don't." The word was almost a growl. It was feral and the intensity of it made her move back just a little. "Don't look at my mouth like that. Unless you want it on yours."

At his words, a flame of desire surged through her. She lowered her eyes to his hand, the one not holding the glass. It was clenched into a fist. Her mouth went dry. She wasn't ready for this. This was too much. The look on his face! His eyes were smouldering pits of fire. If he touched her, she'd explode. She had to get away. She pushed her chair back, sliding the wrap over her shoulders.

~

DALLAS CAUGHT UP with her outside, walking toward his car. Or so he thought. Halfway down the block, she swivelled around and walked the other way, her phone in her hand.

"Priya, where are you going? My car is this way," he walked after her.

"Taking an Uber," she called over her shoulder.

"Why? We're going the same way, are we not?"

"I'd rather take the Uber." She began to walk faster away from him.

Her eyes on the screen, she bumped into someone. Someone

who grabbed her arms so abruptly, she stumbled back on her heels, shoes flashing red.

"Of course the soles are red. She's trying to kill me," Dallas muttered. He raced to her side, shoving the man aside. He took her by the shoulders.

"Don't need your help, Dallas. Can take care of myself."

She shrugged his hands off and walked away. He grabbed her wrist. She tried to shake his hand off. He held it tighter and heard something crack: the glass bangles shattered in his hand and he heard the tinkle of the pieces as they hit the ground. He looked at her wrist dotted with tiny pricks.

"Aw, Priya. I'm sorry. Here…let me," he pulled out a handkerchief from his pocket of his pants.

She jerked her wrist away from his hold. "It's okay. I'm okay. It's happened before. Nothing to it."

He dropped her hand. She finished with her phone and slid it into her purse. She walked fast along the block. Puzzled at her behaviour, Dallas followed her. He caught up with her, putting a hand on her shoulder. She turned and jabbed an elbow into his belly. Hard. Then she raised her arm and something fiery hit him.

"What the fuck?" He crouched, hiding his face. "Priya, what the hell did you do that for?"

She'd hit him with pepper spray!

He was fortunate he was much taller than she was. For there was no doubt in his mind she was aiming for his eyes. As it was, she got him on the chin.

"I'm sorry. So sorry, Dallas. I thought it was the other guy again. Didn't know you were following me. Just wash it out with lots of water. I've got to go."

~

PRIYA DID NOT want to ride home with Dallas. She did not want it to evolve into him coming in for 'coffee.' They'd just had cappuccinos for God's sake! She was not ready for him. Not with that fire in his eyes. She couldn't handle it.

A car sidled up to her as she stood on the curb. Her Uber looked familiar. She got in the back. The driver turned his head and a fierce face with a handle bar moustache stared at her.

"Malcolm! Since when do you do this?" A big sigh of relief shuddered through her body. A respite. She did not have to think about what just happened right now.

"Get in the front next to me and I'll tell you. By the way, I know where you live," Priya sensed his smile.

So she got in the front. "Tell me," she demanded once she was belted in.

"I know you want to hear a heart-wrenching story but the plain truth is: I was bored!"

"And what does Margaret have to say about this?"

"Why don't you ask her when you come in for a Caesar?"

"Right on."

Malcolm stopped in front of his house. Priya ran up the steps while Malcolm was off on another Uber run.

Margaret was on the deck, nursing a G&T. "Wow! Priya! You look smashing." Holding Priya's hand, she made her twirl while she examined her from head to toe. "You been out?"

"Yep. Kind of. Date."

"Oh, do tell. Who was it? Someone I know?"

"You would if you played pickleball more often."

"Yeah, sorry about that. Can't quite fit it in with tennis, bridge and the grandkids. Wait! Don't tell me it's one of the old geezers. Please, please don't." Margaret stood with her hands clasped in front of her, beseeching her to "Say it ain't so."

"It so ain't an old geezer. But why not? You have one."

"Ah, but he belongs in my generation, my dear. You, on the other hand, are one or two below. You're only twenty-eight. You're way out of their-our-league."

"Just by being younger?"

"Let's see...bet you know more about sex than I do."

"Bet you get more sex than I do."

"Okay, let's leave that aside for a sec. You'd have to take control the *whole* time. In bed, I mean. What a bore that would be."

Priya wasn't about to tell her otherwise. She wondered what staid Margaret would say if she told her about her box of feathery instruments, oils and her battery operated friend, BOB. She wondered what she'd say if she found out about Priya's chickening out earlier with Dallas. And most of all she wondered what she'd say if she told Margaret about her hot dreams featuring Dallas and how she *still* chickened out.

"Okay, it's not one of them. It's a young one," Priya turned thoughtful. "Around thirty-four?'

"Now that's more like it. How about a drink?"

"Malcolm promised me a Caesar. I'll wait till he gets back." Priya wanted to postpone the moment she was going to be alone with her thoughts.

"He'll be quite a while. C'mon. What can I pour you?"

"A beer then."

"Coming right up. Tell me more. Go on."

"He asked me out to dinner. I wore this dress. Dinner over, I took an Uber. That's it."

"Guess I'll have to drop in by the courts if I want to see more, then won't I?"

Priya made a clicking sound with her tongue between her teeth. "Guess you'll have to, I'm afraid."

"Won't need you to point him out though. He would stand out among all the grey heads."

"That he would."

The sky was dark and thick with clouds when Priya got home. It mirrored her thoughts. Her mind was nebulous. She was apprehensive. Deep in her heart she knew she had reached a point of no return. It was about to be breached. And once it was, her whole life would change. It wouldn't be hers anymore.

How was she going to face Dallas after she'd attacked him with pepper spray? More importantly, how was she going to face him after he'd said the things he'd said? Only said. He hadn't done anything. Not yet at least. His words terrified her. He wanted so much. More than she was willing to give. And if she did, she'd be lost, swallowed whole by the passion she'd seen lurking in his beautiful eyes: eyes that did not lie, even if his lips had.

Was passion enough? She didn't know. There had been no passion between Simon and her. Simon filled a need in her and she'd been willing to be content with it. But Simon never made her feel like Dallas did. Dallas created turbulence in her feelings. He was beginning to take more space in her life. It bothered her. But then again, she was drawn to him, the urge to lean against him never ending, to feel his body close to hers a recurring fantasy. If nothing else, she would have liked to be held in those strong arms of his, rest her head against his broad chest. He made her feel secure. And oh! To have his lips on hers again!

Yet, she'd attacked him with pepper spray! She'd hurt the one person who made her feel safe. How screwed up was that?

Maybe she could avoid seeing him altogether by not going to pickleball.

How could she do that? Pickleball was her life!

Despite all her intentions of not getting too close to Dallas, Priya had Dallas on her mind. On Taylor Kidd, instead of turning right on Collins Bay road to come home, she'd gone straight. Then had to turn around and come back. She went to Farm Boy without her list and ended up getting only pastries and cookies: her basic distracting sugary kicks. She forgot to check the fuel gauge in her truck and almost ran dry. She forgot clothes in the dryer. Her favourite tank top came out in accordion folds.

Priya got a hold of herself, determined to get on with it. She got to the matter at hand, focusing on lunch. Sustenance. Crucial part of her life.

Her lonely life.

Aargh!

Not that again! No, she was okay with it. Had been until now. Here she was taking her life into her own hands, making lunch. She drained pasta and piled it on a plate. She grabbed the block of mozzarella and began to grate it over the hot pasta, her eyes on the clematis flowers climbing the trellis she could see from her kitchen window. A carpet of big, fat purple flowers covered the climber, obliterating views of the small, green leaves.

She glanced down at the pasta. Good. The cheese was melting, as it should. Strangely enough, the block in her hand melted equally fast too. Which was not as it should. Frowning, she checked the cheese in her hand.

It was squishy, oozing between her fingers. On closer examination, it turned out to be the butter block remaining from the brownie baking session and not cheese.

No matter.

She got cheese out and making sure it actually was cheese, grated some on her plate. Tossing it together, she made lunch, set the table and sat down to eat.

She decided a coffee was in order. A caffeine jolt was just what she needed. She got the coffee from her pantry and switched the machine on. Then went to get into the shower to wash off the stench of her wallowing in despair.

Back in the kitchen, a puddle of brown liquid greeted her.

Fudge! She'd neglected to put the carafe in the blasted coffee machine. No wonder she drank tea most of the time. She spent the next fifteen minutes of her life cleaning up the mess. Wasn't totally wasted though: the kitchen floor was spotlessly fragrant giving off a slight coffee aroma.

It was the first fifteen minutes without Dallas on her mind.

CHAPTER EIGHTEEN

DALLAS SCOOTED BACK to the Green Mango following the signs to the washrooms after Priya ran away from him. Invisible fumes continued to rise from his chin to his already burning eyes. He ran cold water in the sink and doused his face with it. After the tenth time, the burning sensation began to subside. Outside, he let the cool air wash over him, got into his car and drove home.

There he continued the water treatment for a while longer. He hoped the redness would be gone by the next day. His brothers were coming over. He didn't want to explain to them why the woman he had the hots for had hit him with pepper spray. Dallas considered himself lucky when the redness in his eyes and the burning sensations subsided before he went to bed. Only then did he linger over what had happened.

There was no doubt in his mind Priya had not meant to hit him with pepper spray. He let that image go and brought up the others: the way she'd looked at him when he told her about his intentions. She'd looked tense. And the way she'd looked in that outrageously sexy dress of hers and the shoes with the red soles!

Just the red soles did it for him. If she only was aware of the power she had over him. He should have grabbed her right then and there and kissed her senseless.

But no, he wouldn't do that. He'd made a promise.

In the restaurant, he had to keep a tight hold on his hands. They appeared to have a mind of their own where Priya was concerned. His hands wanted to bury themselves in her hair, cup her face and caress the soft skin. But he'd let his eyes do the talking. There was a moment when he thought she felt the same way. The same fire raging in her blood. Then the moment was gone. For a bit there, she'd looked terrified.

When Dallas switched his phone back on again the next morning he saw he had a couple of texts from his brothers. They'd wanted to meet at the Red Rooster, a local pub, the evening before. Now it was a moot point. The following texts postponed the pub outing to the next evening.

"So what happened to you yesterday?" Houston strode back from the bar, balancing three pints in his hands.

"Pickleball." He was *not* going to tell them about Priya in her Monroe dress. "Practicing for a competition with my partner."

"Thought it was done. Cobourg, wasn't it?"

"Another one coming up."

They sat in a booth, Austin lounging back in one corner with Dallas by his side and Houston facing them, all three oblivious to the admiring looks cast their way. It was the way it always was with the Crenshaw boys. When they were together, nothing else mattered. They were completely focused on each other.

"Your partner? Now that has an interesting ring to it. Male or female?" Austin took a deep swig from his pint.

"Male. 60+ A huge Viking of a man."

Houston flicked the screen on his phone. Then he leaned over to Dallas. "This is it? This pickleball of yours?"

A YouTube video came up. Austin twisted Houston's hand so he could see too. The video showed the men's gold medal game at the Minto US Open Pickleball championship.

"Wow! Look at them go! Intense. See how they did that?" Austin's eyes were glued to the tiny screen. "They were first at the base line or whatever and quickly moved up to the net. Then it was bop, bop, bop and smash!"

"Must be quite a workout," Houston put his phone away.

"Reason why I was so bushed last evening."

"'Kay, what are we getting to eat?" Austin beckoned a passing server to their booth. "Sweet potato fries, Buffalo wings and a plate of nachos. That's for three beer-drinking guys, okay? You guys want anything else?" Dallas and Houston shook their heads.

"Think you got it covered," Dallas said. "Oh yes, don't forget the hot sauce, please. The Insanity one, not Tabasco."

The nachos came first. Dallas drizzled hot sauce all over it.

"Enough of that already," Houston took a nacho popped it in his mouth and winced. "You're going to blow my ears off. Not to mention my ass."

Dallas grinned. "This is the good stuff. It will keep flu and cold away."

"Plus impair my hearing. And other vital body parts."

"You have to protect yourself. You have school-going kids. A school is just a humongous incubator for all sorts of infectious bugs just waiting for a chance to complicate your life."

The fries came next. "I got this," Houston swatted Dallas's hand away and refused to allow him to douse it with hot sauce. He sprinkled a bit of sauce over fries then squirted a small puddle of it on the side for Dallas to dip his fries in.

By the time the wings arrived, Houston did not even bother to protest.

"Anything new with Emily?" Under the table, Dallas poked Austin with his leg.

Austin shrugged. "Think we're done. Neither of us is willing to compromise."

"What is she not willing to compromise?"

"Shared duties. She wants the bed made, looking all pretty

with her million pretty mini pillows. Then she wants me to be in the kitchen while she's making dinner, put the seat down on the toilet…blah blah blah. Can't do that."

"Why not? You love her, don't you? Or is it just one of your flings? Again?" Houston contributed his bit, being the married one after all.

"No, I do love her."

"Commitment also means sharing, bro. What's wrong with being in the kitchen when she's making dinner, especially if you're home?"

"That's one of her *other* rules: be home for dinner. So then I gotta be in the kitchen, no?"

"See I told you to learn how to cook. It's enjoyable. And it brings you closer together. She just wants to be with you, dumbass."

"What do you do when she's in the kitchen?" Dallas was betting Austin did the traditional old man thing.

"Watch TV."

"What are you not willing to compromise?" Dallas asked.

"Stop watching TV. Not be in the kitchen."

"So basically, she wants you to do more and you want to do less. Leave the more for her to do. Make the bed for two, cook for two, clean for two and still work five days a week at least at being a lawyer. She's not your maid, for fuck's sake! She's the woman you love. Probably the mother of your children," Houston got really going when it came to commitment.

"What d'you think is going to happen once you have kids? They are babies first remember?" Dallas looked back at the time when Emma and Olivia were babies. "Are you going to get up in the middle of the night when your baby cries? Or are you going to let her get that too?"

"What's the point of me getting up if she's the one with the breasts?"

"Ah, so you have thought about it but just not enough. Guess you haven't heard about breast pumps. She can pump milk the night before, it's stored in the fridge and then when you get up in the middle of the night, you warm it up and feed your baby."

"Oh, fuck! This is too much."

"Yes, it is. So don't just say you want to have kids just for the heck of it. You have to commit to raising them too. You can't just make kids and walk away."

"Anyway," Houston crunched on a nacho, then winced as it was the one doused in hot sauce. "Anyway, what's your problem with having kids? You hang out with Emma and Olivia all the time. You even have them all to yourself twice a month."

"Emma and Olivia are angels. Fully formed angels. I can do stuff with them."

"You can do that with your kids too, moron. You'll see."

"All right, enough about me. What about you, Dallas?"

"What about me? There's nothing going on."

"No special lady on the horizon?"

Dallas shook his head. "I'm taking it slow. It'll happen when it has to happen."

"That's bullshit. You gotta go out there and get some," Austin wolfed down a wing and chased it with a swig of beer.

"Am fine the way things are, thank you bro. Like I said, I have things under control."

Austin raised his glass to his older brothers and snagged another wing. Ripping the meat off the bone of wing, he munched on it before taking a swig. "There's something going on with him," he pointed a finger at Dallas. "Something's bitten him."

"You mean like a bee or a mosquito or a vampire?" Houston wiped his mouth with a paper napkin.

"No, he's hiding something. I can smell it."

Younger brothers were a real pain in the ass and Dallas would have loved to kick him. When did Austin get all wised up? He was Mr. No Commitment, the flirt or whatever. He thought of a curse word he'd only recently learned.

Bollocks.

Well, bollocks to him and Dallas washed the nacho down with cold beer. It sizzled all the way down to his belly.

"Yeah, like you have the energy to stop and smell the roses after plowing through the waves of female admirers."

"And I believe I know who it is," the rascal went on.

"Do tell," Dallas was on the hot seat now, two pairs of Crenshaw eyes pinning him to the spot.

"It's somebody he plays pickleball with," Austin talking to Houston only, leaning over.

Well, duh. He had nothing else that did not include them.

"Somebody we've all seen on stage dancing. Priya. First, there was this sexy beauty jogging down Princess who stopped to chat with my laid back bro here."

Oh, shit.

He'd seen her! Dallas tried to unscramble his thoughts before things got out of hand with Austin. Perhaps a bit of unloading on his part would keep the bastard quiet until they wrapped their evening together.

"Oh, her?" Dallas kept it cool. "Just someone I play with."

"I'll say," Austin chuckled. "I was watching you when she did the dance. And at the beach."

"Really?" Houston being the oldest was always the last to know. Information travelled very slowly up from the lower level. "How come *I* wasn't at the beach?"

"Uncles day, jackass." This was from Austin who was always eloquent when there was a need for it.

"You're an idiot, you know that?" Dallas was going to see Priya again. How, he hadn't decided yet. He was not sure where he wanted this to go. But go it must. And it must be slow.

"This I gotta see," Houston drained his pint. "We getting another round before we get on our Uber or what?"

"Another round to go," Dallas swiped the app on his phone and ordered his Uber. His would be a white SUV.

"You will see, big bro," Austin fluttered his expressive eyes. "Soon, no Dallas?"

Dallas had nothing else to add so he nodded. He was not sure he wanted to share Priya yet with the world. His world. At some point they would collide, of that he was certain. But better later than sooner.

When they were done, they carried their conversation outside while they waited for their Uber drivers. Dallas was grateful his rat of a younger brother saw fit not to broach the subject again.

"So when are you going to see her again? Priya. Spill it, bro."

Dallas had to admit defeat. And for once his younger brother was the reason.

"I'll be seeing Priya soon." He hoped the pepper spray was not the end of it. It deflated him, saying her name out loud like that. He was not ready to share her. Not yet. Not since he was not sure where it was going.

A white SUV came to a stand near them. Dallas wanted to get out of there before Austin and Houston continued their interrogation.

"I'm going to grab this one," Dallas opened the door. "See you guys later." He squeezed Houston's arm and slapped Austin on the back.

"Have fun at the pickleball tournament in Markham," Houston said.

"Bring home a trophy or whatever they give out at these things," Austin added.

"Will do." Dallas got in the front.

The driver had a grey handlebar moustache gracing his face. "Good evening," he said.

Dallas gave him his address. "And good evening to you too, sir," he figured the moustache deserved the 'sir.'

"Did I hear you say 'pickleball' just now to your friends?"

"Brothers. And yes, I play pickleball. Why?"

"It's the strangest thing. I have a friend and she's young like you. She plays pickleball. In fact she's crazy about it. Says it saved her life."

What could have brought on such a drastic opinion? "You do? How strange indeed. But this is a small town. So perhaps not so strange after all. My name's Dallas Crenshaw." It couldn't be! The world couldn't be that small. What were the odds?

"And I'm Malcolm Stevens. Where do you play this pickleball, if you don't mind my asking?"

"In Bath."

"That's exactly where she plays. Her name is Priya. She's this tiny thing with hair up to way below…."

Dallas shook his head as Malcolm Stevens went on describing Priya who was etched in his mind forever. Life was indeed full of wicked coincidences.

CHAPTER NINETEEN

DALLAS HADN'T SEEN Priya on the courts for over a week. Then one day, he found flowers on his porch with a note. Reading it, he chuckled under his breath. She was definitely feeling guilty all right. The flowers reeked of it. The thing was, she'd one-upped him. The hand-written apology was cute and he had to counter with a stronger offer.

He texted his thanks. And then invited her to spend the weekend at the family cottage on Loughborough Lake, after the opening of the Breakwater Park. It took a while for her to reply. She was probably brooding over his invitation. Wondering what the invitation meant and what she was getting into.

JUST YOU AND ME?

PROBLEM?

NO. JUST WONDERING WHAT TO EXPECT. DID MACE YOU.

Sitting in his office, Dallas grinned, Chris Isaak's *Wicked Game* playing in the background. He deliberated whether to tell Priya about it being a family weekend then decided against it. Let her stew a bit. He wanted her contrite and apologetic. He knew exactly where she was going with it. She was making sure they weren't alone. Was she afraid? He planned to send her mixed messages. Make her doubt her instincts.

WATER UNDER THE BRIDGE. AFRAID?

WHEW! NO. I ACCEPT.

Breakwater Park was scheduled to open in a few days. Dallas tried to calm the frenzied atmosphere in the project pool, but it was to no avail. He worked from his office at Hovertek and concentrated on the job of getting all written the documents in order. Plus, the mayor had requested he write the speech for her and so here he was biting the end of a wooden pencil, one finger poised over the keyboard of his laptop.

He found nothing. Not. A. Single. Word.

A wordy train of thought bloomed in his brain only to disintegrate. Visions of Priya sneaked in to send him off on a trajectory involving minor readjustments to his body. He chewed harder on the pencil. Wood chips began to prick the inside of his mouth. There was no way out. He was tethered to his desk.

He flung the pencil across the office where it bounced on the glass wall and rolled into a corner. Rummaging in his bag, he found his MP3 player and stuck in his earbuds. The music cocooned his fuzzy brain from Priya-associated thoughts and it was enough to unblock the word-associated part of his brain. He settled on Beethoven's Third Symphony and set it on a repeat loop. It took him more time since he actually listened to the music but the sound waves gave the wordy part of his brain the impetus it so desperately needed.

It took him two hours but by the end of it, he had what the mayor wanted: a bit of history, a bit about the landscape-architect and engineers involved with the planning and design and how it all fit into the mayor's Master Plan for Breakwater.

He hoped there was some place for pickleball in the Master Plan.

Dallas picked Priya up on Friday evening. She breezed out of her front door, threw her overnight bag on the back seat, climbed in without saying a word, buckled her belt and sat demurely by his side, her hands folded in her lap. She wore a yellow dress under a denim jacket, her fragrance hitting him instantly.

Her gorgeous dark hair was held up in a messy bun, loose tendrils curling down her neck. The few strands kissing the curves of her cheeks caught the light and glowed a burnished brown. Dallas beat down the urge to wrap his fingers around those strands. Sunglasses covered her eyes.

"You okay?" Dallas sent her a glance as he drove to the ramp leading to the highway.

She didn't answer. He drove on the shoulder, stopped the car and turned to her.

"I did answer. I shrugged."

"Well. Seeing that I'm driving and am *not* actually looking at you, it would have to be a verbal answer, I'm afraid." He looked at her, eyebrows raised over the top of his sunglasses.

She shrugged again. "Right. I'm okay. Now can we go on please?"

"Sure."

She offered nothing more, so he filled the empty silence with music. Chris Isaak's *Wicked Game* came over the speakers.

"Why are you playing this song?" Priya asked.

"Not me. Radio."

How appropriate. Question was who was playing the game.

At the lake, after a brief hello to his parents, Olivia and Emma took control of Priya and that was that. Dallas took a step back and was content to watch her play with his nieces while he helped with the food prep.

Priya was a natural when it came to dealing with his nieces. They hung by her side as she matched her strides to theirs. Her melodious voice floated on the breeze toward him. Her laughter mingled with Olivia and Emma's giggles. He smiled as he arranged the condiments on the table. This was going to be a fun day.

Priya wondered whether she had to be on her guard. She had questions but she couldn't and didn't dare ask them.

Were they going to be alone? It would reveal her vulnerability. Chris Isaak's *Wicked Game* over the waves brought an extra depth to her quandary. The lyrics seemed to be talking to her, about her. The singer's gravelly voice gave special meaning to the words.

Seeing his family at the cottage eased her worries somewhat. It was clever and wicked of him to let her believe they would be alone.

"So nice that you could come, Priya." His mother, Madison, said handing her a plate.

"Thank you for having me, Mrs. Crenshaw," Priya helped herself to the potato salad and steamed veggies.

Houston was manning the grill on which hamburgers were laid out in precise rows. Dallas was at the condiment table while Austin was already digging into his hamburger keeping an eye on the girls who were jumping off the dock, Lara by his side. Joe was at the house getting the drinks.

"Maddie, please. Go get your hamburger and then come sit beside me," Madison pointed to the chairs arranged around a rectangular table.

Priya got a hamburger and moved to the assortment of condiments. When she saw the array of hot sauces, she couldn't help salivating. She dressed her hamburger with a large dollop of hot sauce, licking her lips in anticipation.

A chuckle escaped Dallas. "Quite a lot for a little squirt," he murmured, standing a little to the side, hands busy with sticking water and soda in a bucket of ice.

He looked relaxed and completely in his element, all smiles and dimples.

She liked his name for her. She raised her eyebrows and gave him a smile. "You'll be surprised at how much I can take."

With that cryptic remark, she joined Madison at the table.

"So you and Dallas met at pickleball?" Madison took a bite of her hamburger, looking at Priya.

"Hmm yes. He's a great player." She did not want to go into the Turtle Crossing or Hovertek events, things she'd already put out of her mind.

"My sons are very athletic. In school, they excelled at sports. Houston played ice hockey while basketball was Dallas's thing and Austin won quite a few medals for the swim team. Do you have any family, Priya? Any siblings?"

"No. My parents died when I was fifteen and I'm an only child."

"So you're used to being alone. Doing things for yourself."

"Yes. It's second nature to me. I have friends when I want to be with someone. And then I have my catering business, Bollywood dancing classes and pickleball." No need to mention her PI proclivities either.

"Don't forget to eat your hamburger."

Priya put both hands around her burger and took a bite.

Bliss!

"It's delicious, Maddie."

"Oh, I didn't make it. Dallas did. He put in red onions, garlic, grated carrot and minced celery."

Dallas did? Priya took another bite, imagining his hands mincing the red onions and celery. His large capable hands. The same hands wrapped around her, cradling her face. Heat rose up to her face.

His mother was sitting right next to her!

She so needed another dollop of hot sauce. Excusing herself, she got the hot sauce and slathered more on her burger and for good measure on the potato salad too. That would keep her thoughts from wandering.

"Hey, take it easy on the sauces, squirt," came the voice again doing all sorts of things to the state of her body.

"Meh." Priya shrugged.

"Goodness! You do love it spicy," Madison pointed to the food on Priya's plate.

"I'm afraid so."

"Dallas is exactly the same. Well, all my boys too, but especially Dallas. He squirts…"

Priya choked on her mouthful of spicy potato salad, earning a louder chuckle from Dallas, the fink. She refused to look at him.

"…hot sauce on everything. Here, have some water, dear." A helpful Madison handed Priya a bottle of water. "There you are, Joe. Come on, hurry up with the drinks."

"G&T for you, dear?"

Purely out of habit, Priya pursed her lips to make a puking sound but caught herself just in time.

"Not for me, thanks."

"A beer, then?

"Yes, please," she managed to croak the words out.

"Dallas?" Joe called over his shoulder. "Could you please get beer from the house for our guest?"

"Sure, Dad," was the muffled response.

When he brought back a cooler filled with cold beer in a bed of ice cubes, Priya quickly twisted the cap off a bottle and gulped it down so fast, she got a lovely hiccup going.

Joe thumped her on the back. "Now, now. Take it slow. Breathe in deep, as deep as you can go, hold it then breathe out slowly. It usually works for me."

So Priya did as he asked, held her breath and waited. Five seconds later, she was at it again. Only this time, there was laughter mixed in with the hiccups at the expression on Joe's face. He appeared to have been holding his breath too.

"Well, I guess that didn't work."

Laughing and hiccupping at the same time proved quite

painful. Priya got up and left the table, holding her arms over her belly as if that would stop the hiccups. She walked to the edge of the water. Dallas prepared to join her but she waved him off.

"Will pass," she managed to say before the next jolt hit her. "Just need to walk it off." She did not want him close when she was under the influence of hiccups.

But did he listen? Another wave hit her, roiling her insides. She bent over and saw long legs behind her. She let herself fall on the sand.

"Should I rub your back?" The deep voice failed to hide the laughter lurking behind his fake concern.

Priya shook her head. "Don't rub anything." The legs came closer. "Don't," she whispered before another wave hit her. She lay on the sand, hands stretched out on either side of her.

Dallas sat two feet away, his intent gaze on her, not laughing anymore. She closed her eyes, taking deep breaths very aware of his eyes on her. Gradually, the frequency of the hiccups slowed until she was left with a single one erupting as it pleased, coming from deep down within her. It tore at her insides and was quite painful.

She felt him move closer and then his large hand pressed on her diaphragm, stroking warmth into her quaking inside. She quelled her first instinct to shake it off. Feeling the comforting heat of his hand through the thin fabric of her dress, she let it pass. The pressure helped and her hiccups stopped.

She sat up and his hand fell away.

"Okay, now?" he stemmed his arms behind him and leaned back, legs outstretched on the warm sand. His T-shirt tightened across his chest.

"Yeah. All gone."

"That was some attack. What triggered it?"

"Hot sauce and cold beer."

"Good to know."

She jumped up, brushing sand off her dress. "Where are you going?" he patted the sand beside him. "Come. Sit here."

"Going to join the girls." She jumped up and walked fast to the house before she changed her mind.

Inside, she stripped her dress off and got into her swimsuit, grabbed a towel from her bag and went to the dock. Austin and Lara were on the floating wooden platform farther away.

"Come on, Priya, the water is so warm." Olivia said before diving off the dock.

"Emma, you want to hold hands and jump?" Priya offered her hand.

She looked back to where Dallas was still sitting on the sand, legs stretched out, soaking up the sun. Emma nodded, her wet hair sticking to her back. They held hands and when Priya reached the count of three, jumped into the water, Emma squealing all the way down.

"Me too, me too," Olivia shouted.

The next jump was with Priya in the middle, holding a girl by the hand on each side. The girls would have gone on and on had not Priya called a time-out.

"I'm going to join your mom and Austin on the dock over there. Olivia, you staying or coming?"

"Coming," Olivia said and began swimming toward it.

"I want to come too but I can't swim that far alone, Priya," Emma held on tight to Priya's hand. "I'm afraid."

Priya looked to the shore where Dallas was watching them. "Dallas! You want to come with us to the dock? Emma needs help."

Dallas waved, got up, peeled the T-shirt of his body, threw it down on the sand and made his way to the water. When he joined them, they swam out to the floating dock with Emma swimming between them. Once they reached there, they clambered up the ladder and squeezed together on the wooden planks radiating warmth from the sun.

Priya, lying next to Olivia, wished she had her sunglasses on. She so wanted to look at Dallas again: dripping water, flat chest heaving, all abs and pecs and delicious to behold. All she could do was steal glances at him as he pushed his hair back from his face. Austin was a magnificent specimen too and Houston was a close third, but it was Dallas who captured her fantasy and teased her mind.

CHAPTER TWENTY

DALLAS LAY BESIDE Olivia without moving very aware of Priya basking in the sun. If he turned his head, he'd see her, gorgeous in a red one-piece, the tats just waiting for his perusal.

One of the lines from a Sufi poem came to him: The journey is much more beautiful than the destination. It reflected exactly where he was. He was going to enjoy thinking of Priya, wondering how it would be to have her in his arms, imagining his hands on her body, his face in that glorious mane of hers. He was going to enjoy the journey of making her his as much as the act itself. There was nothing more exhilarating than the feeling of acute awareness of Priya.

He was in love.

There was no one else for him but Priya. The revelation ran down his body in excruciating pulsations. When he couldn't take it anymore, he dove off the dock and swam out to the open water.

Later, in the light of the torches, Dallas watched Priya as she made her way toward the fire pit, her hair braided and adorned with wild daisies-Olivia and Emma's touch-hung down one shoulder. A slight breeze ruffled the hem of her dress, lifting it. Anklets jingled softly on her bare legs.

Words refused to come out of his mouth. She stood bathed in moonlight by the water's edge, the white dress making her skin glow. His breath stopped in his throat and he dared not breathe. Time stood still while a fire razed his body. He wanted to wrap her in his arms and crush his mouth to hers. He thought he had it under control. He thought he could be around her and not be swayed by desire. He thought he could go slowly. She was going to test him. Seriously put his iron control in jeopardy.

But it was not the place.

Not with his parents, brothers, sister-in-law and nieces nearby around the fire, roasting marshmallows. Priya refused the sweet treat despite being entreated by Emma. But when Austin dangled a golden marshmallow in front of her, she grabbed it and stuffed it into her delectable mouth. Dallas sat on a tree stump facing her as the fire threw the embers into the air. He was in serious trouble. He was falling for her hard.

When Houston and Lara took their girls indoors to bed, Madison and Joe followed soon after. Austin and Priya strolled down the beach, leaving Dallas alone behind, wallowing in his desires. He saw Austin take Priya's hand. A strange feeling prickled in his chest, his belly tightened and his breath stuck in his throat.

What was his gallivanting brother saying to her?

He had half a mind to join them. Then, taking a deep breath, he pressed his butt tightly to the tree stump, refusing to be swayed by primitive emotions.

~

Priya turned her small hand in Austin's larger one.

"What are you doing, Austin?"

"Realizing how small your hand is. And how powerful a hand it is."

"Powerful?"

"Just now," he jerked his other thumb back in the direction of the fire, "my older brother is sitting tight over there trying to figure out why I'm holding your hand."

"Do tell. I'd like to know too."

"I want to jolt him into action. Has he kissed you yet? No? Then it's time he did."

"Why is that any of your business?" She wasn't going to reveal anything. Not to this handsome devil.

"Because he's one of those go slow guys. No jumping-in-and-let's-see-what-will-happen for him."

"What's wrong with going slow?"

"My lovely, it might be okay for you but it's been over five years for him since he's been in this self imposed dry spell."

"That long?" Priya caught a flash of his teeth as he grinned a devilish grin.

"He shows all the signs of a guy ready to jump in: can't stop staring at you; is not eating much; not talking much and I'm betting he's ready to pop me one in the face right now if I don't release your hand."

They walked past the fire pit. When he plonked down on the sand, he dragged her down with him and pulled her so she sat close to him.

"So let go of my hand."

"No *you* let go."

Priya looked down at their joined hands. Her fingers curled around his relaxed ones and was holding on tight. She released her hold.

"Sorry, didn't know I was doing that."

Austin ran a warm finger across her cheek then patted it. "That's okay. But I really gotta go. He's coming toward us."

With that he got up, turned and went back the way they'd

come, calling out to Dallas as he passed him. "Night, bro. Sleep tight and don't let the bed bugs bite."

Priya couldn't hear what Dallas replied. All she heard was the sound of his deep voice coming closer. She turned to face him. He slowly walked up to join her by the water. He sat down next to her.

"What did he want? What did he say to you?"

"He gave me some brotherly advice. I could always use some."

"Hah! Brotherly indeed! Don't be fooled by him one bit."

They sat in silence, looking out on the water.

"So the Mace is forgotten?"

"Oh, definitely not forgotten, squirt. But forgiven. Understandably, you thought it was that drunk reaching for you."

His soft and deep voice hit her ears, the sound rippling through her chest.

"Thank you, Dallas. After it happened, I was so worried."

He did not press further. "Well, that's behind us. We move on, right?"

"Right."

Move on to what? She was afraid to ask.

When Priya got up, Dallas did too. They walked along the water's edge. The property extended beyond the cluster of dunes, down to the water. Once they reached the dunes, Priya could not see the house or the beach. She sat down near the edge of the water. In the next few minutes, the tide would come in.

Dallas sat close to her without touching her, arms braced behind him. She sat cross-legged, arms in her lap.

"Such a beautiful night," she sighed and lifted her face to the night sky.

"Not as beautiful as you."

Her head drooped. "Dallas…" his name was just a whisper on her lips.

He leaned toward her, cupped her chin in his hand and raised her face to his. Bright light from the moon shone on the stud in her nose. He paused to look at her then he kissed her gently. Softly. And drew back.

Could a kiss have been sweeter?

"I guess I have your permission?" his breath fanned her face.

"More, Dallas." Priya raised her hands, threaded her fingers through his silky hair and sighed softly.

He came closer, his face brushing against hers. The touch of his beard against her skin was exquisite. It was soft as down. There was a sharp intake of her breath before his mouth was on hers.

Not so gentle now. Breaths and tongues mingling, he drank deep.

"Sweet," he said. He let go of her face, his lips still on hers. His arms went around her and he hauled Priya onto his lap. His hands in her hair, he undid the braid first then ran his fingers through it. Cradling her face in his hands, he plundered her mouth, his lips insistent and demanding.

"So beautiful," he murmured as his lips trailed down to the crook of her neck.

His hands on her waist slid up to graze the sweet swell of her breasts.

"The breeze at dawn has secrets to tell you." Priya breathed in his smell. It went right to her hot spot. "Don't go to sleep."

"No chance of that," Dallas said. "Even quoting Rumi is not going to put me to sleep."

"You know Rumi?"

"Why does that surprise you?" He felt her silent, eloquent shrug.

The tide came in, frothy water lapping at them.

Her hands wrapped around his neck, pulling him down to her. Dizzy with the feelings he aroused, her hands found their way under his T-shirt, her touch light as a feather. She felt him quiver. She sat with her breasts pressed against him, arms around his neck, her cool hands moving down his chest.

"Say it, Priya. I want to hear it."

"I want you," she whispered in his ear and he shivered. "I want you like this," she grabbed his head between her hands and murmured against his lips.

"You must ask for what you really want. Don't go back to sleep," Dallas finished the Rumi quote for her.

The water receded and sand took its place.

"What if somebody comes along?" Priya stopped moving her hands.

The tide came in again, swirling around them.

Dallas drank in her sweetness, rocking against her, hip to hip. His arms and his body enveloping her were a safe haven.

"Feels so good. Don't want to stop," Dallas groaned. In the next breath he muttered, "My sweet, I have to stop."

"Why?" she murmured against his chest, lips kissing his skin.

"No condom. Don't have a pocket in my swimming trunks."

She froze as if debating something. She got off him and lay panting by his side while Dallas let himself fall back on the wet sand. They lay there, eyes looking at the stars, willing their bodies to cool down while water came in again, engulfing them in its wet and warm embrace.

Drenched, they made their way back to the house, arms around each other's waist.

When he dropped her off at her place, Priya was almost ready to ask him to come in and finish what they'd started on the beach.

But he made no move to get out of the car. "Listen, Priya," he turned toward her. "Wanted to tell you something. About the Mace..."

"You said it was water under the bridge."

"It is. That's not it." He took her hand in his. "You have these rings, see? This one with the humongous stone? All you have to do is aim this at the face. Aim for the middle. The nose is a good place and it will cause a lot of pain." His teeth flashed.

"You think it's funny, don't you?"

"No, I'm being serious. Just don't forget the rings, that's all I'm asking."

"Anything else?" Priya was surprised when he still made no move to get out of the car.

"I'm going to be out of town for a few days. I'll call you. And text you." He leaned toward her, threaded a hand around her neck and pulled her to him. He gave her a quick kiss on the lips, his fingers just grazing her cheek.

She got out of the car and then he was gone. She stood looking after him.

What the hell just happened?

CHAPTER TWENTY-ONE

A LITTLE CONFUSED BY Dallas's behaviour, Priya felt a bit better when he texted her. He was in Hong Kong, which he'd failed to mention. He'd only said 'out of town.' He was going to be back in time for the Pickleball Club's annual dinner and dance.

It was the time of the year Priya had been waiting for. It was usually held at a stuffy restaurant where there were servers and tablecloths and snowy-white napkins. But one year the chicken had been dry, the next dessert was frozen squares and the third, Bob considered the salad to be at best a 'Meh.'

Moo is better.

Priya agreed and said so. Bob had stuck a finger in his mouth and given an expressive heave. He did offer the gig to her catering company but Priya resisted. She was more interested in the dancing part of the evening and didn't want to be involved with the other details. Plus Bob's offer reeked of self-service. He just wanted more of her spicy food.

She was going to change things. This time she was going to re-invent the annual dinner and dance. She brainstormed with Kelly over cups of green tea-Kelly's choice-and tequila shots-

Priya's choice. Anna was involved from afar. She sent Priya texts about possible halls for rent. Finally, they agreed on a suitable venue with a dance floor *and* a bar.

"Next meeting at my place," Kelly drained her cup of green.

"Why? You don't like my tea? I made you a whole pot. With freshly ground cloves and cinnamon too."

"You're drinking too many shots!"

"So?"

"That's the fourth one. Plus, now I feel like having one too. And I don't do shots. So next meeting will be at *my* place. You're going to have to get into your little truck and drive to my place and back. And there will be no alcohol."

"Didn't know you were such a puritan, Kelly. When did that happen?"

"Alcohol puts crazy thoughts in my head. I do crazy things."

"Like what?"

"Order stuff on line. Stuff I don't want. Stuff I can't afford."

Priya's shoulders shook with laughter.

"You think it's funny? Try explaining to your husband why you need a whole tub of bath bombs! Or fifty pairs of ankle socks. Oh, shucks I forgot. You don't have to do *any* explaining to anyone."

Now Priya laughed out loud. "I'm enjoying my freedom, woman. Wait. Bath bombs? Socks? I thought you were talking about designer clothes. Or jewellery. Or even shoes. Like a pair of Ferragamo shoes. Or even Manolo Blahnik."

"What? You nuts? I go to church every Sunday, Priya."

"What's that even supposed to mean? People who go to church don't wear Blahnik or Ferragamo?"

"No. I meant I'd feel so guilty at having spent so much money on just shoes I'd probably put one shoe in the collection box. And then how will I get home with only one shoe? Plus if they're Blahniks I'd hide them in my closet to look at them every now and then. I'd never wear them."

"You *do* have a pair, don't you?"

"Maybe."

"Okay. Next meeting at your place."

"We decide on the menu right? Check out the take-out places? Will Anna be coming? She might as well, you know. She's right in there with us."

"She won't. She loves to delegate from afar."

At Kelly's place, Priya sipped her green tea meekly. They agreed on Greek food. Pumped up on green tea, Priya had one great idea after another. She beat down the urge to ask Kelly about the Blahniks in her closet. Now was not the time.

"So, we'll pick up the food ourselves. Or should we let some of the guys get it? We could always reel in Bob and Kalle. Better still, we could have it delivered. We'll have it buffet-style, right? Then each person can choose what to eat. None of that dry chicken or frozen dessert crap."

Kelly grey eyes sparkled as she became more animated. "There's an Indian restaurant close by and we can get that syrup-loaded dessert. What's it called?"

"Jilebi."

"And some of the other sweets they have. It'll be great. A change. How about the DJ?"

"I know this is not about saving but it will cost us about half what it usually did. I'll check with the DJ and find out if he's available. Plus, we could decide to donate money to a local charity."

"How about a DJ who can play Indian music? You know, the one we can dance to? Like in…."

"Bollywood?" Priya began to get Kelly's infectious dance fever too.

"That's it! And we can all dress up too. In Indian dresses and things."

"We can do that. Sounds like it's going to be one hell of a party."

"You think the ladies will be into it? To dress up?"

"Why not? We can say the evening's theme is 'Bollywood.' And anyone is welcome to dress up or not. Their choice."

Priya laid out all the layers of her Indian dress on her bed.

Sliding her legs into the narrow, long underpants, she slipped the voluminous skirt over her head and tied the string at the waist. The slightest movement and it rippled out in a pretty swirl, the purple and silver glittering with sequins. Next came the midriff-baring short-sleeved blouse in the same purple and silver. It looked more like a jewelled bikini top. It was held together in the back by beaded strings. She could reach only one pair of the strings to make a knot. She'd have to wait until Kelly arrived to secure the remaining ones.

Over it, came a transparent purple flared tunic with silver embroidery. It had long sleeves and stopped just above her ankles. Three buttons held the tunic closed at the top. At the midriff, it fell open as she moved.

She left her hair open. There was a large ring in her nose and umbrella-shaped earrings hung from her ears. The purple glass and silver metal bracelets on her arms made a pleasant tinkling sound as glass hit metal. An elaborate necklace studded with purple gemstones and silver beads was around her neck.

Her pulse raced as she thought of Dallas. She wondered if he thought about her or if she was just one of his distractions. He'd said he'd be there. She wasn't sure what he wanted. He ran hot and cold. She was probably going to have to up the ante. Play a little offence to get him out of his defensive mode.

The bell rang and she went down to let Kelly in. They were riding together in Kelly's van after picking up some of the food.

Kelly looked adorable in her green ensemble. Apparently she was quite familiar with Little India on Gerrard Street in Toronto.

"You look gorgeous!"

"No, *you* look gorgeous!"

They laughed gleefully, like little girls, happy and thrilled at the same time.

For dinner, Priya made it a point not to sit with Dallas who was dressed in Indian style too. He was at a table with Bob and Anna, looking very handsome and sexy. Priya sat with Kelly, her husband, Tom, Kalle and Milla. After dinner and after the tables were cleared and after the garbage bags were lined-up to be taken out, the DJ started his job. He began with old favourites. Couples danced to slow songs while Priya mingled.

Then the women took over and the music got hotter. They danced, some following the lead of others. Priya was pleasantly surprised to see most of them in Indian dresses. She shouldn't have been for many of them came to Kingston after years in Montreal, Ottawa or Toronto. The DJ got into the mood too and played Bollywood songs. They twirled around until the skirts billowed out. It didn't take long for them to dance in unison following Priya's lead as the men stood around them, watching and tapping their feet.

That stopped as soon as she pulled Dallas to his feet and pushed him into the dancing crowd. He was dressed in an Indian *sherwani* in beige and blue with beige pants. A long blue scarf hung across his shoulders. As a *bhangra* beat thumped out of the speakers, he tied the scarf around his head.

Walking to her table, Priya looked over her shoulder and stopped short, eyes glued to Dallas. He lifted his arms, pointing his index fingers skyward and did the jerky movement with his shoulders. It made Priya weak in the knees.

Right then, Priya fell in love with him. It was a move from her dreams. Nothing was sexier than that move. Heat coursed through her core, up to her head and down to the apex of her thighs. No naked abs or pecs for her. Just the move did it for her.

Hot and breathless, Priya sank into a chair and poured water in a glass. She gulped it down. As she reached for the wine, she noticed Anna talking to the DJ. Probably asking for some song for Bob and her to dance to. Kelly joined her at the table, grabbing her glass of water.

"That was great!" Kelly fanned her face with the end of her *dupatta*, the veil she wore over her Indian skirt and blouse. "I've never seen Tom go so crazy on the dance floor. Everyone is having a great time," she said looking around.

Priya burped audibly.

"Priya!" Kelly admonished her, like the mother hen she was. "That's no way for a lady to behave."

"Sorry," Priya said without meaning it. "Would you prefer a fart?" Then she burst out laughing because just saying fart always made her laugh.

"Oh, stop it, Priya. Behave yourself. Because I'm pretty sure gorgeous Dallas is going to ask you to dance. And none of that burp fart talk any more and don't fucking do *it* either," Kelly said with difficulty as she burst into laughter herself. "No more wine for you." Then she yanked the wine glass from Priya's hand and drained it in one gulp.

"Oh, Kelly, you're priceless. More wine?"

"Kay. Maybe a little more. Tom will be driving."

"No, he's not. You're driving *me* home. Tom came alone with your other car."

"Oh, fuck! I forgot."

"Kelly! Again with the profanity! Didn't know you used words like that so often. Once, I can accept but again and again? I might have to wash your mouth with soap. Won't you have to say ten Hail Marys at church?"

"I can do that in my sleep. Or I'll just throw in my Blahnik. That'll shut them up." With that, she reached for the bottle and poured more wine into the empty glass that had been Priya's.

"You have a pair of Blahniks and not Jimmy Choos?"

"Maybe both. In the back of my closet. Yes."

Okay. Kelly was going to be pretty out of it if she didn't know whether she had a pair of Manolo Blahnik or not. She'd have to ask her about it when she was sober. Priya decided not to have any more wine just in case she had to drive Kelly home.

She leaned back in her chair, her eyes searching for Dallas. She saw him in conversation with Kalle and Bob. From the way Bob was gesturing, Priya was sure they were talking about pickleball. Then sounds of George Michael's *Careless Whisper* began to flow out of the speakers and Priya could not believe her ears. She knew who the culprit was.

How did Anna know it is one my favourite songs?

She was a little nebulous about that. Right, she'd told her. After they'd emptied the bottle of Shiraz. She'd mentioned how she loved that song to Anna, the ratfink.

She saw Dallas break from the group he was with and make his way toward her. When he reached her, he held out his hand, not saying a word. Priya darted a glance at Kelly who was looking very happy with the world. Priya knew then with certainty she *would* have to drive her home.

"Go for it," Kelly mouthed, her lips lingering a bit too long on the first letter of 'for.'

As if Priya needed encouragement. She hadn't seen Dallas in a week, hadn't analyzed her feelings for him yet and couldn't imagine how whatever was going on between them was going to be resolved if neither refused to address it. She wasn't and it looked as if he wasn't going to either.

She put her hand in his, her small one engulfed by his large one. Together they moved to the dance floor, joining other couples. He twirled her around then drew her to him, his hand burning on the naked skin of her waist. Priya almost bit into her lip and looked anywhere but up at his face looming above her head. She fixated on the beige and blue design of his *sherwani*. As they moved, the gold thread in Dallas's suit rubbed against her naked skin. It gave her goose bumps.

When the last notes of the saxophone died, he twirled her out and brought her back to him, close to his chest. She raised her eyes to him and might have winced. She couldn't say. His gaze was unwavering and a slight shiver ran up her spine at the intensity of it. His lips curved into a sweet smile, dimples blooming on his cheeks. If he kept it up, her knees would give away any second. Involuntarily, her fingers inched across his shoulder and up his neck, the goal being to bury them in his hair.

Just then the music stopped and he released her. He raised her hand to his lips and kissed it like a Victorian gentleman. If it wasn't so hot, Priya might have giggled and totally spoiled the moment. She might have curled her fingers around his. Then they rejoined their tables without exchanging a single word.

CHAPTER TWENTY-TWO

DALLAS LOOKED AT the gorgeous woman in his arms. He thought about pulling her into the alcove he'd noticed while coming in and kissing her breathless. Priya's eyes were framed in a smoky green. Black eyeliner followed the shape of her green eyes. Her lips were a deep plum. In the centre of her forehead, was a purple *bindi*. She was smoking hot. His gaze ripped over her then stopped on the humongous ring in her nose.

How the hell was he supposed to kiss her with that thing on her face? Then another wicked thought crept into his mind.

What if she's doing it on purpose?

Was she deliberately making access difficult for him? She couldn't be that twisted, could she?

No. He couldn't believe she'd be *that* devious. He had felt a giggle burgeoning in her chest. It only made him want her more. It was not going to be enough just to touch her soft naked skin right there around her waist. He wanted more of her. He wanted her in his arms, her fingers on him.

Again, there were too many people around.

He wanted her in his life. He loved every facet of her. He knew she had stifled a giggle when he'd kissed her hand. And it was exactly the sort of irreverent disregard for etiquette he found so irresistible. But he'd wanted to put his lips somewhere on her body. Let everyone know there was something between them so he'd opted for a kiss on her hand.

Her skin glowed through the transparent fabric. Through it, he saw a dark shadow in the area of the small of her back. Her hair fell in gorgeous waves around her face. He resisted the urge to bury his nose in it and sniff at the heady sandalwood scent. He felt a quick tug in his belly. How long he was going to be able to keep his hands off her was the question.

Control was his middle name. The mantra rolled around in his mind time and time again. His plan was to make her fall in love with him. But here he was instead, head over heels himself.

PRIYA *DID* HAVE to take Kelly home.

"Tom, I'll drive her home," Priya said, when they were ready to leave. "I'll have to drive your car back to my place since I don't have a ride. And I don't want to call an Uber."

"That's okay, Priya. I'll give you a ride back to your place."

"Great, problem solved," Priya helped Kelly into the car.

Kelly began to sing hymns at the top of her voice.

"Guess she's started atoning for her sins," Tom grinned. "You know, she can't hold her liquor."

"Yeah, didn't realize she had that much wine. It was not even a full glass. Just a couple of fingers worth."

"It doesn't take much to set her off," Tom said. "That's why she avoids it. But one can't be good every second of the day. Life would be too boring. It's good for her to let off some steam now and then."

"But Tom, does she need to let off steam? She's so put together."

"Everybody needs to let off steam at one time or the other.

We've been having a difficult time with her father. He's about to go into a home after the death of her mother and he's not handling it well."

"Oh, Tom, I'm so sorry to hear that. What can I do to help?"

"She loves pickleball. She especially loves playing with you. She's said that often. Pickleball is good for her. Another thing allowing her to let off steam."

Priya didn't know what to say. Instead, she kissed the singing Kelly on the cheek and hugged Tom.

"Let me know if I can help, okay?" Priya got in Kelly's car.

~

IT WAS PAST midnight when Dallas got out of the shower. Just as he pulled on a pair of shorts and a T-shirt his phone pinged with a text from Priya.

HELP. PLEASE COME OVER.

What kind of help could she need?

Heart thumping, he ran barefoot out the patio door into the yard. He put his jointed ladder over his side of the fence and down hers and into her back yard. The moon played hide and seek between the clouds and the summer night was filled with sound: crickets, frogs and laughter from a backyard party still in full swing.

In his hurry, he missed a step, lost his footing and slid down the ladder on the other side. The slide down was accompanied by a searing sensation on his leg.

"Fuck." He swiped at the spot, looking for blood. Nothing. Just a scratch then.

Of course, her patio doors were closed. He ran around the house to her front door.

"Up here, Dallas," she called out when she heard him come in.

He took the stairs two at a time. When he saw her standing in the middle of her bedroom, he came to a standstill. Her bare midriff was visible, the tunic open. The huge ring in her nose was gone.

"The pins are stuck," she pointed to the back. "I'm afraid of tearing it."

"How did you get these pins in?"

"Oh, Kelly was here. We got ready together." She gathered her hair in a bunch and moved it out of his way as he fumbled with the delicate fabric. Being so close to her naked skin made him clumsy. "Ouch!" she yelped.

"Sorry." Her skin was silky. His nostrils flared as he caught a whiff of her perfume. He took out three pins.

She took the tunic off. Her phone buzzed and danced across the top of the chest of drawers. She reached for it, swiped and read the message.

"Have to be at the kitchen early tomorrow. My assistant is down with something. Okay. We'd better wrap this up then. Necklace too, please," her head fell forward, the rose vine tat now beneath his fingers.

He bent his head to access the clasp and got it open. However, strands of hair were entangled with the necklace and his fingers were not made for such delicate work, he soon found out. A few more 'ouches' from her and he had the necklace clear of hair strands.

A chain around her waist was causing a problem too. It was tangled in the sequins adorning the skirt. He sat down on the bed, keeping her between his legs. His head came close to her navel where something glittered.

"There's a jewel in your navel too? Any more surprises?"

"Yes," she turned around with her back to him once again.

Chains of beads held the top together. He undid them one by one, his fingers fumbling more and more. His eyes wandered slowly from the curve of her bent neck to the bare skin of her back and down to the naked strip of her waist. A tat of a fire-spewing dragon peeked out from the small of her back.

He wasn't certain who moved first, but in a slow dance, his arms crept around her waist and circled it tightly. She leaned back against him. He drew her closer to him, his lips reaching for the tender spot between her neck and shoulder. A soft moan from her was next as he dragged his mouth across her shoulder, removing the fabric inch by inch. She raised her arms to rake her fingers through his hair. Her scent enveloped him. His heart thumped in his chest.

Dallas released one arm, running his fingers through her hair, pulling her toward him. She turned her head back toward him. Cradling her head in his hand, he trapped her luscious mouth in a searing kiss and despite the fire raging in his blood, managed to temper it by gentling his kiss into a tender, sweet torture.

His other hand slid under the skirt, sliding over skin as soft and lush as velvet. He felt her belly clenching. His hand slipped down further, the fingers sliding past the waistband of her panties, past the silky thighs. His kiss deepened as his hand moved between her legs. She gasped. Dallas smothered her gasp with his mouth, drinking in her sweetness. She pressed into his fingers, her breathing hitching up.

He was going to make her senseless with lust, see stars explode as she came in his hand.

His tongue parted her lips and plunged inside as his fingers swept through her slick wet folds. Her head twisted from side to side the closer she came to her peak. Her back arched against his chest and she gasped his name into his mouth. He saw her shattering into a million pieces, connecting them together like never before. Her legs sagged, she climaxed and he wrapped his long legs around her to bring her limp body tight against him.

He kissed the dewy skin on her forehead. She was his now.

"If you're trying to seduce me, it worked," she turned to face him and threaded her fingers through his hair, her lips swollen from his kisses.

Laughter rumbled in his chest. "Trying? I had you in my hand. And it was way better than the Mace. Way better."

She bowed her head and hid her face, his T-shirt all bunched around his armpits. "Water under the bridge."

He heard the words form against his chest. "Know what else?" he whispered in her ear. "Am glad you took that humongous ring off your nose."

He took his T-shirt off and because he could, he pulled her close and rose from the bed. His arms snaked around her hips. He lifted her up and captured her lips again, bending his body back. Her legs, circling his waist, tightened. He slowly slid her body down the length of his, pressing his hips to hers, making her aware of his desire for her.

~

PRIYA ARCHED HER back. Dallas covered her heated body with his before going down on his knees, his beard rubbing her skin in wondrous ways. Her breathing picked up a notch, sweet exquisite pleasure thrumming through her.

"Double fudge, Dallas."

Lifting his head briefly, he said, "You must ask for what you want, my lovely. Don't go back to sleep. And don't dream about chocolate."

He was quoting Rumi? Now? There was chocolate too? She didn't know what she wanted.

Yes, she did! She wanted him right there. No was he could make her come again so soon. His silky scruff rasped over her skin. His clever mouth sucked and tugged at sensitive spots, stoking her desire even more. She focused on the stars swirling before her eyes. God, she was going to explode. Did he know what he was doing to her? Her hands threaded in the silky waves of his hair, her lips gasped out his name.

"You are mine now," he murmured softly.

He slid up her body, his beard grazing her skin and locked his gaze on hers. And there was awareness in his grey eyes brimming with fire. Yes, he did know what he was doing to her.

Priya threaded her fingers in his hair and pulled his head back. She brought her lips close to his but did not kiss him. Their breaths mingled, eyes looking deep into each other's. She moved once again.

He winced, lifted his delicious weight off her body, her gaze still locked with his. She saw desire for her reflected in those grey eyes of his. And something else she couldn't quite decipher.

His phone pinged.

"You want to get that?" Priya let go of him. "At this hour, it could be an emergency."

Without saying anything, Dallas picked up his phone, pulling her up with him, one arm around her. She had both her arms around him, her head on his amazing flat chest.

Hmm….she could stay like that forever.

"It's Austin. He's stuck on the highway. Truck trouble."

"Then Dallas, you have to go now. I have to get some sleep. Have early duty at the kitchen." Priya reluctantly tore her lips from his and stepped back from the warmth of his embrace.

"Yeah. Okay. Have a busy day tomorrow. Will text you in the morning."

And with that he was gone.

Isaak's Wicked Game would be just about right.

CHAPTER TWENTY-THREE

DALLAS, ON HIS way to Shanghai to meet with business partners interested in Hovertek's products, checked his flight status heaving a sigh of relief when he saw it was on time. It had been on the books for a while and finally everything had clicked in place. He'd been on the phone all morning confirming meetings with heads of various businesses in China during his week long stay in Shanghai.

"Ni hao, zaoshang hao. Zhe shi…" he spoke into his phone. "Hello, good morning. This is…"

On the last day of his stay in Shanghai, he had room service bring him a bottle of red wine with a bowl of hot noodles. He now poured wine in a glass, raised it to the light and took his first sip of alcohol in seven days.

Still wearing his dark blue Armani suit, he stood at the floor-to-ceiling hotel window, looking at the city before him. He could see the Shanghai tower in the distance. The city was brilliant with lights. It looked so beautiful, so peaceful. He could easily forget this was an autocratic country. Lounging on the love seat, he flicked through the text log on his phone, cleaning them up as he went along. His fingers paused over one labelled 'Draft.'

Shit! It was the one he'd sent to Priya detailing his trip. He sent it again, explaining.

He took off his tie and flung it on the bed. He switched off all the lights, pulled up the armchair in front of the window and took in the sight. His hotel overlooked the Huangpu River, the city lights reflected in its dark murky waters. He should have been exhausted. He should have just flopped on the bed and slept.

Instead, his thoughts drifted to Priya. She'd been there the whole time: during the meetings; during the endless banter and during cocktail hour where he'd only had sparkling water. He'd never had these feelings before with the woman *still* in her clothes. Not even with Kate. Kate who he thought he'd loved and had wanted to spend the rest of his life with.

Then on the beach at the cottage, what she'd done to him. Every touch of her fingers was magic. She'd done something with her hands in his hair, scraping her fingers across his scalp, blowing on his closed eyes. Dragging her fingers in his hair over and over again. Her lips on his chest, trailing ever lower and lower, intent in every kiss until he'd stopped her a with the silly 'No condom,' excuse.

The best part was, she'd played along. It had raised his suspicions. He believed she planned her exquisite torture to take him to the brink with a promise and then let him dangle, gasping for more. He was afraid to analyze it further. What if she was a go-slow kind of woman too? Was this her play at prolonging the anticipation? Why else then would she have agreed to stop?

Then there was that night after the club's dinner. Heat suffused his body now. Shrugging out of the jacket, he hung it on the chair. Undoing the top three buttons on his grey silk shirt, he rolled up the sleeves first, only to slide the shirt over his head. It joined the tie on the bed. He ran his hand over his chest. He very much wanted it to be Priya's.

She'd moved against him, in perfect harmony with his body, her lush dips and valleys complementing the broad planes of his own hard one. Just a touch of her finger on his skin, the whisper of her hair against his face was enough to make him harder than ever before.

He wanted to lose himself in her, in her taste, in all her flavours. It had taken immense control on his part not to give in to his primal urges. Priya made him forget himself.

PRIYA WAS PISSED at Dallas. First he had her all roiled up. All taut and ready to explode with feelings she hadn't had in a while. Then he disappeared without even letting her know.

When Priya's phone pinged with a text from Dallas, her first instinct was to trash it.

Screw Dallas!

Shanghai! It put a smile on her face. He was not avoiding her. He was not even in the country!

She was at Bob's place, having a pop in. She wriggled on her butt, giving Bob a soundless "Yay!"

"What for?" Bob poured cold beer into a frosted glass.

"He's in China! Not avoiding me."

"Who?"

"Dallas Crenshaw."

Bob, oblivious as usual, puffed his cheeks up and blew the air out. At times like these, she wished Bob was a woman. Or that Anna was home.

Anna came home an hour later, when Priya was on her second beer. She was in the kitchen getting spare ribs for the grill. Considering that Priya had to stand on a footstool to reach the lid, the grill waited for Anna to come home to light it. Priya had a sneaking suspicion Bob was not allowed to play with the grill. He just lounged about and did what he did best: bring her cold beer.

The ribs on the grill, Priya got the potato salad out of the fridge.

"These ribs are fantastic, Papillon. What did you put in them?"

"Maple syrup, chili sauce, crushed garlic, black pepper…."

"Okay, stop. TMI. Don't wanna know. I'll just eat them."

"…salt, lime juice, chili powder, ketchup…" she stopped.

Bob, usually so polite and attentive, was actually not listening.

Priya shrugged. Whatever.

"I was talking to Kyle Langdon this morning. He's available to teach. Let's get something together by the end of this week. What d'you think?" Bob was back to pickleball again, his favourite topic.

"Kyle is a great player and a great teacher. I like him. He'll be an asset to the club. Plus he plays with us too."

"His wife…what's her name?...mentioned she could …"

"I don't like her."

Anna gasped and fell back in her chair. "There's someone out there you don't like?" She looked around her, at the ground, under her chair. "Hath hell frozen over?"

Priya stuck her tongue out. "Good one. So good I don't even have a chuckle for you."

"So Kyle without wife it is," Bob said, shaking his head.

"Not too spicy, the ribs," Anna remarked after tentatively biting into one.

"Good. However, I did bring yogurt. Just in case."

"Ha ha! Nice try."

"It's actually quite spicy. I think you're just getting used to it. Or rather your tongue is."

"Whatever. It's delicious. Thanks for the treat, my dear."

WHEN DALLAS GOT home, he had enough of texting. He wanted to hear Priya's voice. So he called her.

"Dallas."

"How are you, squirt?"

"Fine now. But not before."

"Before what?"

"After you left? The before that comes after you left for a week?"

"Sorry about that. Text never left my phone. Got stuck in the Draft folder. Don't know how that happened."

"You should be sorry. After you finger banged me then mouth-banged me, letting you do things I've never let…."

"Wait a sec…finger banged you? Is that what it's called?"

"What would you call it?"

"Pleasuring you."

"So it was all for me then. None of it was for you?"

"You've never let anyone else….?"

His voice turned hoarse and breathless as if he'd been running. Just picturing her delicious little fanny rubbing against his crotch, just remembering the way her hot wetness clenched around his fingers was enough to turn him into wood. He cleared his throat.

"I got the most pleasure out of watching you." Trite but true. He'd never been so consumed by desire before. Never been so completely in tune with anyone else before.

"So we going to keep it to the phone or what?"

"Don't have the strength to do anything but get some sleep. Have a serious jet lag. Flew in to Vancouver from Shanghai. I'll talk to you soon, squirt."

He heard the disappointment in her voice. Yep, he was going to have a hard-literally-time keeping to his plan of cease and desist, particularly the desisting part. Because one look from her sultry green eyes and he'd be lost.

He hoped she was not planning on doing any dancing. That would sorely test his wooden resolve. He wanted to tell her about his true feelings especially the part about her being his and that they were meant to be together. That he cared for her.

He wondered how she'd take it. The other night, when he'd said she was his, it was as if she hadn't heard him. Unless she was ignoring it? Could it be possible?

She wouldn't have let him do those intimate things to her without feeling something, would she?

Fuck! If only he knew. If only he could tell what was going on in that wonderful mind of hers.

~

PRIYA PUT DOWN her phone slowly. Dinner with Dallas later in the week. The thought of Dallas made her body tingle with desire.

But now she had to focus on her day at the shelter.

The shelter for which Priya had organized the fundraiser called her to ask if she was interested in kitchen duty a few times a week. And so here she was at the shelter where there was a new face. She sat in a corner, cross-legged with a cushion to support her back in jeans and boob-hugging top. Nails-both fingers and toes-perfectly manicured and painted with stars. From her vantage point, her large, black expressive eyes followed the staff as they moved around. There was a black bundle next to her.

At the morning meeting, Eva, the supervisor gave them the details.

"We have a new resident, Firdaus. Came in last night. Domestic brought her in with bruises all over her body but none on her face. So we're dealing with someone who knows how to hurt without leaving obvious marks." With each phrase, Eva got redder and redder. At the last one, she looked as if she was about to pop. "Jane?"

"Dr. Aziz was hesitant to examine her," Jane, the nurse began, swiping her tablet. "She's a Muslim just like he is so he knows better. I was able to examine her injuries and reported them to Dr. Aziz. She does not speak much English so that could pose a problem. By the way, the black bundle beside her is her burqua. She just took it off and threw it down on the floor. It was the first thing she did when she came in. Her family in India is well to do, Dr. Aziz says. Firdaus caught the eye of a distant 'cousin' at a wedding. The cousin being from Canada was a plus. A proposal was sent to Firdaus's parents and bada boom! She was married."

Dr. Aziz-it was actually Dr. Aziz Khan-was from Pakistan and spoke Urdu whereas Firdaus spoke Hindi. "Dr. Aziz says that Urdu and Hindi are similar. He said he talked to Firdaus explaining Canadian laws about marriage and divorce."

After the briefing, Priya loaded a tray with sandwiches, cookies and milk and approached Firdaus. She sat down, her back against the wall too, the tray on the floor between them.

"Brought you some food. This sandwich is my favourite: tomato and coriander chutney. Spicy."

The black eyes looked at the tray Priya had put on the floor. Priya saw her swallow. A delicate hand with the beautifully manicured fingers reached for the sandwich. She took a bite and closed her eyes.

"Bliss!" Firdaus said, heaving a deep sigh.

"You speak English?"

"Of course. I went to an English medium school in India. College was in English too. He and his family thought I spoke only Hindi. I let them believe that."

"How did you get into this situation?"

"Oh, we were very stupid, my parents and I. Just because he was from Canada, we thought he was civilized. Instead, he turned out to be a barbarian. A savage beast!" Firdaus chomped down on the sandwich viciously. "I understand traditions. The burqua protects women from predatory males, I get that. What I didn't get was I had to wear it in Canada too! I'd never worn the burqua at home in India, only a veil to cover my head."

"Well, you're safe from him here," Priya bit into a cookie.

"Yes, for the moment. It's enrages me so when people bring restrictive old world customs to the new world. It's a new slate, isn't it? If I were stronger I would so pop that bastard one!"

Priya smiled at Firdaus. Despite her bruises, she still had spunk and was a fighter. "You could always take a self defense class," Priya suggested.

"What a great idea! Yes, I shall do that. I shall arm myself with new world techniques."

Priya didn't bother to correct her. Some of the techniques were from the ancient world.

A few days later, Priya looked up from the pastry dough she was rolling. The kitchen had a direct view to the front door. A big shadow fell over the window by the side of the door. There was a smash as something hit the door. Another smash, followed by the sound of splintering wood and then the door burst from the bolt and swung open.

In the wide reception area, Priya saw Eva swipe her phone then tapping it.

A man stepped into the safe house. He was a huge, brutish-looking man with a thick nose and thick lips.

This was Firdaus's husband. She recognized him from the photographs in the file Eva had passed around. He had a lot of hair right up to his neck, Priya noticed with a shudder. His beard was repulsive. It was full and covered most of his face. This was the moron who made Firdaus' life a living hell. Now, he rushed in wielding a baseball bat. He hung the bat over his shoulder as he looked around.

Isa did not wait. She grabbed a mallet and rushed toward him. It was like David and Goliath. He plucked the mallet out of Isa's hand, threw it away and lowered his shoulder hitting Isa in the chest. The force sent her flying across the room where she hit the wall and lay in a crumpled heap.

Priya's heart almost stopped beating. *He's killed her!*

She did not look at the commotion behind her. All her energy was centred on the intruder.

Looking around for a weapon, Priya saw her knives on the counter. For a second, she debated the idea of using them then decided her aim would not be accurate with a knife. As the man was quick on his feet, there was a good chance the knife would bounce off him.

She saw her pickleball bag on the counter with the paddles sticking out. Thinking of the delicate-boned Firdaus in the hands of this brute, Priya grabbed one of her heaviest paddles. It felt good in her hand. She took a few steps toward the man. It got her out of the kitchen and away from her sharp knives. Bending to the side, she threw the paddle at the intruder, aiming for his legs. Like pebbles twirling while skimming the surface of water propelled, the paddle whizzed out of her hand.

Whizz! Whizz! Crack!

It hit him on his right knee. With a Shrek-like roar he grabbed his knee, dropping the bat. Priya darted forward and got one hand around the baseball bat. Then, oh big relief, she was able to wrap her other hand around it too and get a good grip around the handle. She stood up, wielding it over her head like she'd seen Derek Jeter do. She swung it, brought it down with as much force as she could, aiming to make contact with the same right knee. The momentum of the swing took her out of balance and she took a step forward, missing her target and instead of hitting him, she hit air. It was a major strike out and she lost her balance in the swing.

The moron jumped right at her, took back the bat with no effort at all and swung it with a great whoosh hitting Priya on the head. She sank to the floor without a sound. He kicked her in the ribs not once, not twice...It was terrible to be so weak, to be so defenceless.

Suddenly, the foyer was crawling with people in uniforms.

"Hang in there, sweetheart," Priya heard Jane say. "The paramedics are here."

The police arrived and took the husband away.

After that, Priya heard nothing. The last thing she saw was Firdaus holding Dr. Aziz's hand. He had his other arm around Firdaus, drawing her close. Priya's heart rejoiced at how hope bloomed even in desperate and hopeless conditions. Before everything went dark, she realized there was not going to be a dinner with Dallas.

CHAPTER TWENTY-FOUR

DALLAS WAS WITH his brothers at Austin's place, working on a project. They were going over the plans when his phone pinged with a news alert.

"Hey, Austin can you switch on Channel Three please? There's something going on at the shelter where Priya's working."

'Breaking news from Channel Three. There's been an incident at a local shelter. Two volunteers were seriously injured.'

In the ticker across the bottom of the screen, Priya Keelor's name marched then across before it slowly disappeared.

"Got to go," he managed to blurt out. His mouth dry and his heart thudding, Dallas grabbed his keys and made for the door.

"No problem, bro," Austin called out. "Go and see if she's okay."

At the hospital, Dallas did not get to see her right away as she was still undergoing tests.

He paced in front of the grey double-doors, head swirling with images of the night of the dinner dance. That last dance, the slow one, was one he'd never forget. How wonderful it had been to hold her in his arms. He'd twirled her around, oblivious to everything else but her, the smouldering green eyes never leaving his face. Each step she took was accompanied by a soft jingle.

Then he'd fallen apart later. Falling in love with her had not helped either. There would be no more going slow for him. Not since that night. He wanted all of her, all at once and the sooner the better.

The double doors whooshed and swung open. Her body was covered with a white sheet, her hands on the cover. His step faltered, shocked at how still and listless she appeared. Her eyes were closed. When she was stationary in her room, he approached the bed with trepidation.

He took her hands gently in his and wrapped her small ones in his. They were cold and dry. He held them between both of his, infusing his warmth into them, like he'd done once before. Her cheeks were pale, the freckles appearing in sharp contrast. There was a bandage around her head.

He ran his finger down one cheek and her eyes flipped open the pupils wide and dark, engulfing most of the lighter iris. Meeting his concerned look for a brief moment, she turned her head away. He cupped her chin with his hand and turned her head toward him.

"What happened, squirt? Who did this to you?"

She swallowed, closing her eyes briefly before opening them again. "A brute," her voice was a whisper. "Water, please."

He reached for the metal stand beside the bed where a pitcher with water and a glass with a straw stood. He poured some water in the glass. He didn't know how to raise the bed, so he slid his arm under the pillow and raised her upper body so she could drink, his actions reminiscent of another night when he'd given her water to drink just like this.

She barely had a sip or two when she said, "Thanks."

He put her down slowly. "Where're you hurting?"

"Ribs. Not broken, but it pains when I breathe or swallow. And the head."

He captured her hand in his again. He did not want to let go. "How long are they going to keep you here?"

"Just a day or two."

"Then you're coming home with me. I'm taking you home."

"No, Dallas," she took a breath, closing her eyes briefly again. "Have to do this on my own. Please don't make this difficult for me."

"I'll take good care of you." He couldn't believe she was putting distance between them. Not after that night in her bedroom.

"Dallas, I need time to heal. Surely you can understand that." A weary look came into her eyes.

Of course he could. Maybe. But it was not what he'd envisioned. He hadn't imagined something like this would push them further apart. Crisis was supposed to bring them closer.

The fire in her eyes dulled. Her lips drooped. The pallor of her skin turned grey. He saw her falling apart right in front of him. Perhaps it was not right of him to want things from her when she was clearly unable to give them.

He had to admit defeat and step aside.

"Yes," he admitted with great reluctance. There was nothing he could do about it. "Do you need anything?'

She took a breath and winced. "All I need right now is to lie here and think of nothing. Thanks for being so understanding, Dallas."

"So I'll see you later?"

She nodded, closing her eyes.

He bent down and touched her lips with his. Gently. Like a whisper. And then he left her.

Outside, Bob, Anna, Kalle and Milla were waiting, standing around, looking lost and dejected.

"How is she, my Papillon?" Bob darted forward.

"She's doing okay. Just in pain. Has a few bruised ribs where he..."

"….I can't imagine someone doing this to that tiny body lying over there. What kind of a fucking-pardon my language-monster was this? And where was the damned security in that blasted place? Huh?"

"Apparently, they were short handed." Dallas's chest heaved as a deep sigh escaped him. He did not want to think about it anymore. It hurt too much.

"She's on painkillers, I hope," Anna took his arm, squeezing it. "She'll be fine, my dear. She's a tough one. It'll take more than a brutish man to take her down."

"I want to go in and see her," Kalle said, brushing his cheeks. "Can I?"

"Sure," Dallas tapped him on the shoulder. "See you guys later."

They said their goodbyes and Dallas left, his heart heavy and his mind reeling. He felt she had indeed slipped away from his fingers.

~

Priya had no broken bones. She had bruised ribs and an egg growing out of her head. Physically, she'd be all right in a couple of weeks.

Mentally was a whole another can of worms.

Bob and Anna were there to take her home when she was discharged from the hospital. She hobbled from the bed into the wheelchair.

"Oh my dear, oh my dear," Anna couldn't stop tears from dripping down her cheeks. "What did he do to you?"

"I'm getting better. Just need to go home," Priya winced as Bob, being as gentle as he could, helped her into the car seat.

Bob did not say a word. His mouth was tightly set and his jaw clenched. When he buckled her in, he took her hand and kissed it. Then he took her home.

"There's food in the fridge, my sweet," Anna said. "Am sorry can't hug you right now."

Priya tried to smile and failed. "I know. Thanks."

"Let me know if you need anything today. I'll see you tomorrow."

"K. Bye."

Then Priya was alone with her thoughts.

Gingerly, she eased into days where she just sat either on her deck or in her living room doing nothing. She was still on painkillers and sleep aides. Without the former she couldn't get through her days and without the latter she couldn't get through her nights. It was like being in a warm fuzzy cocoon. As the days wore on, she got number, her thoughts rambling around in her head.

She refused to think about Dallas.

A week into her convalescence, Marie Nilsson came to Kingston and took her back with her to Toronto. Afterward, Priya could not decide whether it had been a good thing or not.

In Toronto, the change of pace and scenery did her good. Or so she thought. She was sleeping better and decided to go off the sleeping aide. Her ribs and head still hurt, so it was difficult to find a pain free sleeping position.

It was even worse than she'd imagined. She began to re-live the attack. Over and over again. Night after night. So she began to read late into the night, then let sleep overcome her with sheer exhaustion.

As with everything on this earth, life moved on, nothing stayed the same. Whatever was happening in her head began to change. Even if time did not heal her wounds, timely distance put a different spin on her perspective. It was the past. And she was, after all, a woman who went with the flow where it took her into the future. The nightmares faded. She even began looking forward to sleep. For it was the only time when the images did not dance in front of her open eyes.

She found herself on Marie's couch one morning. She'd drifted from the bed to the living room after waking up trembling and drenched in sweat.

"Bad night?" Marie pressed the button on the coffeemaker.

"Yes. Again." She rubbed the butterfly tat on her wrist. It covered the scar right beneath it. Marie, her bestie since her school days in England, had been there too the time she got the scar.

She'd just received news of the death of her parents. It was delivered in the cold matter of fact voice by Mother Superior who sat in her office, behind her massive desk while Priya sat opposite in the huge plum leather club chair, her back straight up, feet together on the ground. She would have liked to lean back into the softness and had begun to slide her butt back slowly. Just as slowly, her feet left the ground to accommodate the depth of the armchair. The only way to get somewhat comfortable would be to tuck her legs under her and that would not do. So she sat straight up with both feet on the ground, hands folded in her lap, giving off the illusion of calm acceptance when her mind was ablaze with images and thoughts.

She listened stone-faced, the emotions rioting through her mind leaving no marks on her face. "Nothing is going to change for you, Priya. You will have to be in Canada in a bit to meet with your solicitors. And be back in time to sit for your finals."

Mother Superior's pink-cheeked face was framed in a white coif and wimple as rigid as she was. The dull grey eyes stared down at Priya without warmth. After she left Mother Superior's office, Priya went to the library and hid in a corner, arms tight against her body, hunched forward, rocking to and fro.

Solicitors. Canada. Finals.

Her life for the next few months plotted out.

And then what? Would she go to the house in British Columbia? The house she barely remembered since she'd spent so little time there? Live there alone? But wasn't she alone anyway? Still, there had been a mother and a father regardless of how absent they were. They were the adults.

"Hey, hey," Marie Nilsson snaked an arm around Priya's shoulders. "It's going to be all right. It will be. I know."

And Marie did know for hadn't she gone through the same thing three years ago? Being a year older than Priya, Marie had all the wisdom of a sixteen year old. But her parents hadn't died. They'd divorced.

"But they're dead, Marie. Dead. As in I'm-never-ever-going-to-see-them-again dead."

"Mine are just as good as dead. I never see them. I've never spent a holiday with them. Divorce is just the same as death."

Priya knew in her heart of hearts it was not the same. That night, Marie smuggled in a flask of whiskey and they took turns at it. Before she knew it, Priya dozed off, mind blank and in a bubble, empty of all morbid thoughts.

But the waking up after a few hours of sleep was awful. When she opened her eyes, the room spun like crazy and she was forced to keep her eyes closed. Her mouth was dry and a horrible headache split her head in two. Squinting over to the other side of the room, Priya heard a soft snore come from Marie's bed. She stifled a groan and lifted herself off the bed. Then reality hit her.

She was alone. Her parents were dead.

DEAD!

What was she going to do? Would she have to go into foster care? That's what they did, didn't they? When there was no family to take care of minor children? She'd done some research at the library and it appeared to be the case.

Oh, God! Go to live with strangers? What if they turned out to be pervs?

Priya stumbled into the bathroom. She flinched when she switched on the light. At the sink, she ran cold water and splashed it on her face. She cupped her hands and drank from it in big gulps. After letting out a solid burp, she took a peek in the mirror.

She looked ghastly. Her eyes were puffy and swollen, her face blotched and her hair hung in listless strands.

Good, she looked as ugly as she felt. No pervs were going to get their hands on her. Her eyes fell on the stuff Marie had left on the counter: her bath sponge, a bottle of shampoo and a razor. In a split second she'd made a decision. Priya slid the blade of the razor out of its holder and sliced at her wrist, right where the blue vein ran under her pale skin. The next second, awareness of what she'd done hit her.

But the deed was done. It was fascinating to watch. A scarlet drop-why was it only a drop?-bloomed on her wrist, ran slowly down her arm and dripped into the sink.

A gasp behind her broke the fascination and she turned around.

"Fuck, Priya. What did you do?" Marie's screeching was so loud Priya raised her hands to block her ears. "Let me see."

Breathing as if she'd just completed a marathon, Marie grabbed her wrist. Priya dropped the blade. It fell into the sink with a metallic tinkle.

"Don't want to go live with pervs," Priya said, sinking down on the cool tiled floor.

"Pervs? What the fuck are you talking about? Okay, okay, the cut is not deep." She heaved a big sigh. "You silly bitch. You just nicked your skin. Thank God. Oh, thank God," Marie pulled Priya by the shoulders and held on tight.

"Can't breathe," Priya whispered.

"Good. Because I could kill you. Whatever gave you this idea? And what's this about pervs?"

"My parents are dead so I will be placed in foster care as I'm still a minor. They could be pervs, the foster people. My parents are dead."

The words repeated again and again in her mind.

"First things first and you listen to me carefully. First, you did not nick the vein. Just a surface scratch. No need to go to the infirmary. We'll stick a Band Aid on it and it's done. Second, whatever gave you the idea you'd go into foster care? Your parents were rich. Stinking, fucking rich. You probably have a half a dozen solicitors getting rich looking after your affairs as we speak. You'll stay here until you graduate and then you're free to do as you please coz you'll be an adult."

Eloquent as always, Marie did know how to get her attention. "Stinking rich? Fucking stinking rich? How do you know?"

"Yeah, baby. As in filthy rich. I'm older so I'm wiser. No foster homes for you. Money will probably go into a trust fund and your solicitors will get rich off you managing it all. So rich that when you snap your fingers, they'll ask how high."

Marie pressed on the nick made by the razor and as if by magic, blood stopped seeping through. Then she slapped a piece of Band Aid on it and that was that.

Now, Priya fingered the scar beneath the butterfly tat. It was a reminder and a lesson of past stupidity.

"Can I have coffee too, please?" Priya leaned against the granite island.

"Sure. What kind? Vanilla mocha? Thought you drank only tea."

"Today I feel like coffee. Vanilla sounds good. And sugar too. The works."

Marie got out two mugs into which she poured coffee. Priya tossed three spoons of sugar and stirred the coffee. The aroma was tempting and the taste was a jolt of sugared deliciousness with a wallop of caffeine. She hooked a bar stool with her leg and sat on it. Marie did the same on the other side.

"So talk to me, babe. What's going on in that head of yours? This isn't like when your parents died, right?"

"No, it isn't. I wasn't a witness when my parents died. But this one...I can still see that brute of a man swinging the bat. And Isa lying in the corner." Priya took a ragged breath.

"Isa is fine. Just a small bump on her shoulder. Unlike you. So tell me more. Get it out of your system."

So Priya told her about the brute. The section was short. And somehow Dallas and the kiss on the beach came up too. But she did not spill the beans about the night of the pickleball club's dinner dance. She wanted to.

Badly.

Until then, they had told each other everything.

"All right, here's what you do. You get back on your horse and skedaddle out of here. Get hold of this guy of yours, Dallas, for whom you obviously have the hots for, knock his socks off with more than just a kiss and see where it leads. Live a little, woman! What are you saving yourself for? This is it. This is the life, the only one, you have. Forget Simon. From what I hear, this Dallas is quite something. I'd like to meet him someday. And for that to happen, you have to go home. Your home."

Dallas.

Yes. She'd have to face him again. Question was, how? And more importantly, was she ready for him? Once she let him into her life again, there would be no going back. Dallas was too intense, too passionate and too focused. He would not let go of her. She was certain of that.

"Guess you're right."

"As usual. You forgot to say that. And Priya, use some of that Tantric knowledge you have. Shouldn't let it go to waste."

"I already did. On the beach."

Marie squealed. "No, you didn't. How did it go?"

"Well," Priya began in a whisper so low Marie had to lean across the counter and put her ear to Priya's lips.

Marie's jaw dropped and her eyes got wider. When Priya was done whispering, Marie fanned her hand in front of her face. "Good fucking grief, girl. He must have been putty in your hands.

How was he even able to resist you? Especially that blowing in his…"

Priya clamped her hand over Marie's mouth. "Not in, on. I had to stop because he didn't have a condom in his swimming shorts."

Marie laughed. "Right, if you insist. But aren't you on the pill?"

Priya shook her head.

"Yeah, forgot. Don't you wear an Intrauterine Device? An IUD or something? Yes, that's it. And he agreed?"

"It was his suggestion and I went along. He's this go-slow kind of guy. Kind of Tantric too, in a way. You know, prolong the anticipation." It was her turn to fan her face. "All this Tantric talk is making me hot."

"There's a better word for it. It's called being horny." Marie bent over with laughter spilling out of her. "So don't think about the other brute. Think about sexy Dallas."

"I will be thinking of him. Thanks for the advice. But I'm not ready to meet him yet. I need a bit more time."

"Well, don't wait too long. Grab it while you have the chance."

"I shall listen to you, then. And skedaddle out of here."

"Wonderful," Marie drained her coffee and stowed the mug in the dishwasher. "Not that I don't love having you here. But you got other things to do. Serious stuff. And I hope it leads to a lot of great sex."

"Oh, Marie. You always hope it leads to sex."

"Sorry to say this, my dear, but sex does make the world go round. It has for thousands of years. By the way, you have to teach me some of your Tantric stuff. Please say you will be my Guru."

"If I do, what do I get in return?"

Marie scrunched up her face and looked into the distance. "How about a fabulous day at a fabulously expensive spa? Just you and me?"

"That should do it. You're sure you want to spend that kind of money?"

"It's an investment. It'll to be totally worth it. And by the way, does Dallas have a brother? Unattached? If so, I'd love to meet him. Then we can compare notes."

"As a matter of fact, he does. Austin, a heartbreaker. A marketing guru and a landscape architect."

"Marketing, landscaper *and* an architect? Wow! Triple fudge! Jot me down then for one Austin some time in the future."

"What about Jason?"

"Oops! Yeah, right. Can't do Austin after all. You want me to drive you back? Or you going to take the train?"

"Train. I will leave today."

"But you will teach me the Tantric stuff so I can make Jason crazier? Promise?"

"I promise."

CHAPTER TWENTY-FIVE

PRIYA WALKED TO the bus stop and hopped on a bus to take her to Union Station. In a few hours, she was home. Without waiting to get comfortable, she packed another suitcase, stopped at the grocery store to load up on food and drove to her cabin on the shores of Green Lake. It was a small lake, separate from the others and not linked to any water way at all, keeping noisy boaters away.

It was her refuge. The place she came to when she was at her wit's end, the place with no memories of her parents. Only hers.

She spent her days and nights drinking in the play of the sun and moon on the water. The nights were what she longed for. The quiet solitude, the dark embrace of the dewy air and the warm sand mended the broken bits inside her better than medication. Even better than the bottle of red she kept on the counter ready if she needed the oblivion it promised.

She hadn't reached that stage of want yet.

If she were a poet, she'd write reams of poetry. If she were a painter, she'd paint her heart out. But she was none of those. Her hands were idle while her mind tried to put itself together.

She could listen though. Music filled her whole being, it

became her solace. It was what she longed for. Nothing else but the strains of Dvořák, Beethoven and Ravel, all long dead and Ravi Shankar not dead for that long yet all still alive through their music, to keep her spirit sated. With music in her ears keeping her brain busy with absorbing the harmonious melodies, the pain began to recede bit by bit.

Her life had been a cocoon cushioned with the wealth her parents had left her. Parents she'd barely known. They'd been this unknown entity pulling the strings of her life from afar. Even after their death, her life had not changed in any perceivable way. She'd known there was a world outside her cocoon, but had not actually been aware of it.

Until the shelter.

For the first time in her life, she became aware of how privileged and inconsequential her life was. She had to change that. She had to make her life mean something. Giving her time to the shelter had seemed like a good idea. She still thought it was. She hadn't changed her mind about that.

As the days wore on, her mind emptied itself of the memories keeping her chained to the past. And more and more, images of a broad chest and a tall, dark-haired man with gorgeous grey eyes began to slide ever so slowly into her mind. With no Marie to egg her on to grab on to life, Priya went with the pace her heart set.

She loved him.

It was plain and simple. But did he love her? And not just the promise she held? Would she be enough for him? Even if she couldn't give him what he wanted?

She had to be sure in her heart what she wanted. And if it was the same thing as what she was prepared to give. That night after the dinner dance, that glorious night, he'd walked away from her without losing his cool while she'd been in a puddle at his feet.

No, in his hands.

What kind of a man did that?

Oh, there had been passion all right. As intimate and hot as it could only be between two people willing to take it forward.

So she had to be sure before she saw him again. Because once she did, all her resolve would shatter. One touch of his lips and she'd want more. One look from his dark, fiery eyes and she'd melt into his arms, ready to be consumed by his passion.

And she couldn't have that.

DALLAS, FLOUNDERING IN his emotions, sat in his living room, oblivious to the beautiful night outside. Stars were out, littering the dark velvet sky with jewels. The lake glittered in the moonlight. He had his phone in one hand and a bottle of beer in the other. He had yet to take a sip from it. Elusive fingers of sleep hid in the dark shadows of his brain. It refused to shut down.

He wanted *her*. He wanted all of her. It was either Priya or no one else. He wanted to press his lips to the hollow of her throat and taste her. He wanted to drink in her sweetness, to smell her skin and bury his nose in the fragrance of her body. Feel the ecstatic squeeze of her body around him, and not his fingers, draining him before that final burst when he died a little.

A shuddering breath heaved through his body.

He could not accept that this was it. That they were done. That she was done with him. Where was she? Why had she run away? He still heard her husky whispers as he drove her up to her peak before she shattered in his arms. Hadn't it meant anything to her? The memory was so sharp it sliced through him, the thought of losing her cutting the breath off in his chest. He searched desperately for some relief while his mind grasped at the last wisps of sanity.

There was no life without Priya. How could she do this to him?

His phone pinged. Texts from Houston and Austin. His family. He couldn't be with them. He needed Priya.

"Priya?" her name fell from his lips, hunger flooding his throat, desire welling up in his body.

He didn't have a clue where to look for her. He'd exhausted all avenues and short of hiring a private detective, he couldn't think of anything else. A month had gone by with no word from her. His messages went either unanswered or straight to voice mail. He didn't even know if she was still in the country. Maybe it *was* time to bring in a private investigator.

He looked for her on the pickleball courts. Which was useless anyway. She'd just had a traumatic event. Pickleball would be the last thing on her mind. Then he asked Kalle. Kalle didn't know. Or he could have been refusing point-blank. His answer was ambiguous which puzzled Dallas. Kalle was straight up if anything.

"Can't, dude. Just can't, if you don't know already. I don't know where she could be."

"Can't or won't?"

"The same for you isn't it? One way or the other, it doesn't change."

"Do you know if she's abroad? Have you seen her?" Kalle shook his head. "What does it mean, Kalle? You shaking your head? Have you seen her or not?"

"Did you check with Anna?"

"She will be my next stop. D'you have their address?"

Driving to Bob and Anna's place, Dallas hoped they were home. He let out the breath he was holding when he saw both Anna and Bob's cars in the driveway.

Bob answered the door, in shorts and T-shirt, his feet bare. "I know where she is," honest Bob said. "Can't tell you though. Need her permission."

"What, you her therapist or something?"

"Something like that."

What the fuck? But Dallas steadied his rising frustration. "Why can't you tell me? Please, I'm begging you."

"She needs to be alone right now."

"Is that your decision or hers? She's been alone for more than a month, Bob. I have to go to her. I love her."

Bob nodded. "Yes, I could tell that. I've watched you two together. Anna's somewhere weeding. Tell you what, I'll talk to Anna and…"

"Please talk to her right now. Please? I can't wait. This is torture." He plowed his hands through his hair.

"Why don't you come in? Have a beer." Bob led Dallas through the side of the house to the patio in the back. "Grab a beer. It's in the fridge."

Even though Dallas did not want a beer, he got a cold bottle. He sat down then stood up, paced, tapping his sunglasses against his hand.

"Okay here it is. I've made an executive decision," Dallas had to smile. Bob's executive decisions were always for the underdog. "Priya's at her cabin. It's on Green Lake. And here's the address. I've just sent it to your phone."

"Thank you, Bob. I've got to get her back. Can't live without her."

"So go tell her that. And best of luck. You should know Priya will exact her revenge some time. And hopefully Anna will not exact *her* revenge."

Dallas entered the address into his dashboard and let the GPS do its job. Then it was up to him. He couldn't live without her. But he couldn't just have her and leave it at that. He wanted *all* she had to give. And more. He remembered her saying she was a drifter with no desire to anchor down somewhere. He was going to break through that resistance of hers. This was for keeps.

He wanted her to dance for him and him alone in those gorgeous outfits. She was the one for him. He had to make her understand they were made for each other. He wasn't going to let her go. Not this time. He wanted it all so badly, his head spun. He had to find her and tell her that.

~

IT WAS A beautiful moonlit night. Stars were out by the gazillions. A night fit for lovers. But Priya was alone. Reality was waiting for her and she had to face it one way or another. She'd get back to pickleball sometime in the future. A future without Dallas. It was not going to work with him. He was too focused. He had it all planned whereas she was content to let it drift, one day at a time.

He wanted a wife. He wanted children. All things she could not give him. He would make a great father. But not with her. Whatever sexual interaction she'd had with him had been great. She couldn't call it making love. It was just sex-orgasmic no doubt-but still. She did not want to be a cog in *his* wheel of life. Not the way he expected. It was too much pressure. She didn't do well under pressure. If anything, she avoided it.

Truth was, she loved him. Was deeply in love with him. Perhaps would always be. There was no other man for her. But she was a fiercely independent, modern woman who carried Mace and wore nose-breaking rings on her fingers. What she needed was someone who'd love her back the way she did, someone who was intent on a life together as a couple first. Everything else would come after.

Once children came into the picture, the dynamics between a couple changed forever. From being lovers they'd migrate to being parents without identities of their own. They would disintegrate into nothingness. *She* would disappear.

With Dallas, she'd have to take his family into her life too. The Crenshaws were part of the deal. With noisy, loud get-togethers, certainly no more alone time at Christmas. That would be a thing of the past.

On the other hand, she'd have a family, a large one to see her through thick and thin. They'd be a comfort during life's darkest hours and a joy to share life's brightest days.

No, they wouldn't work. They were too different. Maybe they had pickleball in common. But that was not the glue for a shared life! It was just a game after all. She could not envision giving up her single life. She was happy with her single life. Well, maybe not happy but content.

Like how she was right now, at the bottom of the dune, sitting on a blanket surrounded by a ring of tiki torches, watching the play of the moon on the waters and the night sky. It was a glorious sight. But was it enough? Glorious sights were a dime a dozen on this planet. They happened all over the world.

She heard the hum of a motor before she saw lights flashing on the windows of her cabin. Even in the light of the moon she recognized his car.

So he had come!

Who spilled the beans? Kalle or Bob? The rat!

The one she'd repay with a cholesterol-rich bland meal and the other with a few of her fiery dishes, upping the Scoville units by a few hundred thousand.

As she waited for him to come to her, every logical argument she'd gone through just moments before, dissipated. Instead, she was suffused with desire. It radiated from her heart and enveloped her whole being in its warm glow. Doubts trolling inside her head evaporated. This was right. She loved him and she'd take whatever he offered. His family, his plans for the future, all of it. All it had taken was a glimpse of him. All it had taken was his proximity and she was spilling over with need. She'd never needed anyone like this before. No one else made her feel so wanted, so safe.

On the outside, he was all hard muscle ripped in perfect harmony with the rest of him wrapped in irresistible pheromones. On the inside, he was gentle and considerate and sweet.

God, how was she going to resist all that? Did she have to? Yes! Otherwise it was goodbye to her contented life, the end to her placid drifting uninterrupted by waves.

And now he was here. She wanted him.

In her life. Forever.

CHAPTER TWENTY-SIX

DALLAS SLIPPED OFF his Birkenstocks, letting the soft, still-warm sand envelop his feet. Sounds of Beethoven's Third spilled out of the open door and windows. Somehow he knew she would be by the water. A row of tiki torches led the way over the dune. He crested it and paused.

She stood away from the glow of the tiki torches watching as he walked slowly and deliberately toward her, sand impeding each stride.

She wore a long light-coloured dress. Could be white. Could be beige. Moonlight swallowed whatever colour it was, washing her in its silvery glow. The hem fluttered in the breeze. Her hair was bundled high, held together by chopsticks. Shadows jumped on her face.

She watched him approach her, her eyes never leaving his face. She stood with her arms loosely folded in front of her. The thumb of her left hand rubbed her right wrist, just over the butterfly tat.

When he reached her, she looked up at him, her eyes wide. Light from the torches illuminated the green in her eyes, the golden reflections flickering through like ripples on the lake. Her lips trembled and she looked away.

He lifted her chin toward him with one finger. "I've been looking all over for you. Where have you been? I've been going crazy not knowing."

Her eyes closed. "Now you know how it feels."

His hand cupped her cheek. His other hand slid up from her waist and up the column of her throat to cover the back of her neck with its warmth. He pulled her to him holding her tight, feeling her nipples harden through the thin material of her dress. He felt her shiver. Or maybe he was?

"Is that what this is? A tit for tat?" His lips lingered on one smooth cheek, dropping kisses as they trailed across to her ear. He drew back, eyes searching hers.

Her eyes glittered. He felt rather than saw the tears. "No, Dallas, of course not. What d'you take me for?"

"There is no me without you, my sweet. Has never been since the day I met you. You should know that by now, know the power you have over me. I'm never going to let you go."

Cradling her face in his hands, he gently wiped her tears with his thumbs. Then he wrapped his arms around her and drew her into the warm comfort of his embrace. He tucked her head beneath his chin where she fit perfectly. Dallas closed his eyes, his lips resting on the top of her head, inhaling the sensuous fragrance of her, feeling her tense body relax and soften in his arms. He pulled her closer still to his heart, the fabric of her dress fluttering against his bare legs, their hearts beating as one.

In tiny waves, the fragrant summer air swirled around them, replacing the cool earthy one with hot. Gradually, the relaxed feeling began to change. Like a tropical storm, heat met lush moistness to create one molten core.

Dallas lifted her chin up with a finger. "Guess I have your permission."

Blood flowed hot and fast, as her hands reached under his shirt to caress the smooth skin on his back then moved to his belly, her palms moving in circles. He quickly yanked his T-shirt over his head. She pressed her lips to his chest and her soft sigh pierced his heart. She sighed like no one he knew. It conveyed so much.

Her fingers explored the flat, broad expanse of his chest, the touch and feel of her was exquisite. He groaned low in his throat and her hips moved closer to his. Bending down, he lifted her. She knotted her legs around his waist.

She brought both hands around his head, running her fingers through his silky hair and bent his head back so she could access his mouth. Their lips met just as Beethoven's Third reached a crescendo. There was hope and despair in the meeting of their lips, passion and desire. Above all, there was a connection deepening with each intimate move.

Her soft hands moved over the hard lines of his body: his shoulders, his chest and his back, her touch inflaming his senses. The scruff on his face grazed the valley between her breasts.

Making quick work of stripping off his shorts and boxers, he grabbed her by the hips and lifted her again. Capturing her mouth again with his, he was in the warm water in three strides. Her dress billowed out, lifting away from her body. He was now skin to skin with her. It was not enough. He wanted all of her against him.

Her legs tightened around his waist and she moaned his name. He kissed her until his senses were spinning. The water was everywhere he was not and he was going to change that soon. She tried to lift the dress over her head but the water was having none of it. The wet fabric clung to her curves, refusing to relinquish its hold. Somewhere along the way, she lost the sticks holding her hair up and it swirled around her, undulating with the movement of the water, a mermaid in his arms.

A goddess. His goddess.

"No," the goddess in his arms whimpered when he removed his lips from hers.

"Priya," he breathed against her ear, then again as he crushed his mouth to hers. "Touch me."

He lifted the dress, rolling it as he went along, his lips following her bare skin it left behind. She was naked underneath it, her breasts glistening in the moonlight. His mouth went dry despite all the moisture around him. His mind went blank, all thoughts of being the master of slow dispersing in the warm water.

He dragged them to deeper water, until he hit a sandbar, and lifting her, he bent his head to kiss her breasts. Lifting her legs, he entwined them around his waist.

"Now, Dallas."

Her words were his command.

He forgot all about being Mr. Go Slow. A nagging voice in his head prodded him about something important he'd missed. He shoved it aside as he lost himself in her. Threading his fingers in her hair, he lifted her face to his, his grey eyes looking deep into her green. Then his lips came down on hers, drawing in all the sweetness she had to give.

His hands held her to him, as he moved against her, her soft breasts rubbing against the hard planes of his chest. Her body pulsed and a velvet fist grabbed him. His heart pounded and he shuddered as he came, hard and fast. He groaned and let go.

~

THE WORLD FELL away. All Priya felt was Dallas. All her senses filled with him, around her, against her, in her.

Her climax came in a gush of hot waves. The soft sand she stood on dropped beneath her. Sensations spun and eyes glazing over, she saw only the stars he made her see. They floated, the silver water creating a silken shroud mingling with their essences. She floated, sensations building up inside her, buoyed by the silent embrace of the water.

Then he murmured against her eyes, her cheeks and her lips. If she hadn't been so focused on him, she'd have missed it. His voice was soft, almost a whisper, sending a shiver through her body.

A promise.

A hope.

Priya drooped in his arms like a wilting flower. She was replete. She was where she wanted to be. She had come home. It was so much more than she'd imagined. She was sated. Feeling Dallas stirring to life again, she smiled the secret smile of a woman who knew her power and how to wield it judiciously.

Dripping wet, he carried her inside the cabin. He had to kick open a couple of closed doors before he found the bathroom. Priya slithered out of his arms. She ran water until it was hot. Then stepped in, dragging Dallas in with her. She let him kiss her breathless before she trailed her fingers over his chest, over the smooth texture of his biceps and shoulders. She gently traced the outline of his nose and lips.

She filled her nose with him, his scent and his shape. She felt a ripple go through him as she brought his scruff against her nipples. Eyes closed, he stood without moving, hands braced on the wall on either side of her.

When her hands left him, he flipped his eyes open, the grey lighting up with tiny flecks of flame. She reached for the soap, squeezed a bit on her palms and began to lather him from bottom to top: his long legs, up his thighs, around the back and to the front again.

That was as far as she got. In one swift move, he had her braced up against the wall. "Like I said, touch me like that and you're at my mercy." On those heated words, he looped her legs around his waist and he was no more going slow.

Just as quickly, he paused and groaned out loud. Her legs slipped down his body.

"What now?"

"Guess what?" He trapped her legs between his.

"Bet you I can. No condom?"

"How…?"

"I have protection. An IUD."

"Isn't that against missiles?"

God, he made her laugh.

"Yes, yours," she rested her head against his chest and giggled, almost choking on the water rippling down her face.

"Don't be vulgar, squirt." A soft chuckle from him.

"Maybe you're thinking of the obsolete SCUD. This one is called an intrauterine device and has no ballistic capabilities at all. It's lodged in my uterus so you don't have to worry about your boys lodging there."

"A brochure. Okay." He grinned, his dimples showing on his cheeks. "*Now* you tell me. You could have whispered it in my ear that night on the beach."

"*You* stopped. *You* wanted to stop. All I did was agree. You wanted the slow dance."

"Ah, yes indeed. Thanks for reminding me."

"Would it have mattered?"

"Probably not. I had a plan I was following. Now to my next plan: I think I need to find that elusive bed."

She grabbed a thick towel from the shelf and threw it at him. Then tied another one around her and made her way to the living room.

"Thought we had something to finish here," Dallas knotted the thick soft towel around his waist.

"It can wait."

She could see he was playing along, fiddling with the knot around his waist gaining time before his next move. He made a grab for her, drew her to him and looked down at her, his scorching gaze riveted on her mouth. He did not kiss her, just let those eyes brimming with hot desire look his fill of her face, lingering over the flushed planes of her cheeks, his thumb grazing softly on her lower lip. His arms knotted around her waist and brought her even closer to his body. He pressed his face in the crook in her neck and took a deep breath. Then he released her.

Priya took an awkward step back, stumbled and hit the arm of the plump sofa on her way down. Before she hit anything further, a strong arm broke her fall and braced her against a broad chest. It was Priya's turn to breathe deep. She clung to him, both arms around his neck, feeling his heart pound next to hers. Mixed in with their heaving breaths and pounding hearts, rose a rumble from her stomach.

Reality hit her with another growl from her stomach. "Food. Need to eat," she mumbled between rasping gulps of air.

Priya picked up a remote from the coffee table, punched a button and beautiful music evocative of mountains and green valleys hit her ears.

"What's that? It's gorgeous."

"Dvořák Ninth symphony. I'm starving." Priya turned to the fridge.

Out came a basket of plump strawberries. Dallas took it from her hand, went to the sink, rinsed it and dumped it on a plate. He then proceeded to hull the berries while she took out a block of dark chocolate from her tiny pantry. She melted it in a bowl, whisked in a bit of maple syrup and heavy cream until she had an unctuous dark liquid, the aroma of which had her salivating. She dunked a strawberry in the hot molten chocolate and took a bite.

"Hmm. Heavenly," her lips closed around it and she closed her eyes.

Then she fed Dallas the next strawberry. And the next. That did it. Her energy level shot up again watching his lips close around the succulent berry.

. . .

There had been another time she'd felt like this, the sense of spinning out of control. The time when the world around her had crashed. Then rewarded her. She'd paid a price for that reward.

It was when she'd taken the razor in her hand.

But this time she was with Dallas, with his strong sense of loyalty and equally strong sense of family and friendship. She felt loved in his arms. Safe. He was invincible. He looked at her like she was the only thing he cared about and it made her feel cherished.

He looked at her like nothing else mattered.

She heard his breath rasping against her body. His flat chest pressed against her: body to body, soul to soul. This time when her world crashed, Dallas would be there to keep her safe with his glorious powerful body, a solid wall of male strength.

The missing piece.

~

BRIEFLY DALLAS WONDERED if that anti-missile thing up her body would bite the most sensitive part of his very vulnerably exposed anatomy, for it *was* guarding the gates of her womanhood.

He had come home. She was his safe harbour. He drowned in her, losing himself in her as she began to pulse. He was hers just like she was his. Her utter surrender to the onslaught of his desire and her fiery touches branded him to her, tearing at his defences, smashing it to bits.

"D'you know what my name means?" she whispered in his ear later.

"Loved one. My love," his lips barely a whisper away from hers. His fingers brushed her wrist just above the butterfly tat. "Now tell me about this scar, my sweet."

So she told him.

"Marry me?" he said. It was simple and succinct.

"Okay," her reply was even simpler and more succinct if that were possible.

"Trip to India? I want to take you there."

"Okay."

"Didn't know you were a woman of few words."

"Right now, I am."

EPILOGUE

Kochi, Kerala.

Dallas rented a houseboat on the backwaters of Kerala, India. The air was fragrant with cloves and cinnamon, rich with smells from the outdoor fires. Priya wore a *munduh* and *veshti*: a two piece ensemble, one to wrap around her waist like a sarong and the other, tucked in her waist, around it and over the left shoulder. She wore a short sleeveless blouse with it, her tats causing quite a stir among the local kids. She had henna on her feet and hands, anklets jingling softly.

She lay stretched out on the bow, hand trailing in the water.

There were jasmine flowers in her hair. It was the most sensuous fragrance to hit his nose. He could stay with his nose buried in her hair all day, waiting for darkness to fall when she would be his and his alone. There was something magical about the tropical darkness. It was not the sweet, slow dusk he was familiar with. Like everything else here, it was opulent in its darkness. One second it was day and the next, it was not. A cape of velvet from the ground up to the sky littered with millions of stars.

Patience was his forte. He *was* Mr. Go Slow. He knew the power of his touch. His fingers. His lips.

But he'd met his match. She had a suitcase full of fabulous Indian dresses. Diaphanous ones and silky ones in jewelled tones. He was going to his do best to keep it all together. He only hoped he could hang on to wherever she was taking him.

Chris Isaak's *Wicked Game* played softly through her iPod. They'd discovered it was one of their favourite make out songs.

Dallas covered her body with a transparent red veil. Her skin glowed, the red stud in her nose glinting in the flickering light of the oil lamps. A nothing of a blouse covered her chest. Riding low on her hips was a red skirt, covered with sequins and mirrors. He stuck his nose in her jasmine scented hair and breathed in deep. The dark silky waves feathered across his face, the long black strands linking themselves to the short scruff on his cheeks.

"Priya. Beautiful Priya. You make my head spin. And I want more."

He felt rather than saw the hint of a knowing smile bloom on her face. She kept her hands to herself. He wondered what erotic surprise she had for him. And, more importantly, when she was going to reveal it.

He ran his hand down the length of her body, down her legs, to the anklets and toe rings. He lifted her foot with his hand and kissed the hennaed arch.

She jerked her foot away. He took it back. So she was ticklish there.

"So, Priya. There's a pickleball club here in Kochi. There are a couple in Mumbai too."

"What?" she squealed and he grinned. "Dallas, let's go there. Now?"

"It's midnight, squirt. We'll check it out in the morning." After he had his way with her.

It was in Kochi that Dallas felt the stirrings of a book in his mind. It was still vague and tenuous, the ideas still fuzzy and cloudy. But he was thinking about it more often. He thought he'd get a notebook and a pencil. And see where it led him. For once, go with the flow.

He was taking Priya to the land of Bollywood...Mumbai. Then it was off to Agra, Jaipur and Udaipur, land of the Maharajahs. They were meeting Houston, his family and Austin in Jaipur.

All in all, it was promising to be one hell of a trip.

THE END

ABOUT THE AUTHOR

Nalini Warriar dreamed of being a writer then forgot the dream for a bit as she went on to garner a Ph.D in Molecular Biology. While in her lab, the dream came back and hit her on the head and she's never looked back. After more than a decade in cancer research, Nalini returned to the creative part of her soul and now devotes her time to dreaming up the perfect alpha male and feisty woman to appear in her books. Her novel, Fireflies in the Night, was a Foreword Reviews Award finalist and won the Next Generation Indie Book Award in 2017. Karma's Slow Burn, a contemporary romance was released in February 2020. She's working on her next romance, a Bollywood romance, to be released later in 2020. Look for Book 2 from the Crenshaw Brothers series due out soon.

Join the Warriar Squad!

Did you enjoy Dallas and Priya's story? Do you want to stay in touch to be informed of releases, giveaways, free books, excerpts and sneak peeks? If yes, LOL, do sign up on my website here: www.naliniwarriar.com

If you love posting book reviews, join the Warriar Squad Beta reader and ARC teams here:

nalini@naliniwarriar.com

AUTHORS' NOTE

Thank you for reading Mr. Go Slow. In 2017, I was able to breathe again largely due to pickleball, a sport which features prominently in Mr. Go Slow and mostly because Fireflies in the Night won the coveted Next Generation Indie Book Award for Best Fiction. Pickleball gave me my life back. It brought me in touch with people who have become my family. While you cannot choose your family, you *can* choose your friends.

If you prefer literary fiction titles, please consider my books The Enemy Within, a portrait of a marriage and love; Fireflies in the Night, a coming of age novel set in 1960s India, Winner of Next Generation Indie Book Awards 2017 and Foreword Reviews Finalist. And yes, it got a starred review from Kirkus Reviews. But what can I say, I want *more!* Karma's Slow Burn is a sizzling contemporary romance about a baseball pitcher and a journalist.

If you're an avid reader like me, all you want now is to move on to your next book. I get it. But…guess what's coming next? If you enjoyed my book, my request would be to leave a review. Reviews are crucial to an author's career. They not only dissemi-nate word about my books to other readers but also help

Amazon show my book to readers. Please use this URL or use the book title to get to the book page. https://www.amazon.com/review/create-review?&isbn=1777401306

As always, I'm grateful to those who have already reviewed my books. Mr. Go Slow is Book 1 in the Crenshaw Brothers series with Book 2, Mr. No Commitment coming up soon. If you'd like to be the first to get news of my next books do drop me a line here

nalini@naliniwarriar.com
https://www.facebook.com/authornaliniwarriar
https://amazon.com/author/naliniwarriar
twitter.com/nwarriar
instagram: nwarriar

PLAYLIST

Playlist for Mr. Go Slow

I write to music. My taste is eclectic. It's classical when I'm creating, blues and rock follow and then it get's fuzzy. Music inspires me and certain parts in Mr. Go Slow are written under the influence of specific harmonics in my ears. Do check them out!

Beethoven: Symphony #3 Eroica Opus 55, Marche Funèbre, Berlin Phil, conductor Herbert von Karajan

Dvořák Symphony #9 The New World, Opus 95, LA Phil, Conductor Zubin Mehta.

Not classical: **Chris Isaak** Wicked Game

Metallica Until it Sleeps

The Tea Party Temptation

Blue Rodeo Dragging On, Falling Down Blue, Cinema Song, Sad Nights, Bad Timing, Till I Gain Control Again

Dire Straits Brothers In Arms

Staind It's been a While, Outside

Gerry Rafferty Baker Street

Red Hot Chili Peppers Californication, Scar Tissue, Other Side

Soundgarden Black Hole Sun
Duran Duran Come Undone
Def Leppard Love Bites

GET A FREE BOOK!

https://dl.bookfunnel.com/zxcncddx5h

Download a free copy of my novella 'A Man of Substance.'

- Nimmy, a trauma surgeon, does the unthinkable. She chooses an arranged marriage . What she doesn't count on is falling for the guy.

Printed in Great Britain
by Amazon

53013518R00152